HENRIETTA CLANDON

POWER ON THE SCENT

With an introduction by Curtis Evans

DEAN STREET PRESS

Published by Dean Street Press 2020

Copyright © 1937 Henrietta Clandon

Introduction Copyright © 2020 Curtis Evans

All Rights Reserved

First published in 1937 by Geoffrey Bles

Cover by DSP

ISBN 978 1 913054 91 5

www.deanstreetpress.co.uk

HENRIETTA CLANDON
POWER ON THE SCENT

VERNON LODER was a pseudonym for John George
Haslette Vahey (1881-1938), an Anglo-Irish writer who
also wrote as Henrietta Clandon, John Haslette, Anthony
Lang, John Mowbray, Walter Proudfoot and George
Varney. He was born in Belfast and educated at Ulster,
Foyle College, and Hanover. Four years after he graduated
college he was apprenticed to an architect and later tried
his hand at accounting before turning to fiction writing
full time.

According to the copy of Loder's *Two Dead* (1934): "He
once wrote a novel in twenty days on a boarding-house
table, and had it serialised in U.S.A. and England under
another name . . . He works very quickly and thinks two
hours a day in the morning quite enough for any one. He
composes direct on a machine and does not re-write."
While perhaps this is an exaggeration, Vahey was highly
prolific, author of at least forty-four novels between 1926
and 1938.

Vahey's series characters were Inspector Brews, Chief
Inspector R.J. "Terry" Chace, Donald Cairn (as Loder) and
William Power, Penny & Vincent Mercer (as Henrietta
Clandon).

With a solid reputation for witty characterisation and
"the effortless telling of a good story" (*Observer*), Vahey's
popularity was later summed up in the *Sunday Mercury*:
"We have no better writer of thrill mystery in England."

HENRIETTA CLANDON MYSTERIES
Available from Dean Street Press

Inquest
Good by Stealth
This Delicate Murder
Power on the Scent

STRING PUZZLES BY THE COZY FIRESIDE

The Mysteries of Henrietta Clandon

Who is "Henrietta Clandon"? We don't know—we wish we did!" Anyhow, "she" has written one of the best murder novels we have read in a long time.

--newspaper advertisement by Geoffrey Bles, publisher of the Henrietta Clandon detective novels

TODAY we know, as the coy "she" above hinted, that Golden Age mystery writer Henrietta Clandon, author of seven detective novels between 1933 and 1938, was in fact a man: John George Haslette Vahey (1881-1938). Women mystery writers adopting the guise of masculine or sexually ambiguous pseudonyms was a common enough practice during the Golden Age of detective fiction, as it had been with their Victorian and Edwardian sisters. Margery Allingham wrote a trio of mysteries as Maxwell March, Americans Dorothy Blair and Evelyn Page five as Roger Scarlett and Lucy Beatrice Malleson over three score as Anthony Gilbert, while the names Ngaio Marsh, Moray Dalton, E.C.R. Lorac and E.X. Ferrars--the latter three respectively pseudonyms of Katherine Mary Dalton Renoir, Edith Caroline Rivett and Morna Doris MacTaggart, aka Elizabeth Ferrars--left readers in doubt as to the authors' actual genders and male book reviewers often referring, in their early years, to the excellent books by Messrs. Marsh, Dalton, Lorac and Ferrars. When in doubt, assume it is male, so the thinking then seemed to go. (More recently the late scholar and mystery fan Jacques Barzun referred to Moray Dalton as a "neglected man" while another, Jared Lobdell, speculated that "Moray Dalton" might have been yet another pseudonym of prolific British Golden Age mystery writer Cecil John Charles Street.)

It was commonly believed, in those days, that men were more credible to readers as writers of detective fiction. It also was presumed that readers of detective fiction were predominantly male as well. "[T]he detective story . . . is primarily a man's novel," emphatically declared a woman, American Marjorie Nicolson, then serving as dean of the English department at Smith College, in "The Professor and the Detective," an essay originally published in the *Atlantic Monthly* in 1929. "Many women dislike it heartily, or at best accept it as a device to while away hours on the train. And while we do all honor to the three or four women who have written surpassingly good detective stories of the purest type, we must grant candidly that the great bulk of our detective stories today are being written by men."

This was an attitude which began decidedly to change, however, with the rise of Britain's so-called four Queens of Crime in the 1930s: Agatha Christie (first mystery novel published in 1920), Dorothy L. Sayers (1923), Margery Allingham (1928) and Ngaio Marsh (1934), not to mention a slew of additional talented British women detective writers, such as the aforementioned Anthony Gilbert and others like Patricia Wentworth, Moray Dalton, Gladys Mitchell, Annie Haynes, E.C.R. Lorac, Joan Cowdroy, Molly Thynne, Helen Simpson, Ianthe Jerrold, Elizabeth Gill, Josephine Bell, Mary Fitt, Dorothy Bowers, Harriet Rutland and, coming along a bit later in the 1940s, Christianna Brand and Elizabeth Ferrars. (In the United States there were, aside from Roger Scarlett, an admittedly minor player in the world of Golden Age detective fiction, the hugely popular Mary Roberts Rinehart and Mignon Eberhart and their many followers.) By the late Thirties and early Forties readers and reviewers alike had concluded that classic detective fiction was a form of fiction at which women excelled as much as, if not more then, the male of the species. It was, indeed, the men who might have been well advised to watch their backs, for fear of fatal feminine thrusts from wicked-bladed letter openers or jewel-encrusted hatpins.

It is this altered environment which led to the appearance, with the novel *Inquest* in 1933, of another purported woman crime writer, one who was emphatically a lady in tone, if not in fact: Henrietta Clandon. In the hands of Dorothy L. Sayers and, I would argue, Agatha Christie, with such novels as *Strong Poison*, *Have His Carcase*, *The Murder of Roger of Ackroyd* and *The Murder at the Vicarage*, there had arisen so-called "manners mystery" murder fiction, filled not just with corpses, crimes and clues, but witty and sardonic observation of people and social mores. (Male authors Anthony Berkeley/Francis Iles and C.H.B. Kitchin were also signal contributors in this regard.) Margery Allingham would follow suit in 1934 with the marvelous *Death of a Ghost*, accompanied by Ngaio Marsh's debut novel *A Man Lay Dead*, but Henrietta Clandon actually had already anticipated the two younger Crime Queens with a fully developed manners mystery in 1933.

When he created Henrietta Clandon, John Haslette Vahey was no new hand at mystery mongering. Born on March 5, 1881 in Strandtown, a district of Belfast, Northern Ireland, Vahey was the middle son of Herbert Vahey, a superintendent of Inland Revenue (i.e., tax collector), and his wife Jane Lowry Vahey, a daughter of a wealthy Belfast watchmaker and jeweler. Like his contemporary, author and crime writer E.R. Punshon, "Jack" Vahey, as he was known, after walking away from careers in business around the turn of the century (in Vahey's case insurance and accountancy), had started writing fiction professionally. Vahey published his first novel in 1909, while residing at a Bournemouth boarding house with his elder brother, who also wrote fiction, and he began turning out mysteries in the classic mold by the late 1920s, primarily under the pen name Vernon Loder, whose work recently has been highly praised by vintage mystery authorities Nigel Moss and John Norris. (Moss calls Vernon Loder "a paradigm of the English Golden Age mystery writer.") Jack Vahey's other known pen names—those besides his two most notable ones, Vernon Loder and Henrietta Clandon--are John Haslette, Anthony Lang, John Mowbray and the hobbit-ish Walter Proudfoot; under the entire tribe, whose output included mysteries, mainstream, adventure and espionage novels, and school tales, he ultimately produced sixty-five books, making him a prolific author indeed. Vahey boasted that he once composed a novel over a span of twenty days at a table at the boarding house, afterward serializing it in both the United Kingdom and the United States under different pseudonyms.

By 1933, when Jack Vahey at the age of fifty-two created Henrietta Clandon, he had as Vernon Loder already published eight detective novels in five years, and no fewer than three additional Loder novels would appear in print in 1933. Many of the Vernon Loder titles were published in both the UK (with the prestigious Collins Crime Club) and the US (with Morrow, publisher of Christopher Bush and, shortly in the future, Erle Stanley Gardner and Carter Dickson.) Why, then, one might ask, did Vahey start publishing under yet another pseudonym?

When one reads the Clandons, the "why" becomes readily apparent, for Vahey with this new line clearly was attempting to do something different, and more ambitious, with his crime fiction than he had with Vernon Loder, et al., as pleasing as some of the Loder novels are. The Henrietta Clandon novels are the most carefully crafted mysteries that Vahey ever wrote, models of manners mystery which present to the reader wittily epigrammatic and cuttingly sardonic murder in its most deceptively cozy British guises of country houses and villages—quintessential malice domestic, as it were. Critics responded favorably to the Clandons, sensing an enticing new spice of mystery in the air, one which seemed exquisitely feminine.

Dorothy L. Sayers herself welcomed Henrietta Clandon's *Inquest* in the pages of the *Sunday Times*, where Sayers was the crime fiction reviewer from 1933 to 1935, as "an attractive and promising piece of puzzle making." She added that the "book is very well written, the dialogue being quite exceptionally fresh and well-managed, and the characterization good," before adding encouragingly: "This appears to be Miss Henrietta Clandon's first detective story; I hope we shall hear more from her again." Score one for the ladies!

Of a later Clandon novel, *Rope by Arrangement*, Sayers keenly pronounced, employing a most apt image, that the novel's merit lay "in a kind of quiet tortuousness; to read it is rather like working out an intricate little string puzzle by the fireside. . . . the tale makes very agreeable reading." Nor was Sayers alone in her praise of Clandon. Concerning *This Delicate Murder*, Torquemada (noted crossword puzzle designer Edward Powys Mathers) in the *London Observer* praised its "wit" and the "nearly watertight impeccability" of its puzzle. For his part crime writer Milward Kennedy, Sayers' successor at the *Sunday Times*, in reviewing the superb inverted poison pen mystery *Good by Stealth*, which recalls not only works by Francis Iles but ones by Anthony Rolls and Richard Hull, lauded the author's "gift for irony in the depiction of the criminal's mind." An able literary limner like Henrietta Clandon, observed Kennedy admiringly, "can suit style to subject, and even enable us to see character in its true colour though revealed by colour-blind eyes." Perhaps Anthony Berkeley, reviewing crime fiction as Francis Iles, summed up best when he declared that "Henrietta Clandon's novels are always welcome. She has developed a style of her own in crime fiction."

Sadly, the steady series of Clandon mysteries was abruptly halted after the appearance of the seventh Clandon novel, *Fog off Weymouth* ("quite charming narration," pronounced Torquemada), which was published in March 1938, just three months before Jack Vahey's death at age fifty-seven on June 15. I do not know what killed the author, but only three years before his death he had flippantly boasted, in a letter to the *London Observer* signed "Vernon Loder," that "I have not spent a day in bed in thirty-two years," despite the fact that "I add great quantities of salt to my food, and vast quantities of sugar to tea, coffee and lemonade." As a remedy against the chronic throat inflammation he had suffered between the ages of fourteen and twenty-one, he had taken up smoking eucalyptus cigarettes (forerunners of menthols, recently banned in the state of Massachusetts). Salt, sugar and cigarettes—perhaps Jack's death should not have come as a surprise. It will be recalled that thriller writer Edgar Wallace, who died from a diabetic coma and double pneumonia in 1932, consumed copious amounts of sugary tea.

At the time of his untimely demise Vahey resided with his wife, Gertrude Crowe Barendt, formerly a music teacher from Liverpool, at a flat in affluent Branksome Park in Bournemouth (today Poole). A final Vernon Loder, *Kill in the Ring*, a boxing murder tale far removed from the milieu of Henrietta Clandon, was published in October and, after that, Vahey, who left no children, was largely forgotten. His elder brother, Herbert Lowry Vahey, a more peripatetic author than Jack, survived him by two decades, but though he wed as well, he left no children. Jack's younger brother, Samuel Lowry Vahey, an insurance executive who migrated to Canada and later Houston, Texas, predeceased Jack by a decade.

Where did Jack Vahey get his mind for "delicate murder," his ability to compose a quietly tortuous mystery resembling "an intricate little string puzzle"? He was educated at Foyle College, Londonderry, Northern Ireland and in the city of Hanover in the state of Saxony, Germany (which perhaps helps explain his later marriage to an Anglo-German wife), and his favored hobbies were shooting and fishing, but perhaps he carried within himself something of his canny Scots-Irish maternal grandfather, John Lowry, who died in Belfast in 1886, when Vahey was five years old. Old John Lowry was a highly respected maker and retailer of watches and chronometers (a time measuring instrument used in marine navigation to determine longitude), who owned a big shop in the High Street and did regular business as well in London. Pieces which Lowry designed are highly sought collector's items today. (For example, the website of David Penney's Antique Watch Store offers an exquisite "top quality" nineteenth-century chronometer by Lowry with gold hands and a "very rare sapphire roller.") At the old man's death, he left an estate that was valued at, in modern worth, some 470,000 pounds (over 600,000 dollars), indicating that he was a top person in his field.

A well-plotted Golden Age mystery, after all, resembles not only a string puzzle or Rubik's Cube, but a clock--whether or not unbreakable alibis and railway timetables are involved. Vahey's grandfather John Lowry possessed more than the consummate skill to construct intricate mechanical devices, however; he had, as well, personal experience with criminals. In 1867 Lowry, sounding like detective writer R. Austin's Freeman famed medical jurist sleuth Dr. John Thorndyke, testified at the criminal prosecution of one Bernard O'Kane for allegedly passing counterfeit coins around Belfast. At the trial, it was reported, Lowry established that the coins at issue were fake, being made of "base metal." Eleven years earlier, burglars had daringly invaded Lowry's shop at 66 High Street. The watchmaker had spent the evening and early morning hours on the roof of his house, where he had been engaged in "comparing his time by transit observations of the stars" until one o'clock in the morning. During this time he heard noises on the roof, but took this to be merely the nocturnal perambulations of a cat. Later that morning, when the entire household had gone to bed, a felonious party took a pane of glass out of a skylight and with a rope descended into the house. Fortunately, "the shop being well secured, the goods locked in a large safe, a party well-armed sleeping in a room connected with the shop, and doors properly barred inside, the robber or robbers could get no farther than the kitchen and back room, from which they took several articles of dress and even some eatables," departing without detection. It is the sort of setting that with embellishment might have inspired Edgar Wallace's famous mystery *The Clue of the New Pin* (1923), in which a shady businessman who keeps all his spoils hidden away at his home in a massive basement vault, securely locked up at night to make it impregnable, is found shot to death, inside his own locked vault. There is no gun anywhere to be found, merely a single pin. . . .

Great outré stuff for a classic Golden Age mystery (though in violation of the rules of Father Ronald Knox and the Detection Club, a mysterious "Chinaman" lurks), which might have been just the thing for that earnest fellow Vernon Loder. In Jack Vahey's more up-to-date and sophisticated Henrietta Clandon tales, however, finical readers should rest assured that murder is something altogether more refined, a delicacy which can be served to polite society in the drawing room, along with buttered scones and tea. Just keep an eye out for arsenic and acid bon mots.

Inquest and *Power on the Scent*

INQUEST, the debut Henrietta Clandon detective novel, has as its setting that most fabled of locales in Golden Age mystery fiction: a house party at an English country mansion. The mansion in question is Hebble Chace, Wiltshire residence of Anglo-French Marie Hoe-Luss, widow of recently deceased English businessman William Hoe-Luss. It is said that William Hoe-Luss expired during a house party at his French estate, Château de Luss, from the accidental consumption of deadly death cap mushrooms; and now his widow intriguingly has reassembled all of the original guests from the fatal French house party for a second time, this time at Hebble Chace, with the addition of Hoe-Luss' English physician, Dr. Eric Soame, the narrator of the tale. When one of the houseguests at Hebble Chace falls to his death from an upper story window, after announcing his belief that there were no death cap mushrooms on the grounds of Château de Luss, the question arises: Did this person fall or was he pushed? Added to this question is another highly pertinent one: Was William Hoe-Luss actually murdered? Read on and find out in the novel which Dorothy L. Sayers hailed, when it was originally published in 1933, as "an attractive and promising piece of puzzle making."

Certain fictional Great Detectives, like Wilkie Collins' Sergeant Cuff and Rex Stout's Nero Wolfe, have famously had rather a nose for blooms, but in Henrietta Clandon's sixth novel, *Power on the Scent*, it is the murder victim—if victim of murder he is—who was a prizewinning grower of roses. When stockbroker Montague Morgan--renowned among flower fanciers as the originator of the "Rennavy Rose"--is found mysteriously dead in the garden at his rural residence in the English village of Malpertuis (pronounced Malpert), attorney William Power, familiar to Henrietta Clandon readers from three previous novels, is called into the case on behalf of his client, Morgan's dismal and disgruntled nephew Charles Sibbins, who would make an almost book perfect suspect in his uncle's death, if that death, as seems likely, indeed proves murder. For, Gertrude Stein notwithstanding, a rose is not always a rose—or, more exactly, a rose is sometimes something more than a rose, at least when that rose comes dusted with cocaine, like the prize specimen that was found in the dead man's lapel!

Power invites his good friends (and Clandon series characters) the Mercers, Penny and Vincy, insouciant husband-and-wife detective novelists who are ever eager for real life "copy," to Malpertuis to help him investigate the matter of Morgan's strange demise, which implicates as well beautiful widow Mrs. Davy-Renny and the several men who hovered around her, like bees to the most fragrant of flowers. Also on the scene are series professional sleuths Inspector Voce and Sergeant Bohm of Scotland Yard. With all this sleuthing power on the scent, murder surely will out!

Curtis Evans

CHAPTER I

Human beings, unlike eggs, are not more digestible when hard-boiled, Vincent often says. But he is old-fashioned, if cynical, and the modern fashion which awards praise and admiration to those who preserve an appearance of calm in the presence of bad morals, bad manners and bad art, does not appeal to him.

People who do not know Mr. Power wonder why Vincent and I admire him. It is easily explained. To continue the egg metaphor, you can't judge how long one has been on by the look of the shell. We knew that Power's apparent moral toughness was no more than a hard shell which covered a soft white.

For Power, in spite of his relentlessness as a pursuer of criminals, is a sound man. He is also a lawyer, and if a lawyer has no respect for the law he lives by, it is a sad thing. As a partner in a firm of solicitors, who on occasion deal with criminal cases, he undertakes some work more often dealt with by professional detectives.

He has been extremely successful, I must say, and as a result his firm have been consulted by various people who required defence, or asked to have investigations made to prove their own innocence, or other people's guilt.

After his successful investigation into the plague of poison-pen letters at Lush Mellish, he told us he was inundated with clients, but unfortunately, of a type he was not at all anxious to defend.

"I thought you fellows defended anyone," Vincent said to him.

Power grinned: "Only the worthy, my dear man," he replied. "Your wife knows me better than that."

"I do," I said, "I am ashamed of Vincie. His anxiety to be funny is no excuse for slandering members of one of the finest professions in the world."

"There," said Power, "that's a testimonial, Mr. Mercer, which would be perfect, if it wasn't so dashed sarcastic. Well, all I will say is that I haven't any sleuthing to do at the moment. When I have, I'll let you in on the ground floor, and you can put it in one of your books."

We saw him often enough during the next few months, but it was June in the following year before he was able to provide me with the promised material for a novel. Vincie wanted to do it, but as he was halfway through what was to prove later his most successful book: *Mine Eyes Dazzle*, I protested to Power, and edged my husband out.

We were sitting at home one evening, Vincie reading a novel he had to review, and myself darning one of his socks, when Power came in, greeted us cheerfully, and accepted a cigar. They were good cigars, my husband told him, and came from a famous author known as a good judge of everything but his own work. And they were the last he ever sent Vincie. They came to us just before the man's newest novel was published, and it was obvious later that he did not think the labourer had proved worthy of his hire.

"Still enjoying the common law, Power?" my husband asked him, "I mean to say, no really juicy cases for Penny here?"

Power grinned at me. He knows that my nickname is "Penny," and told Vincie once that it must be because I was wise.

"Well, I have, and I have not," he replied. "A suspended inquest is rather like suspended animation; it may end very soon, or come to life with a jump."

"Are you on the jury?" I asked.

"No. I don't quite know where I am, but it's not on the jury, Mrs. Mercer. The fact is that we represent the next-of-kin."

"Be definite!" Vincie said. "Next-of-kin to whom?"

"To a retired stockbroker, who passed away in his rural residence at Malpertuis (pronounced Malpert), Mercer. He had looked rather dickey for a month, but had not called in a doctor, or complained. Then he suddenly conked out. The local doctor didn't like the look of him. He hadn't attended him, you see, and did not feel prepared to sign the death certificate. So there was an inquest."

"What was his name?" I asked.

"Montague Morgan, aged sixty-five, suffering from osteo-arthritis in his left knee, which rather immobilised him, if you will allow me to be so military."

"Do you die of arthritis?" Vincie said.

"No; but sometimes you wish you could," said Power. "It used to be thought a form of rheumatism, but is really due to degenerative processes in the joint. Otherwise the gentleman's corpus appeared to be fairly sound."

Thankfully I finished darning the largest hole in a sock, and put my materials away: "There seems to be no good reason for killing a stockbroker," I murmured, "a financier, a share-pusher, yes; but not a stock-broker."

"Not an inside-broker, you mean," said Vincie. "An outside broker, or a bucket-shop proprietor, comes up high in the list of those-who-ought-to-be-killed."

"But why killed?" Power asked, with his head on one side.

"Do they suspect suicide, on account of the chronic disease he suffered from?" I asked.

"It has to be taken into account," Power replied, "but I admit that I think that's a mistake. He had retired, had plenty of money, a nice house and garden, a butler, a cook and housemaid, and was very cheerful to the last. He left no last message saying that he was going on to see if he could do better elsewhere."

"Possibly insured," I said.

Vincie shook his head: "My dear, a whitewashing verdict of suicide-being-merely-accident, does not legally compel the insurers to pay up."

"Apart from the fact that he was not insured," Power said brightly. "His house and furniture are, normally enough, but he had let his life policy run for many years, and then collected the surrender value. So that isn't it."

"Who is your client?" I asked.

"A nephew, Charles Gailey Sibbins, I understand. But he went to Africa last year to shoot a bongo, and is either still on its trail, or huffed by the beast itself—whatever it is."

"The bongo does sound predatory," Vincie agreed. "Meanwhile, did the first sitting of the coroner dig up anything relevant to the cause of death?"

"No. They sent several organs to the Home Office pathologist to dig into. He is still busy, as far as I know."

"I presume you saw the local people?" I said. "Did you visit the police?"

"Yes. I had a talk with Captain Hollick, the Chief Constable for the County, also the superintendent, who is a village constable writ large. I also saw the county's detective-inspector, a very superior bloke, of whom they are very proud."

"Hendon?" I asked.

"You ought to know better, Mrs. Mercer! They have only just burst on the official world, and will be sub-station inspectors, the Hendonites. No. Inspector Kay is a son of the late Colonel Hepsey Kay. He joined the C.I.D. in London, rose to be sergeant, got asthma, saw a specialist, and was told that one cure was a change of scene and air. He applied to Captain Hollick who had been a subaltern in the colonel's regiment, and was transferred to the county force."

"Did they like him?" said Vincie.

"They did. Believe me, country policemen are not so snuffy as people imagine about men of education and rank coming into their force. In fact the superintendent down at Malpertuis was inclined to boast of their phoenix. But why this anxiety to know all about the brood of country bobbies?"

"I was wondering if they told you anything?" I said.

Power took another of our *buckshi* cigars, and lit it.

"Not exactly. The only odd thing I learned came from the local G.P. He wondered if Mr. Morgan doped."

We both started. "Doped?" I said, "but surely there are ways of knowing that?"

"Yes, decidedly, but as none of the tests and reactions acted, that was why the doctor wondered."

Vincie laughed. "If there was nothing to prove it, it seems rather an idiotic suggestion for him to make."

Power puffed at his cigar for a moment or two. "H'm. He found some traces of irritation in the nasal passages. There was nothing to show that the dead man had been suffering from a cold. In fact, his household staff said that he boasted that he never had a cold."

"Then what?" said Vincie.

"Well, the G.P. had been a major, R.A.M.C., in the war, and had come in contact with some U.S.A. troops who had acquired the dangerous habit of snuffing snow."

"Cocaine?" I said.

"Yes. Our doctor wondered if Morgan had got the habit. In that case it might possibly be that the man had snuffed-out through it. But as I said there were no other symptoms to suggest dope. The police, naturally, sent Kay over to have a look-see. He found no drugs in the house, except a liniment called Ethidol, which you rub on, and a small box of zinc ointment, also a bottle of aspirin tablets, which sufferers from arthritis find relieves pain to a certain extent."

"Nominal aspirin, zinc ointment and liniment?" I said.

"No. Actual, Mrs. Mercer. They were analysed, and found to be what the labels said they were. So that cock won't fight."

"What about the state of the throat passages, Power?" my husband asked.

"Well, the mucous lining is more or less coterminous with that of the nose, Mercer," was the reply, "but a short length serves for the passage of food and drink, as well as air. Drink, liquid of any kind, would, of course, tend to wash off anything which might otherwise adhere."

"I see what you mean," I said, "but the doctor evidently suspected that the poison, if it was poison, was administered via the nose. It could be, I suppose?"

He smiled. "Yes, granted certain conditions. Say the dead man took snuff, which was mixed with a poisonous powder. In that case it would have to be a poison he could not detect in the snuff, either because he had an insensitive nose, or was one of those people who don't bother much about scents or flavours.

The soluble powder might be carried into the pharynx, and so downwards, I think. The snuff would be sneezed out."

"Then snuff is not soluble?" Vincie said.

"Not to any great extent, I imagine, if at all. Tobacco snuff certainly isn't, and medicated snuffs are generally prepared so that they stick to the mucus lining, to stop irritation. There was no sign of nicotine action, for the man did not smoke."

"People like printers, who are not allowed to smoke at work, often take snuff as a substitute," I said; "I've seen them."

"Quite. But no one ever saw Morgan snuff, there was no container for it, and if he snuffed regularly there would have been some staining in the nasal passages."

"I believe Mr. Power has something up his sleeve," I cried. "He has a sort of mock humble air that tells of discovery in ambush."

Our visitor looked hurt. "My dear Mrs. Mercer, I am the most candid man in London. It was not something up my sleeve, but something in Mr. Morgan's button-hole that provoked to wonder."

That beat us both, and Mr. Power went on, when we failed to connect that link. "Yes, he wore a rose in his button-hole. It was not more than a day old. The idea of a suicidal person decking himself out with flowers was another argument against the theory of suicide."

Vincie put down his own cigar, and looked thoughtfully at Power. "The idea, of course, is that Mr. Morgan sniffed at the rose, and involuntarily inhaled something which had been put upon it. What colour was the flower?"

"The white flower of a blameless life."

"I see. Then that suggests a white powder, soluble in liquid?"

"Not necessarily. Just as Whistler in the famous case said that a Symphony in F. was not all F.F. F—fool! No offence meant, of course. A white rose is not all white. Frequently, the centre, into which one dips one's proboscis, is pale yellow. And if there is any pollen in roses, it is there, it is there, it is there!"

"Have you got the rose?" I said, for it would be like Power to remove something he thought relevant to have a better look at it.

"No, I handed it to the local superintendent. Curiously enough, he is not interested in flowers. Most country coppers are. So I had difficulty in getting him to take and inspect it."

"But surely you only went down for the inquest?" I said.

"Yes, but when Morgan was undressed, his coat was hung up in the wardrobe. When I found that the doctor was up to snuff, I asked to see the coat."

"Pure nosiness, I suppose?" said Vincie.

"On the contrary, my dear fellow, the snuffer has no mercy on his coats or waistcoats. I had an idea the police might discover some grains or traces of snuff on the material of either."

"But they didn't?"

"No. Not on the clothes."

"Where then?" I asked.

"On the rose," said Power. "The superintendent then gave me a lecture on bee-keeping. It seems that he only regards flowers as bee-fodder. When I informed him that I was aware that bees fertilised flowers by carrying away pollen on their stamens—I beg your pardon—on their legs, and so on, I begged him to have the stuff analysed. When is pollen poison? roughly speaking. He thought me an ass, but buzzed the rose off to the Home Office fellow, all the same."

I felt quite excited now, for Mr. Power rarely speculates without some useful evidence to help his guesses. "What you have in your mind is the possibility that someone put poison on a rose, and Mr. Morgan sniffed it up?" I asked.

"On the face of it, that is the idea at present."

"If so," I said, "it should be easy to discover several things."

"And the first, O Wise Woman?" he said, with a little bow.

"Was Mr. Morgan in the habit of wearing a daily button-hole?"

"Yes, he was."

"A rose?"

"No. Or not always."

"Secondly, you have not mentioned a gardener."

"Daily from the village."

"Did Mr. Morgan grow white roses?"

"Malpertuis, Mrs. Mercer, for some reason not well known to me, is not a place where roses grow to perfection."

"Lack of clay," said Vincie.

"Lastly," I said, "where did the roses come from?"

"They were brought to the house by a maid, at ten in the morning. Mr. Morgan was found dead in the side-garden about half-past twelve. He had collapsed on a garden chair."

"Whose was the maid?" I asked.

"She was employed by Mrs. Davey-Renny."

"And who is Mrs. Davey-Renny?" Vincie asked.

"Ah," said Power, thoughtfully, "now you're asking me something."

CHAPTER II

WHEN you hear that you are "asking people something," it is tactful on occasion not to press for an answer.

"Purely rhetorical that question," Vincie said. "Nothing more."

"I admire your delicacy of feeling," Power replied, "the more so that I have no information about the young woman."

"Except that she is young?" I said.

"I saw her, and take her to be thirtyish," he murmured, "a very pretty thirtyish. She lives about two miles from Morgan's house."

"In the country then?"

"My dear Mrs. Mercer, if 'Fair Rosamond' came to life and wanted a fresh bower, she would undoubtedly have chosen 'Fairlawn Cottage' in the county of Loamshire."

"Remote and secluded, hemmed about with trees," Vincie said dreamily.

"I mention Fair Rosamond without prejudice," Power smiled.

"No one can, and no one does," I said. "Your lawyer-like tricks won't avail you here. Be honest and not insinuating."

"I was thinking of the qualities of a bower," he replied. "I saw the perfect one in Surrey in the course of an afternoon's drive. The owner was in the garden; large, raw-boned, wearing sandals and shorts! The horsehair with which a wren may line her building doesn't turn the affair into a mare's nest. What I wanted to explain is this. Fairlawn Cottage was originally built in a corner of Lord Bogan's park. In process of time it became surrounded by a thicket of silver birch—still 'fairest of the trees,' in spite of the Shropshire Lad's plea for the cherry."

"Obviously lawyers read poetry," Vincie said to me gravely, "but I suspect that Power was chiefly interested in the criminal side of the poetic proceedings."

"I want to hear about the bower," I protested. "A lovely little Tudor thing, ringed in by silver birches. Go on!"

"And hedges of yew, path-edgings of box, a macrocarpa maze, two herbaceous borders thronged with tall flowers."

"You might be editor for nursery garden catalogues," Vincie murmured. "Did you see all this?"

"No. I heard about it from Captain Hollick."

"So he has ventured in the maze?" I asked.

"Apparently. He and his wife called when Mrs. Davey-Renny arrived. But let me go on. There is a gate in the high wall of Bogan's park, and from that you wend your way across a corner of the park itself, and enter a wicket gate in a yew arch. And there you are."

"Now why all this?" my husband asked reflectively. "Is it relevant, or have you gone all poetic by accident?"

"It is relevant to a promise I made your wife," said our guest, "I have hopes that there is a story for her in this. I may be wrong, of course, but if not, local colour will be helpful."

"Vincie's jealous because I bagged the next story," I said.

"I am not jealous," Vincie replied. "My attitude is represented by that notice the Germans were said to have put up on the walls of one of their favourite Belgian ruins: *'Nicht ärgern nur wundern.'*—Do not be angry, only feel surprised. What troubles me is the omission of any reference so far to Mrs. Davey-Renny's roses."

"You heard that it was a bad district for them," I said.

"Mrs. Davey-Renny's roses?" said Power. "There, of course, I am at a loss. No doubt she has them."

"If she shares her treasures, she must have," Vincie said.

Irritating Mr. Power shook his head. "The idea of a woman sending roses to a man is so unusual that I boggle at it."

"In these sentimental, modern country-books a man with a new cottage often receives fragrant bouquets from local residents," I suggested.

"Ah," said Power, "but there are always spinsters of lavender fragrance, of indeterminate age, quaint speech, and no mission in the world except to provide novelists gone to grass with sentimental figurines."

"Mrs. Harrises in short?" Vincie said, "but I feel unusually deductive this evening, Power. I have an impression that Mr. Morgan's rose did not come from Mrs. Davey-Renny's rosarium."

"It struck me like that," Power replied. "I don't know a primula from a polyanthus, if indeed they differ at all, and roses only in connection with St. George's Day. At the same time, if Malpertuis is bad for roses, I thought Morgan's rose too good for Malpertuis."

"Mr. Power," I said, "reminds me of those sixth-form lads, who use obscure and involved phrases with a view to being thought either funny, or clever. Simply put, he wonders if the rose was a rich stranger."

Vincie nodded. "He boggled just now over a woman sending roses to a man. But one was sent. By the hyphened lady, he says, her maid being the bearer. Let us hear about the maid."

"I inquired about her, and, of course, I saw her at the inquest. She is a local girl aged twenty-five, engaged to the postman, not ill-looking, but not flighty. She is a good cook, and adores her mistress, who treasures her."

"I suppose the advent of the postman daily has resigned her to the quietness of her home?" I asked.

"That, and Mrs. Davey-Renny's good nature. At nine, Mrs. Davey-Renny has breakfast; at one, lunch; at four, tea; at seven, a light dinner. At eight, every evening if she wishes, and on condition—implicit but not on paper—that she is with the post-man, Mary is allowed to be absent till ten. As the postman is ardent and decent, and Mary a quick worker, who is also in love, she is generally out every evening."

"We come now to the exotic, what Penny calls the 'rich stranger rose,'" Vincie remarked. "Herrick has something to say of the shortness of human life coupled with rose-buds. As Mary took this one to Morgan about ten in the morning, which hints at a quick, breakfast wash-up, and a cycle, that rose either came from the Bower garden, or reached the Bower itself pretty late the previous evening."

"That's obvious. I saw the girl for a few minutes, and asked her about it. Her story is this. The day being warm, she left the house at eight to meet her Mercury, Sam Collins. Her mistress was then lying in the hammock in the side garden, which has a macrocarpa hedge nine feet high. She was reading *Trumpeter, Sound*, which she had asked Mary to bring out, and smoking a cigarette from a box Mr. Morgan had sent her. Mary returned at ten to find that her mistress had gone to bed. She went to bed. Next morning she found that there were some fresh roses in a vase in the drawing-room. As her mistress is very proud of her hands, does not garden, and never cuts roses, she took it that they were a gift. Mary never gossips. They say her fiancé does, so it is just as well. A garrulous postman, with a gossiping wife, would be a worse terror in the country than any fabled monster."

"The sixth-form lad will not construe!" Vincie said firmly.

"I see it's no good trying to impress you hard-boiled folk," Power observed with a sigh. "I mean that Mary asked no questions, and when her mistress gave her some shopping to do, she also handed her a rose from the vase, nicely packed up in tissue paper, and told her to give it to Mr. Morgan. Mary went."

"She handed it to the butler?"

"No, Mr. Morgan was limping past his garden-gate when she cycled up, and took it from her. That was all."

There was one point that still puzzled me. "Look here, Mr. Power, you represent the next-of-kin. Do you represent the interests of the late Mr. Morgan too?"

"Am I his lawyer? No. He transferred all his business, when he left London, to a Mr. Brown, who lives between Malpertuis and Baston, and has his office at the latter place. We represent Sibbins, whose father was a client of the firm sixty years ago. He is now dead. His son, hot on the trail of the bongo, is a bad hat, but a good shot. In Africa he is a hero to his gun-bearer; at home he is an extravagant, ill-mannered nuisance."

"Rich?" I said.

"No. His father was. The son wasted the substance in every foul way, and is now what is called a 'hunter'. It is really an American who wants the bongo, and Sibbins is to shoot it for him, and then photograph him sitting on its midriff."

"And now he'll have more money to waste," said Vincie. "Will it be much?"

Power looked doubtful. "As Brown has now disclosed the terms of the will, and the papers may publish it in the next day or two, I may say that Morgan left no more than forty thousand pounds. Of that sum, seven thousand five hundred goes to 'My friend Mrs. Davey-Renny'."

"No wonder she sent him roses!" I said, "even expensive ones."

"But that," said Power, wrinkling his nose in a way he has, "was the only rose she ever sent Morgan, as far as I can hear."

"There is a language of flowers, though I do not know if it applies to particular species, or the tribe generally."

"Let us return to the roses," Vincie suggested, "for this modern Borgia business interests me quite a lot. In the morning, Mary discovered roses. Obviously they had not been there when she left on the previous evening. If not, they had been culled in the garden, or brought by hand, between the hours of eight and ten."

"When Mary was away," Power agreed. "But Mary couldn't see what took place when she was away, apart from the apparatus of park walls, yew and macrocarpa hedges, and what not, inside the little silver ring of birches. And she made no secret of the fact that there might be callers to see her mistress during the summer evenings. *Honi soit. . .* was the motto of mistress and maid."

"Let it be ours," I said. "In any case it should not be difficult in a quiet country spot to say who were the lady's visitors. It's generally too easy."

Power agreed. "I gathered from Inspector Kay that he knew her."

"A policeman should know everyone in his manor," said Vincie.

Power crossed his legs, and looked delicately at the ash on his cigar, which was now creditably long and symmetrical. "Socially, Mercer, socially! It makes a difference."

Of course it did. Inspectors in the R.I.C. (which was a semi-military body, I believe) had a position in the society of their district, but inspectors of a County C.I.D. in England (unless they happen to be those imaginary Cambridge graduates, who jest with assistant-commissioners) might easily gain a black mark with their hierarchy, if they set up to invade the circles frequented by Chief Constables.

"Of course he is the son of a regular officer," Vincie said, "but we know that discipline is discipline, especially in places where they make a song-and-dance about precedence."

"He is about thirty," said Power, ignoring our protests, "clever, I should say, and decidedly attractive, but in some ways ingenuous."

"How did you detect that?" I asked.

"Like the man in *La Poupée*, his blush was like the rose," was the reply.

"You said that was white," Vincie remarked.

"Any rose, not the exhibit in the case, Mercer. It struck me that he might be in love with the lady."

"Evidently the service is pursuing its old way, to the dogs," I said. "If it had been the constable and the cook, it would have been in the old tradition. Didn't you say that the inspector went down to the country because he suffered from asthma when in town?"

Power glanced at me sharply. "I did. Is that a snapshot, or just conversational padding, Mrs. M.?"

Vincie and I exchanged glances. Mine had certainly been an idle question (if any question is really idle), and our wits were not sharp enough to get at the meaning of Power's strange remark.

"It was just decent curiosity," I said, after a pause, "but how like you to see a fly in the transparent amber of my conversation."

Power smiled. "Ah, now I can let my cigar go out in peace. That ash was getting on my nerves."

He laid down the cigar carefully in the ash-tray, the ash gently tipped off, and a thin blue spiral of smoke rose in the quiet air. Power put out a finger to point at this ephemeral spiral pattern.

"Does that suggest anything to a medical mind?"

"No mind is more provoking than one that enjoys scoring silly points," Vincie grumbled. "That means you, Power. A medical mind might think of nicotine, and imagine you were trying to tell us that Mr. Morgan was slain by snuff. But you have already said that he wasn't."

"Look again!" he said. "Has it no medical, or therapeutic, suggestion for your two great minds."

"A bronchitis kettle!" Vincie almost shouted. "Am I right, sir?"

"No, certainly not. You are 'warm' as regards the disease, cold in regard to the cure."

"Bronchitis," I murmured, "and cognate complaints? Mr. Power, it is asthma."

He grinned. "Why, I practically handed it to you. Yes, in my early days I had an uncle, and he had a stuff called Himrods. He burned it, and inhaled the fumes. I don't think it cured him. But he had it, and I remember. *Cannabis indica*, or Indian hemp, was another of his fancies. *Bhang*, as the anti-narcotic agencies call it. It made his heart dickey, and he dropped it later."

"Occasionally leads to mental derangement," Vincie supplied a fact, "I know the stuff. But is not likely in a sniff to slay a healthy stockbroker. So why drag in the asthmatic inspector."

"I'm not dragging him in, my dear fellow, I may have to drag him out. I may be quite wrong, but I have a vague idea that he was Mrs. Davey-Renny's visitor the evening before Morgan conked out."

We were both rather impressed, for Power rarely has vague ideas in our sense of the word, or, if he has, he does not often air them. He has them aired, and dried, and ironed out, to a certain extent before he passes them into verbal currency.

"Why should you think so?" I asked.

He smiled like the Cheshire cat when it began. "There was a rose-leaf on the back seat of his car, a fresh scratch at the base of his thumb, and a green-fly, scientifically known as an *aphis*, had died on the back-door handle."

"You're a picturesque liar, Power!" said Vincie.

"Quite so. I grant you that. Actually, it was the blush, conjoined with the fact that there were tyre-marks in the lane near Mrs. Davey-Renny's gate. To his shame, Kay drives an ancient bus, with the tyres of yesteryear, regrooved, high-pressure, unmistakable. There had been a slight shower the previous day, about four o'clock, one of those short and sharp affairs in summer which some people call 'sun-showers'."

"You said the inspector was ingenuous," I intervened. "Now you have made him out the complete idiot. He buys a bouquet, dopes a blossom, which the lady herself may very well put to her nose, inhale, and die."

Power got up. "I told you the man was in love. A man may be jealous. His motto may not be *honi soit*. If it is, he isn't jealous. But, from first to last, I do not suggest that Kay slew Mr. Morgan. I merely say that I may have to drag him out of the fumes of gossip which will eventually arise, if the coroner brings in murder."

CHAPTER III

I OFTEN feel that coroners are unnecessarily abused. They are, after all, human beings, with a certain amount of education, not dumb beasts of the field, who have no wish or right to get to the hearts of mysteries a little ahead of other people. It is true that they do not always recognise the basic principle of English law, which is that a man must be tried in some rigid way, and allowed to go free if any undue flexibility in the trial is detected. The fact that the man is guilty has nothing to do with it. Everyone should realise that justice is not the essential, or perhaps I should say justice out of leading-strings is not essential. Not only must the man be guilty, and the evidence prove him guilty, but even the indictment must be technically correct. It is because coroners sometimes forget these basic principles that they are regarded as men with low minds, and nosey tendencies.

Fortunately for the reputation of the coroner who presided over the Morgan inquest, he showed no desire to decide hastily who killed the stockbroker. He ordered an adjournment for a fortnight. Meantime, the police must get on with it.

The police did. Getting on with it is one of their chief virtues. But Inspector Kay was not in charge of the case. Captain Hollick gave him a week's overdue holiday, and called in Scotland Yard. Our friends Chief-Inspector Voce and Sergeant Bohm, professionally known as the "Cat and Kitten," who specialised in country cases, went down.

As a rule publishers are better read, and not seen. Authors in the flesh alarm them. I don't wonder, from what I know of our tribe. But mine is a fairly agreeable man, and since I began to sell well, he is not nearly so nervous. Women authors, he once told me, are dreadful, and sometimes terrifying. They want so much. They cannot be bluffed. They speak their minds. He says they rarely have nice minds, or wholesome thoughts. He did not refer to morality, but their habit of suspecting their publisher's accountancy, and their anxiety to know why all the advertising appropriation is not used for their own books.

As Vincie and I always spend much more than we have, I decided to see my man about the prospective book. I told him about it, added that I wanted local colour, found it expensive, and would he help us to camp out in Loamshire for a while? To be really redolent of the soil, it would be necessary.

The good man promised me an advance for a substantial sum. I love advances. The only trouble about them is that you have to deduct earned royalties from them afterwards. But you can't get away from snags in life; for there is always a catch somewhere.

A publisher who gave all his authors advances, and made no deductions afterwards, would be a most popular man. He would not last long, but I repeat that he would be immensely popular.

When I reached home, Vincie was tremendously pleased with me, and the prospect of a little holiday at Malpertuis, and, as he added, there is no better way to spur your publisher to frenzied effort on your behalf than to obtain a large advance. All publishers are rapacious, according to Vincie, except his own. He has something of an affection for him, which is strange enough.

Mr. Power does not often make a slip, but this time either he or the local doctor was at fault. He made up for this by writing and telling us so. It was just a short note, to remark that the poisonous powder dusted on the rose was of a narcotic nature. "Not large enough to have much effect, unless he was a terrific snuffer, and also had an idiosyncrasy against it," he added. "As you know, dosages which do not affect one person may have a fatal effect on another. Infants take doses of some poisons which would do no good to a grown-up."

"We do know what an idiosyncrasy is, thank you," Vincie said when he had read the note. "But does the man think that Morgan was a sybarite in his dubious pleasures? I mean to say, it seems ultra-luxurious to spread dope on flowers before you take it."

"Has he ever seen an anaesthetic administered in a children's ward?" I asked.

"My dear, he was a stockbroker, and a bachelor, not a surgeon," he replied, "and as for child addicts—"

"There was one famous anaesthetist," I said dryly, "who was remarkable in his successes with nervous children. As far as I remember, he put a little of the stuff on a flower first, and asked the child to sniff it."

"Very pretty indeed," Vincie agreed, "but I think we may take it that cocaine would have to be snuffed up in very considerable volume to kill a man, and unless it was a determined suicide, the idea is ridiculous."

"Did it occur to you how ridiculous the whole proposition is?" I asked, as if it had occurred to me days before—"I mean the powder on the rose?"

"Can't say that it did. It even sounds feasible, and actually the powder was found there."

"My dear boy," I protested, "I was darning a wicked hole in one of your socks the night Mr. Power came in."

Now my husband looked intelligent. "Ah, I see. The sock was whole once, and not so long before you took it to repair."

"Remember Power's metaphor about the horsehair and the mare's nest," I said. "Who put it there, and how, and where? The point here is the progression of the rose from X., the unknown visitor to Fairlawn Cottage, via Mrs. Davey-Renny, to the maid."

"Who was apparently handed the floral offering, as undertakers unnecessarily call it, fastened up in tissue paper."

"How else?" I demanded. "If I buy flowers in a shop, they are handed to me wrapped up in paper. Don't waste your mental strength on trifles, my man. The cottage is off a lane, not the main road, and the maid has a cycle. X., or Mrs. Davey-Renny, puts cocaine on a rose, in the form of powder. She hands it to the maid, who cycles off for two miles."

"What ho, she bumps!" said Vincie.

"She would," I said, "it is years since I rode a bicycle, but I dare any rider to deliver a charge of very fine powder, dusted on a rose, to a man two miles away."

"Perhaps she put the rose in a handbag."

"Power must see it in that case; it will be either nicely whitened, or perfectly clean. If the former, and the maid was not the murderess, she will explain how that came about."

Vincie patted me on the shoulder. "You are trying to establish the presumption that the rose was dusted after delivery."

"I am considering it. Meantime, I think we must see the place, and you can ring up the village post office, or an agent at Baston, which is the county town, and inquire for rooms surrounded with rose-buds, two rooms; board, including country cream and butter, honey, and things like that. If you offer four guineas a week, we may have strawberries as well."

Vincie rose at once. He is always glad of an excuse to move about. It keeps his brains fluid, he says, and the only trouble is that it requires fluid currency to achieve it often.

I settled down to work for a little, and when Vincie came back, I saw by his smile that he had clicked.

"I've got a lovely landlady and delightful rooms," he said, with an air of triumph, "also saved half a guinea each on your extravagant estimate. It is the Old Rectory, midway between Malpertuis and Fairlawn Cottage. Every rural luxury, a Guernsey cow kept."

"But how do you know that the landlady is lovely?" I asked.

"By her name," he said, "Mrs. Evadne Jennifer."

"Pretentious!" I said. "Also, if you read novels, you will see that all Jennifers are passionate, and dark Devonians. They get mixed up in intrigues."

"She sounded fiftyish, and past the age of intrigues," he replied. "Dark, maybe; the remains of a beauty, perhaps; but I never knew a woman given to affairs and passion who was so keen to inform a prospective lodger that the sheets were always aired, and no bright young society taken. I said we were married, neither bright nor young, but novelists on holiday. She said she had never taken writing folk, but did not mind them, especially as we were on holiday."

"What did she mean by that?" I asked.

"We might be temperamental when at work," he said. "Authors in the country, you see, often act like trippers on the Continent. Especially those authors who write, but aren't read."

"Can we go down to-morrow?" I asked.

"Any old time, my dear. I took the rooms from lunch-time to-morrow. Now carry on with your work, and I'll ring up old Power, and put him wise."

He did not get Power at once, but came back half an hour later, and stared at me. "Penny, it's a question if he *was* poisoned."

I jumped up. "What? Mr. Morgan?"

"Yes. Power is not very sure of his facts yet, but he gathers that the pathologist scouts the idea that the small amount of narcotic taken could have caused death. From internal evidences, he is inclined to think that a blow on the abdomen was the immediate cause of death. There have been cases where no external bruise was apparent."

"What a beastly idea," I said. "Then Morgan must have been killed in his garden?"

"Unless he fell over on something, say the iron of the garden-seat," Vincie suggested. "But that's the latest, anyway. I told Power we were going down, and he kindly remarked that he would be glad to consult with us at times."

"Which only means give me new material," I said. "I was just wondering if Mr. Morgan had good teeth."

We both tried to imagine ourselves rather gifted detectives at times (for we are as inwardly conceited as the rest of our tribe), and I could see Vincie's face light up with the pleasure of an amateur Holmes who has grasped the meaning of an allusion.

"If he hasn't," he replied, in the quiet voice one uses to suggest modesty when one is not feeling at all modest, "Power will certainly interview his dentist."

I felt faintly disappointed. When you hit on some rather subtle point it should be received with a flattering demand for elucidation. "What do you mean?" is a useful example of tact in auditors. Of course it may also cover gross ignorance.

"In any case he may prefer gas?" I said, still hoping that Vincie was thinking of something else.

"Even then, my dear," he replied in a husbandly voice, "apart from his dentist's foibles—and some do prefer nitrous oxide—he may have asked for it, on account of his idiosyncrasy, say, against cocaine."

"Is it cocaine nowadays?" I asked.

"Eucaine and novocaine are surely derivatives," he said, and spoiled my last hope of scoring. "What's the dangerous dosage, if he has this intolerance?"

"Under a grain, I think, has caused death," I said. "I believe there was once a case of a dentist who stopped a painful tooth temporarily with some stuff containing a twenty-fifth of a grain; which produced an illness, or rather, was suspected of it. The jury decided against it. In any case, Vincie, the pathologist would have known in this case if cocaine killed Morgan."

"Absolutely," he agreed. "Harking back to asthma, Penny, what about stramonium—datura-poisoning is an eastern habit. And it is smoked, I think, for asthma."

"My dear boy," I protested, "all the best detective stories make the criminal the least suspected person, but we can't jump on the poor inspector because of that. As for his complaint, which is now cured, there may be a dozen asthmatics in Malpertuis."

"We may hear of all sorts of hyoscine, or atropine, theories." Vincie ignored my protest. "But your idea about the folly of expecting powder to stick on a rose while it is taken two miles on a bicycle, blows that up. There remains the delicate matter of Morgan's tummy."

"Agreed," I said. "Considering the amount some people stuff, and continue stuffing, into it, we may say that it is a most useful and enduring organ. But it has its sensitive points. For example, when a man has a big meal, and takes a bathe afterwards, he may conk out as a result. Did Morgan prove British, or take a roll and a cup of coffee at breakfast?"

"I think a stockbroker would have eggs and bacon, and, perhaps, kidneys or haddock as well, not to speak of toast and marmalade—I may be wrong." Vincie shook his head, as if doubtful of that but determined to be fair. "That, however, is my impression. It's as firm as the belief that the literary aesthete is usually a good trencherman."

I nodded. "There is a current feeling that members of the Stock Exchange are hearty fellows. Did you ever see a cadaverous stockbroker on the stage? I haven't."

"Let's take it as an hypothesis," I added, "that Morgan ate a very hearty breakfast—"

"Wait a moment," Vincie said. "His arthritis, my dear?"

I laughed at the idea. "This acid in the system, darling, is all a part of the old theory of rheumatism and arthritis. It is the sad fate of some arthritics that they live well, look well, have a good colour, and a bad time, all at once. A bilious sufferer gets more sympathy because he looks yellow-green—I'm all for having Mr. Morgan as lusciously fed."

"Be it so. Now, he has had a big breakfast, and should really sit still, and upright, for a while. Instead, he goes into the garden with the high macrocarpa hedge. By the way, why is macrocarpa grown so extensively in Malpertuis?"

"Stick to the point," my husband replied. "The fact that he and the lady both favoured that quick-growing cypress is not relevant here."

"Very well then," I resumed. "He feels faint, or dizzy. He has a garden-chair made of battleship teak—"

"How do you know?"

"I feel it," I said. "Or else with one of those iron frames, which have projecting knobs at either end, and wooden slats to sit on. He falls across a knob."

Vincie got up. "I suppose it is possible. A jab in the tum after a big meal, what? Still, I think we had better wait till we get down to the place and scout round."

CHAPTER IV

MRS. Jennifer turned out to be rather more than fiftyish. She was very plain, but a woman of extreme refinement. She made us feel coarse and urban. But she spoke very little at any time, so her refinement did not trouble us so much as we expected at first, and she certainly was a marvellous cook. It was a gift with her, and a joy. She had two maids, but luncheon and dinner were both cooked by Mrs. Jennifer.

The Old Rectory was one of those large houses which afflict rectors, and destroy their wives. The present rector lived in a cottage near the church. It was a dream of a place, and had a fine garden. True to Malpertuis type, it was almost surrounded by—no, I will not use that hateful word again—a cypress hedge. We heard afterwards that the late squire had first imported the pest. Now it was commoner than privet, and three times as high.

"An admirable shrub for a forger, or counterfeiter's, garden," Vincie murmured, as we took our first tea in the Old Rectory grounds. "No one can see over or through, or under it. Yews are all right to surround dark deeds in poetry, but give me the—"

"Cypress," I said hastily.

"The cypress for practice," he added.

We had mentioned Morgan's death to Mrs. Jennifer. She admitted it; for death is refined, though the details are not. If we expected her to dilate ghoulishly on the subject, and so pick up some clues, we were disappointed. Let it be to her credit that while we were there she never gave utterance to any local gossip. For her, Mrs. Davey-Renny in her bower did not exist. She only once mentioned a local resident's name, and that was Mr. Pollaby. She said he was interested in trilobites.

That was one pond we could not fish in, but we were both determined to acquire local colour, and the man who came twice a week to do Mrs. Jennifer's garden knew all the secrets that hid behind cypress hedges.

He also knew Mr. Morgan, and Mr. Morgan's garden, giving us the impression that he had laid it out forty years ago.

"What? Not the garden in which Mr. Morgan was found dead?" I said, very guilelessly.

"Aye, that were the grass garden," he replied. "There be three in all, ma'am. There's the vegetable; there's the herbaceous, as you may call him; and the grass."

"Special grasses?" Vincie murmured.

"No, sir, not that I knows on. Cumberland turf were laid down for a gent who liked bowls. Hedge weren't more'n five foot high that time, but, lordy! he's grew since. Ten foot it'll be, trimmed atop."

"Mac—" Vincie began.

"Cypress," I suggested.

"One o' they cupressus," said the old man, "cypresses they call them for common. Four-foot thick it be, and you never did see such a hedge."

Vincie ultimately got the old man to make a sketch of the gardens, and it did prove his claims to have done a little landscape gardening.

As we sat and smoked in the sun, and inspected the plan of the gardens, we could see that there was one-half enclosed by the cypress hedge which might easily be hidden from the house. The arch in the hedge through which one entered the garden was at the end nearest the road. At the other side a two-foot terrace had been grassed, and two seats placed on it. I imagine a spectator or two might sit there and watch the bowls on the smooth turf below.

"I think," said Vincie, when we had looked our fill, "we might drag ourselves out for a walk. It is hot, but I am curious to know what, if any, windows there are on this side of the house."

He pointed to the line the old man had shaded in, and I went indoors for my hat. Then we left the garden, and with every appearance of leisureliness, went off to see the stockbroker's mansion.

In the High Street, we came, of all people, on the "Cat"—Chief Inspector Voce. He was dressed in striped flannels, looked very festive, and not at all official. He came on, looking at us with a growing smile. When we met, he raised his hat smartly, and opened his mouth.

"Think better of it!" Vincie said sternly, before any words could come from our friend. "You were going to suggest something about the vultures gathering together, weren't you?"

Voce grinned. "Nothing so rude, sir. How are you, madam? The birds were pheasants last time, I think. Now, a remark about pheasants would be more like me."

"Golden pheasants," I said, well aware that he was referring to the murder of a neophyte shot, and popular author, with which we had been mixed up. "A much more pleasant simile."

"You were guests last time," said Voce, accepting a cigarette from my husband's case, "if I remember right."

"Meaning that we are now unauthorised snoopers?" said Vincie. "No, we just happened to hear from Mr. Power that there was a nice boarding- I mean paying-guest place, the Old Rectory. But I forgot to ask how is Sergeant Bohm?"

"Splendid," said Voce. "He will be pleased to see you both again I am sure. By the way, Mr. Mercer, the house is down the second turning to the right."

"What house?" I asked innocently.

"Mr., the late Mr. Morgan's"; he raised his hat, and added: "I expect I shall see you both again."

"Is that the man who—" Vincie began to call after him.

"That's the one, sir," he called back. "You'll easily find it."

We strolled on, and followed his directions. We might have expected to find Sergeant Bohm there, and we did. He was in the front garden, and when I called to him, he turned and beamed, as if we were a most welcome sight.

"Fancy seeing you and Mr. Mercer here," he said in a most unconvinced voice, and shook hands over the gate.

"Mr. Voce sent us round," I remarked, turning the direction to the best advantage, "we were asking how you were."

"In the pink, ma'am," he replied, opening the gate. He looked quite nice in a navy-blue suit, and velour hat. "I suppose he thought you might like to see the garden."

Vincie has a bias against bowls, but I assured Bohm that he was a fervent player. "Skipped something, or somewhere," I added.

Bohm plays bowls in his spare time in North London, and grinned. "I believe there was a green here one time. But it hasn't been played on for years. It'd be slow."

"We never know when we may not move into the country," I said.

"That's so, ma'am," he replied with a knowing air.

"And this house may come into the market," said Vincie.

"Come along, then," said Bohm, "I was just going back to the Red Crown, where Mr. Voce and I are staying, but I can spare a few minutes."

Followed by us he led the way down a path, and through an arch in that formidable hedge. We crossed what had been the bowling-green, and mounted to the grassy terrace. And there, sure enough, were two battleship-teak seats.

"This is the seat on which the poor gentleman was found collapsed," he said. "Fell across it like."

Vincie nodded, and went back a little. "Look, Penny," he said, with a gesture, "you can just see a bit of the house over here."

I looked in the direction indicated. Bohm came over and smiled.

"Very private this place, sir. Can't be seen from the ground-floor windows, of which there are two, and the only bit of the upper wall has no windows."

"When you've finished thought-reading, Mr. Bohm," I said severely, "I should like to know if the house is empty."

"It will be this afternoon, ma'am," he replied cheerfully, "I had to have a little chat with the butler, cook, and parlourmaid, but they go at three."

Assuming quite correctly, but unnecessarily, that this was the only part of the garden we wished to see, he led us out again to the gate, merely stopping for a moment in the archway to show us that there was another narrow break in the hedge at the far corner.

"Gives on to the vegetable garden, which has a gate to the lane behind, Mr. Mercer," he remarked.

"Wasn't it sad about the poor man?" I said, as we reached the road. "I suppose you have both had to be very busy. By the way, did you know that Mr. Power represents an heir or something?"

"Yes, ma'am," he said simply, "I believe he has to come down to-night to some sort of conference with the other lawyer—Mr. Morgan's."

"How delightful," I murmured. "Quite like old times, sergeant. Now, my husband and I are going to think hard, and see if we can help."

"That will be nice, ma'am." He saluted, and observing that he was sure to run across us again, went on his way to the inn where he was staying.

"That settles it," I said, as we looked after him. "He and Voce are still on the job, so it isn't accident or suicide. I wonder who could tell us if Mr. Morgan did live fatly."

"Power," he said. "I hope he is refined enough for Mrs. Jennifer. I am sure he will come to us."

The gift of prophecy was evidently on Vincie that day, for when we reached the Old Rectory again, Power's car was on the gravel before the door, and Power himself was in the driving-seat, preparing to drive it round to the garage. He greeted us with enthusiasm.

"Ready for the legal conference?" Vincie asked, a few minutes later.

"I knew you'd know," said Power. "You're right. I dine this evening with my legal friend, and confer after. I have had tea on the way, so when I've put the bus to bed, we can all sit in the garden and have a chin-wag. Seen Voce yet?"

"Voce and Bohm, and the fatal green," I replied. "Do hurry! We are very keen to hear the latest."

"Has Mrs. Jennifer approved of you?" Vincie asked, as Power started the engine.

"So far as I know. I didn't mention that I knew you," was the reply. "It may make a difference, but I'm not proud."

When we were all sitting in the garden ten minutes later, and I was sipping some of Mrs. Jennifer's home-made lemonade, my husband asked the question on which we laid so much stress.

"Morgan was a full-blooded man—did himself well, and so on?"

"So I heard from the doctor. He was not fat, just comfortably filled out for his height. But he was a gourmet after his fashion. A sedentary life, plus most of its good things to eat, tends to adipose. In his case, it didn't."

"I can see him at breakfast," I said, half closing my eyes. "He has bacon and eggs, a devilled kidney or two, a bit of fish. He tops up with toast and marmalade—Oxford marmalade."

"Too bitter," Power said, "I gather that he had a sweet tooth."

"Then you have been questioning the cook too?" Vincie said.

"No, but if I had, why 'too'?"

"Bohm was, to-day."

Power laughed. "I was in the house and about once, but I had no pow-wow with the cook. I saw her coming out to empty stuff she was clearing away. Now what goes out of a house by the back door, is often more interesting than what goes in by the front. The hasty criminal still inclines to let the local refuse destructor do its work."

"If you ever tried to destroy letters or papers in an ordinary grate, you'd understand," I said. "And what came out?"

"Half a dozen circular boxes of thin wood; chip stuff, you know, with labels atop."

"Preserved lemon and orange slices?" Vincie guessed.

"Turkish Delight," said Power, "or what passes for it. Now what do you know about that?" he asked me with a grin.

"It ruins your clothes," I said, "that is, if you are greedy. Don't tell me, Mr. Power, that the dope smugglers have found a new way to deliver their goods?"

"Throw away the sweet glutinousness within, and collect the white powder?" our friend mused. "H'm. Talking of white powder, I hear now that the chemical traces of dope found contained chemical traces of boric powder."

"What does that suggest?" Vincie asked.

"Adulteration, my dear fellow. As the addict is avid and finds it hard to get the stuff, and the seller finds it expensive, and also hard to get, he often bulks it out with some adulterant. Which is a form of cheating that has its good points."

"What are they?" I murmured.

"Lower strength of the drug, and smaller effect on the ass who snuffs it, Mrs. Mercer," he said.

Vincie smiled. "To get back to the boxes of delight. Penny's suggestion is ingenious."

"Very. I'll tell Voce to try to retrieve some of the boxes. This is Tuesday. I am afraid they will be ashes by now—ashes of delight. How poetical! Meantime, my inferences did not extend so far. I asked cook who ate the stuff, and she said Mr. Morgan had been very fond of it. He was one of those people who defy indigestion and eat between meals."

"Then my idea still holds good," I said. "If Morgan was a Turkish Delight addict, and someone dusted his sweetmeats with cocaine, it would account for his not being so well of late; also, if you allow the idiosyncrasy, for a small dose having topped it off, and slain him."

"As a novelist, of course, you have imagination," Power admitted, "but the analyst who succeeded in finding little in little would surely have found traces of the finely-powdered sugar as well."

"True," said Vincie, looking at me reproachfully, and lighting another cigarette, "if the Turk drank brandy as a connoisseur does (and of course the Prophet forbade him to drink it at all), he might warm the liquid with a palm round the glass, and inhale the bouquet before he sipped. But I do not think that Turkish Delight is sniffed, even in Anatolia."

"Very well," I said, "tell Voce anyway! Meantime, powder so finely precipitated as that on the sweet, or the rose, does get diffused about when you sniff it, or open a box. If I were Voce, I should have all the man's clothes sent to the Home Office person, and also collect all the dust and stuff that could be scraped off the grass by the suit."

"Some trouble," said Vincie.

"Scotland Yard never makes a trouble of anything," Power remarked, "I give them the highest marks for that. Dear old Voce has already had your brain-wave—which he negligently calls routine stuff—and sent the suit to be beaten and shaken by an expert. What the fellow at the other end will make of all this valiant dust, I know not. But you can bet your next week's laundry that it will keep some microscopes busy for a while."

"I suppose," Vincie observed, "that that sort of scientific beating and sorting will bring things out of a suit its owner thought long dead and gone?"

"It will. I saw the operation once, and the snows of yesteryear, notably so prone to vanish, were nothing to the traces which returned."

"Meanwhile, why have a rose, if there was an easier means of conveying cocaine to the palate?" He asked.

"And who would have access to cocaine?" Vincie added. "A dentist?"

Power shook his head. "My dear fellow, you must be careful that you don't libel anyone here. Not intentionally; not at all. The dentist is a prominent member of the local dramatic society. He has curly, fair hair, and big blue eyes, an ideal *jeune premier*. He is unmarried, twenty-six, and is said to be rather *épris* of Mrs. Davey-Renny."

CHAPTER V

MRS. Jennifer excelled herself that evening at dinner. Imagine a delicious soup, sole from Dover, *petits poussins*, and a trifle which was an epic, all included at four guineas a week.

Power congratulated us. "You are in clover," he said. "The last test is coffee. In America they use cream. Shall we—shall we, have cream?"

The answer was yes. Power sipped his nectar with a dreamy look. "This lovely cream might have been mated with unlovely coffee," he said, "or excellent coffee, defiled by mere milk, might have been the alternative."

Chief Inspector Voce was reputed by hardened criminals to turn up when least expected. I have a feeling that our hostess would not have approved of policemen as visitors, but she had gone out the moment she made the coffee, and the maid announced our friend, and made no bones about showing him into the drawing-room where we now sat. His striped flannels certainly gave him an air.

Power promptly ordered another cup to be brought. "Curse you, Voce!" he said, when our visitor was seated, "someone will go short of a cup of this marvellous coffee. Couldn't you wait till we have guzzled all the cream?"

Voce looked at him sombrely. "We policemen have few enough pleasures, sir."

"That's right. Be plaintive!" Vincie observed. "There is no more tear-inducing sight than a copper sitting up to beg."

The cup came and was filled, and Voce sipped and rolled his eyes.

"Ah, that's coffee, sir!" he said unctuously.

"It *was*," said Power. "Take it easy! You won't get any more."

But the cup was empty, and Vincie passed his cigarette-case. "Now, Chief Inspector," he commanded, "what's the news? Your flair does not extend to aromas in a house off the roadway."

"No, sir, but I'm glad I came. I heard Mr. Power was here, and I wanted to—"

Power jumped up. "Great Scott! The fascination of you young people! I was to dine with my confrère, and here I am, sitting idling. My fellow lawyer will have me disbarred."

"But—" said Voce.

"Tell your tale to our friends," said Power, "It will filter to me when I get home, but—"

The maid entered suddenly. "You're wanted urgent on the phone, Mr. Power."

Power thrust her aside, and darted out, the door closed behind both, and Voce looked at us.

"Looks to me as if the coffee is all I'll get this evening."

"And the pleasure of our society," I said. "Apart from that, we have lots to tell you. I have a solution of the poison difficulty, and my husband is anxious to put you on the clue of the snuff-stained lapel. Please don't go!"

Of course he didn't want to go. Your policeman likes a chat and a smoke in his leisure hours. Vincie also explored the coffee-pot, while I shook the cream jug and discovered enough for another cup.

"The gluttonous lawyer has left you his heir," I said, as I poured it out, and handed it to Voce.

"While you sip that—for it really is the last, I'll explain my theory about Turkish Delight."

Voce's wondering eyes surveyed me over the rim of the cup for a moment, then he gulped, put the cup down, and used his handkerchief politely.

"Almost forgotten what it's like," he said in a deep voice. "Lemme see. Ah, I know."

"Then I don't need to labour the powder," I said. "Lots of it, smeary and sticky, unless you're careful."

"That's right. Well, Mr. Power discovered that Mr. Morgan had a weakness for it. I at once deduced either narcotic or arsenical dust, but he seemed to think it unlikely."

Voce did not turn the idea down at once, he nodded his head twice, and replied reflectively. "It's an idea, anyway. And like all ideas it has two sides. Take it you've eaten Turkish Delight with these chemical trimmings on it voluntarily, you are anxious to dope yourself, or poison yourself, or you have no sense of taste. That happens! I read a detective story some years ago about that. Atropine was the poison. But suicide by arsenic is rare, and nasty. Cocaine, I think, would taste bitter. A man with a sweet tooth would hardly like it."

"Suppose," I said, "that the general sweetness of the confection toned that down, and the eater took it to be a new flavour, to give it piquancy?"

"Or that the boxes came from a dope pedlar, who found it a good way to avoid the police?" Vincie asked.

Voce smoked again, and looked unconvinced. "The pathologist does not think that he was poisoned."

"In any case you have to account for the trace of cocaine?" said Vincie.

Voce did not deny it, but he remarked mildly that he had noticed that two of Mr. Morgan's teeth had been recently removed. "I had a talk with the young chap who did them," he added conversationally. "I suppose gas extractions are not so common as they were? was what I asked him."

"Oh, I think they are," I said.

"So did he, Mrs. Mercer. I know some dentists prefer it, and some don't mind either way. He said, for ordinary extractions, he gave an injection; for certain others, on request, gas; and for long ones ether. That is common practice. What did he give Mr. Morgan, if he ever pulled out a tooth for him?"

"Then he wore a plate?" Vincie asked.

"A small one, with one tooth more recent than the others. Well, my dentist said gas. Why? Because Mr. Morgan told him that he had had an injection for his first tooth extracted, and had felt funny. The man who gave it said it was an idiosyncrasy."

We exchanged smiles.

"We thought of that," I remarked. "Which makes it all the more odd that he should snuff up some."

"Voluntarily," said Voce.

"Admitted," I said. "There was the rose, of course."

Vincie ventured to fish. "You know what gossip is, Voce. In the circumstances, don't you think it hard lines that Mrs. Davey-Renny should have tried to say it with flowers?"

Voce grinned. "It's hard to see how powder could stick on a rose, or the sender expect it to. It might, of course, be brushed on as a solution and dried *en route*. I have heard of people putting an aspirin in water to freshen, or preserve, cut-flowers, but I don't know what effect a solution of cocaine would have on the petals."

"But she would be an ass, even if she knew the secret, to send her maid with the rose," Vincie said.

"Not necessarily," Voce replied. "It was Mr. Power's gift for seeing things that put us on to it. As a rule, you don't examine a dead man's buttonhole. And she would know that. No; her trouble, as you surmise, will be gossip. Let her be pure as snow, and so forth, and half the population will wonder audibly why she sent Morgan a rose; who she is; who her friends are; and so on. By the time her name is removed from the roll of suspects, it will be so covered with mud that it will be illegible. Unless we can do something," he added doubtfully.

Vincie gave him another cigarette. "Too true. Who is she? Now isn't that the source of many of the troubles of life in small communities? And none of us," he looked hard at Voce, "knows who she is."

"Ah, that's the question, sir."

I smiled at our guest. "Vincent put that clumsily," I said. "Of course we are both dying to know. But we must not expect you to dole out inside information to us."

"I heard someone say once that Expectation was the little brother of Hope," Voce murmured.

"Well, I don't deny we have a bit on his little brother too," I admitted. "I suppose it is all bound to come out."

"Yes, one time or another, and I am happy to say that there is nothing very secret about her at present. What will cause trouble locally is the fact that some Malpertuis people are in love with her, and called at times at her cottage. It would have been wiser if she had taken an old house in the High Street."

"Instead of behind high hedges," I suggested. "It isn't fair to potential neighbours to have none. And in the town the visitors could not have called without being spotted, recognised, and timed. Disappointment at not having seen things will inevitably add gall to the gossip."

"There is no limit to what people will say and think," Vincie remarked virtuously. "Even the local inspector's holiday may be a focus for gossip."

Voce shook his finger at my husband. "Now, sir, I've been long enough at this game to know what I may tell, and what I can't. Before he went away, acting on Mr. Power's advice, he was asked about those roses. And he was frank. Policemen are—with other policemen. It's no shame to a good man and decent officer if he falls in love. He admitted that he drove into Baston the day before Morgan's death and bought a dozen fine roses. Eight were red, four white."

"Something symbolical about that, perhaps?" I suggested.

"That, madam," said Voce with a formality which was redeemed by the twinkle in his eye, "is outside my manor. All I can say is that he gave the lady a bunch of roses."

"Since you know what you can tell," said Vincie impudently, "have you interviewed her?"

"Yes. She said that she had started life—that is business life—as a secretary-typist in Mr. Morgan's office. After five years there, she married a stockbroker. He was a friend of Morgan's. He and she lived in Surrey, thirty miles from town. She lost sight of Morgan who, oddly enough, seemed to be annoyed that his friend had robbed the office hen-roost."

"Though he didn't want to marry her himself?" I asked.

"No. There is no suggestion of tender passages between them. He was either a dog-in-the-manger, or she was a superlative typist. They are, I hear, rare in the City."

"We are vastly interested," said Vincie. "Carry on."

"At that time," said Mr. Voce, looking demurely at the floor, "Mr. Morgan was a rose-grower; an amateur, but an amateur of parts. He was a connoisseur. His roses, or his gardener's roses (it is often the same thing), were his pride, and others' envy."

"What a nice literary style Voce has!" Vincie murmured to me. "'The fairest roses on the border's side, were others' envy, and their owner's pride'."

"He was not only a grower, and a connoisseur," said Voce calmly, "but an inventor, or originator, or whatever you call a man who produced a new rose. The 'Rennavy Rose' is, I think, a proof that though he did not visit the married couple, he became reconciled later to the idea of their marriage."

"Davey-Renny='Rennavy'," I said. "So that was what the rose was?"

"Yes. When the lady's husband died two years ago, Morgan went to the funeral. He had just come here, and apparently recommended the place for her retirement. In fact, he took the cottage later on her behalf, and has since visited and been visited by her."

"But not sub-rosa?" said Vincie.

This was too obvious a pun to amuse either of us. Voce ignored it. "The upshot of my interview was this: Mrs. Davey-Renny confirmed the inspector's story of the bunch of roses. When he had gone, she put them in water. As she arranged them, she noticed four 'Rennavy' roses. She did not want to spoil the gift, so just selected one next day, and sent it to Mr. Morgan."

I saw the point at once. "She was returning the compliment," I said.

"That's all," he agreed. "He appreciated the reminder of past times, and put it in his button-hole."

"All very sensible and normal," Vincie remarked, "but one thing does make me wonder. That a gardener, a noted grower and connoisseur of roses, should move to Malpertuis, where they don't grow well, and then give up the hobby, which was also a gift, is strange."

"Not a bit of it." Mr. Voce poured deserved cold water on him. "It's a fact that people who do a thing supremely well sometimes get tired of it. They say there is a trout fisher in Hampshire so clever at it that success bores him stiff. And as for your second point, it has even less substance in it. A common grower, of common or garden roses, is glad to have a few ordinary blooms to show. A man like Morgan would as soon try to grow roses where the flowers would be inferior, and undistinguished, as a billiards professional would be to spend his time practising on a Gilbert and Sullivan table."

I must say here for us both, that neither Vincie nor I really expected to get ahead of Voce in the matter of clues and their interpretation. After all, the business of a detective has to be learned, and as Mr. Wallace's late secretary very wisely wrote somewhere, the amateur author has never solved, and is never likely to solve, actual crimes. Frankly, Vincie was out to help me, and I was engaged on getting material for the "story" Power had seen in the death at Malpertuis.

We had no illusions either about Voce forgetting his professional oath and either giving away secrets he shouldn't, or imagining that we could act as skilful auxiliaries, unpaid. We might get to know something which was new to him, but we would get nothing from him which Scotland Yard desired to be kept secret. And he knew we knew that, which made for the pleasantest relations.

"Did it ever strike you, Mr. Voce," I suggested, "that when we stand up on a platform with many others, we have an idea that all eyes are concentrated on us?"

"I do myself," he said genially, "there's always a danger of mistaking what I might call the focus of attention."

"Now that bromides are seemingly fashionable," Vincie added gravely, "what about this one? When there are two or three mistletoe bunches hung about, don't expect to find all the kissing under one."

"Very true, sir," said Voce, rising to his feet. "There is a tendency to find the lady, even in sharping circles. We won't be led astray by that."

When he had gone, Vincie remarked that these detectives were rather like some of the old regular generals. You had an idea they were not too bright and brainy, before you got to know them.

I quite agree. Men like Voce are not only full of common sense and very sharp in the uptake, but nowadays, at least, they are surprisingly well educated.

"Evidently he hasn't made up his mind that Mrs. Davey-Renny or her suitors are actually involved," I said. "Is the rose a red herring?"

"Or a white lie?" said Vincie.

I smiled. "That's not so bad, my boy. But I see you have the same feeling about it. So I won't praise you any more."

CHAPTER VI

WE ARE all snobs at heart, but some of us wear our hearts on our sleeves. Mrs. Davey-Renny, partly because she was a stranger, by country standards, and partly because she was a friend of a retired stock-broker, had never been taken up by the first circles in Malpertuis.

But she had, in a surprisingly short time, attracted the attention and secured the friendship of half a dozen men. There was the dentist, Mr. Edwards; Mr. Morgan, now dead; Inspector Kay; Mr. Paul Bone, a local artist; Mr. Everard Jolson, a bank manager who had come into money from a wealthy client and promptly retired; and Mr. Tressy Withers, who lived in a fine old house in the High Street, and was supposed to gamble largely. He was the handsomest, and perhaps the least encouraged, of Mrs. Davey-Renny's acquaintances.

Mr. Power returned at ten. He had had his talk with the other lawyer. But the news he had to tell us was more intriguing than we expected. It concerned his own client, young Sibbins, who had addressed a letter, by accident or design, not to his own lawyer, but to the solicitor who had Mr. Morgan's affairs in his hands.

"In short," Power added, when he had mentioned this, "it seems that the young waster has been in England for some weeks."

"Leaving the bongo to its fate?" I asked.

"Apparently. He writes in to ask when he can get the money. Mr. Family Lawyer is very indignant. I gather that he wrote a very stuffy letter back, and will certainly not try to hurry probate through. I got the blighter's address—a hotel in Piccadilly. I shall want to see him and so, I think, will friend Voce."

"On the question of motive?" I said.

"And a hotel in Piccadilly for one who rarely had a bean. But now I am going to bed. To-morrow morning I see Mrs. Davey-Renny."

"You do?" we cried together.

He nodded. "My confrère has given me a letter of introduction. He is uneasy. His fine, old, fruity firm have never had the remotest connection with a crime. A case which may hint at an intrigue, past, present, or to come, makes him tremble. He does business for the best people."

"Do the best people never have sordid intrigues?" I asked.

"Very frequently," said Power, "but divorce only becomes squalid when the parties thereto are of no social importance. It's narrow-minded to decide that peers must be monogamous. But the Commons must mind their p's and q's. Joking apart, the old boy said Mrs. Davey-Renny would like to see me. As she is easy to look upon, I am anxious to see her. Good night."

"I'm ready to bet," said Vincie, as we got ready for bed that night, "that Sibbins did not kill or slay his uncle."

When I thought it over I rather agreed with him. "No. He's too much in character, my dear," I said. "All right for a novel, but as life is never like novels, I bar him."

Vincie inspected a growing bald patch on his hair-brush. "Quite. A waster and ne'er-do-well, heir to a rich uncle, been hunting big game in Africa, mysteriously returns to England when his uncle is murdered, and after taking up quarters in an expensive hotel, writes to ask when he gets the wages for his crime."

"Don't scowl, Vincie," I said, "you bought that brush exactly five years ago. I told you it was getting weary. As for the heir, if it turns out that he hasn't got a perfect alibi for the date, we can be sure he is innocent."

Next morning Vincie, finding that Power had risen with the lark, and vanished into thin air, set out to wander about and collect impressions for me. I myself, forgetting that I was supposed to be on holiday, got out my portable, and tried to begin a sheet of data I could use later on.

"CAUSES AND CONTACTS AT MALPERTUIS."

Rosa Rennavy.—Morgan's button-hole, and original production, was bought in a mixed bunch by Kay (inspector local C.I.D.), given to Mrs. Davey-Renny by him, sorted out and sent, per maid, to Mr. Morgan.

Question.—Rose dusted with cocaine?

Cocaine adulterated boric powder?

Mr. Morgan.—Rose-grower and expert, once. Hearty eater, and fond of Turkish Delight. Item, powder thereon. Senses of smell and taste intact?

Question.—Idiosyncrasy against cocaine?

A. Yes, on evidence of dentist.

Edward Smith.—Dentist on occasion to Mr. Morgan. In love with Mrs. Davey-Renny.

Question.—Jealous of Inspector Kay, or Morgan, or both?

Question.—Do dentists use or obtain cocaine in powdered form? We may cut out novocaine or eucaine, and similar synthetic stuff, since cocaine was found.

Question.—Would a dentist, if he had crystals or powder, buy stuff adulterated with boric powder?

A.—Unlikely unless he was peddling dope, which is unlikely too.

Inspector Kay.—Obviously a suitor, but not necessarily involved. A man of superior type for his post, but even superior people may be jealous.

Question.—Did he suspect the former relations of Morgan and the woman with whom he was in love?

Here I stopped and had a faint passage at arms with Mrs. Jennifer. There was no trouble about my typing but (in more refined language) I was given to understand that policemen coming to the house gave it a bad name. I replied wooingly that policemen vouched for a house if they visited it, that Mr. Voce was not a policeman proper (and certainly not improper), but a big noise from Scotland Yard.

"You are, of course, aware that the Assistant Commissioner is often a gentleman," I said. "Even your inspector here is the son of a colonel in the regular army, and Mr. Voce is much higher up than he. In fact," I lowered my voice and added, "you have never heard of General Voce?"

"Never," said Mrs. Jennifer, and, of course, I haven't either. But I could see, by her expression, which was softened, that the progression: Inspector, Colonel's son, Chief Inspector, General's son, seemed right and natural.

On the maternal side I was not far wrong, as Vincie said later, for Mrs. Voce had been a general in the household of a nice family in Ealing. His father, and that is where I was wrong, had been a sergeant in X division.

Vincie came back in an hour or two, and looked at my notes. "I think that's a good point about the commercial cocaine," he said; "I imagine few dentists now use cocaine, and if they did, it would hardly be powder; soluble crystals, I think."

I marked that answer provisionally. "Did you hear anything?" I asked.

"Well, it seems the refuse-bins would be cleared the day the cook put the boxes in one," he replied. "But you must remember that the man was dead before that. If there was anything nasty about them, you would think he would have cleared them out one by one during his lifetime. What puzzles me is this: if there is the faintest idea that Morgan was buying dope for himself, or for others, and getting it in these sweetmeat boxes, would he just tell the servant to tip 'em in the bin?"

"Did he?"

"So I hear. She often threw these empty boxes into the bin, and as you know, they're generally covered inside with this clinging white powder."

"It is quite possible," I suggested, when I had thought it over. "A maid takes stuff to the ash-bin. Do you think she stops to examine it, or to lick the stuff that clings to the boxes? The day when Dickens's 'Marchioness' collected orange-peel to infuse a drink from are gone."

He nodded. "H'm, yes. It would be as safe a way as any, while, if he was seen taking precautions to destroy the boxes, it might arouse suspicion."

"Meanwhile, all the containers have been incinerated?"

"Yes, I met Bohm, dear thing, and he had made inquiries at the refuse department."

"If this had been a detective story," Vincie added, "a convenient cat, rat, or dog, would have licked the boxes, and fallen dead. I always love the ones where someone pours out a saucer of milk, and the domestic cat goes all rigid."

"What is Bohm doing about it?" I asked practically.

"He has been inquiring at the grocer's, and sweet-shop. They neither stocked nor ordered that high-class kind. It seems that Mr. Morgan got it through a Greek importer in town."

"Why Greek?"

"I think the Greeks still do some of the business of Turkey," he said. "And that bit of Asia Minor is rather given to the dope racket."

"Is Bohm following that up?"

"Yes. He telephoned S.Y. to-day for inside information about the importer. Since Morgan got it from an importer, not a retailer, Bohm thinks the man may have been a friend or business acquaintance. As a rule wholesalers won't supply private individuals."

"Have you heard anything about the flies round the honey-pot here?" I asked. "The male ones?"

"A spot here and there. Everyone is anxious to talk about the case, and everyone has heard that you and I dined Power, and had a visit from Voce last night."

"Evidently," I said, "Mrs. Jennifer didn't think it quite nice of us to have a tame policeman on the premises. Lowered the tone, I think was the word."

"It's a marvel to find a good cook so refined," Vincie murmured. "I would have expected to find a conjunction of moral and spiritual and physical attenuation. Why didn't you say Voce collected Trilobites?"

"I gave her the impression that he was the son of a general," I replied. "Simpler and just as effective. But get on with the news."

"Mr. Bone, the artist, has a cottage outside the town. He has a short pointed beard, a taste for liquor, a weak head for it, and would be a great artist in oils if he were not so frequently oiled."

"You're getting as bad as Mr. Ivor Brown, Mr. Gould, and the other critical gentlemen, with your puns," I said. "These revivals are in bad taste."

"Well, that's what I hear. When sober, he is mild and nice, and a good worker; when he has a drop of liquor in him—and it is, I hear, not much more than a drop—he is contentious, pugnacious, and possessive. He began a portrait of Mrs. Davey-Renny, and it has been in progress ever since. The object presumably, like ca' canny, is to prolong the job. A strain of infantilism in his make-up has so far prevented Mrs. Davey-Renny from gently detaching him. In his cups he has been indiscreet enough to suggest that he is hers and she is his, and a marriage will take place one of these days. It is said, though not on the best authority, that Kay ticked him off about it, and so on."

"What about the fellow 'oiled, curled and perfumed like an Assyrian bull'?" I asked. "That is the impression one gets when one hears about Mr. Tressy Withers. In fact, when I had made my peace with Mrs. Jennifer just now, a man was looking impudently over the gate. She bridled tremendously, and said it was Mr. Withers."

"He's heard that Power is here," Vincie said. "Some of the townsfolk have a vague idea that you're a London police-woman in disguise."

"Did you see anyone else?" I asked.

"Just talked to Captain Hollick, the Chief Constable, who came on me and Bohm. Bohm got away, and left me to it. In the High Street at this time of day you see most of the residents. One, Mr. Everard Jolson, was pointed out to me by Hollick."

"The bank man?"

"Retired. He had a dear old client, who had no relatives, no head for figures, constant trouble with her income-tax returns. He has a bedside manner, a kind heart, had a weakness for the aged. He is single and lived with his mother till she died at the age of seventy-five. At any rate, his aged client passed away, and left him thirty thousand pounds."

"Lucky man!"

"Then, at forty-five, he wanted a wife to console him in his retirement. There were plenty of offers, naturally. But they all rebounded off his head, and then Mrs. Davey-Renny turned up. Morgan put her up for the tennis club. Mr. Jolson 'fell' for her."

"And Mrs. Davey-Renny?"

"Doubtful what her feelings are, my dear," he said. "Of course, as a bachelor for years, and now madly in love for the first time, and condemned to see rival moths round the flame. Mr. Jolson is a jealous fiend. Mr. Bone, Inspector Kay, Mr. Withers, and Mr. Morgan spoke to each other occasionally when they met, tolerantly, indulgently, or scornfully perhaps, but they did speak. Mr. Jolson no sooner saw his hopes of marriage threatened by the rival ruffians, than he lost flesh, became irritable, and low-spirited, and went in for all the rigours of the game of love."

"Having exhibited all these horrid signs," I said, "he is the least likely man to murder his rival. Too exhibitionist, my dear."

Later in the day Power came in. He had had a chat with Mrs. Davey-Renny and an excellent tea. He said with some conviction that you could never trust a murderess to ask if you like China or Indian. Like ourselves, he regarded drinkers of China tea (if not valetudinarians) as lacking in robust imagination.

"I may be mistaken," he said, "but I always see the aesthetes drinking China tea, and smoking Turkish cigarettes. I am sure they are the nicest people; but not solid, not solid."

"Well?" I asked, when he had described the tea, "having doped you into acquiescence in her innocence, what did she say?"

"She said," Power remarked with gravity, "that Morgan had been an outside broker."

"That's torn it!" said Vincie. "And nobody knew?"

"Not here," said Power. "Stocks and shares down here are sold or bought by stockbrokers; not all belonging to that great and glorious body which does not advertise. So Mr. Morgan got the credit for being 'In' when he was technically 'Out'."

"After all, it may not be so bad," I objected, "or did your friend hint at a bucket-shop?"

"No, not like that. She didn't give me any hint of disgruntled clients. It was simply that Morgan hadn't a 'Seat,' but merely offices and a staff. According to her, he was an honest man."

"And who would know better than his secretary-typist? I gather that is what she was?" said Vincie.

"So did I!" Power replied thoughtfully. "In fact I asked her. I even went further, for I wanted to know if Mr. Morgan was the kind of man who made love to his employees. She assured me that women had no part in his life."

"Then why was he so angry when she left to get married?" I asked.

"Sheer laziness," he replied. "Though she said it as shouldn't, Mrs. Davey-Renny told me that she knew so much about Morgan and his ways that he was able to transact his business with the minimum of mental effort and disturbance. When she had gone, he had to train seven girls; or at least start to train them. His blood-pressure went up. Some of them could not write shorthand as fast as longhand; some could only type every third word correctly. In short, his life became the lazy man's hell."

"Sez she!" Vincie murmured vulgarly.

"In the absence of further evidence, Mercer, we may take it that it was so," said Power. "I always believe a lady's word, if I can't avoid it."

CHAPTER VII

WE ALL had a kind of hope that Voce would drop in to see us after dinner that evening. As Power says, Voce grows on one. But he did not grow on us that day. Instead, while we were having our coffee, Mr. Sibbins was announced.

"You must see him alone, Power," my husband said. "Just give us a moment to swallow our coffee."

Power shook his head. "Stay put, dear people! Let the wild hunter come in here," he added to the maid.

"The wild hunter, sir?"

"Mr. Sibbins."

If anyone wished to understand the meaning of that passive, military "crime" known as "Silent Insolence," he could not do better than take a good look at Power's client, Mr. Sibbins.

When he came in, he nodded to Power, and looked silently at us. Then he bowed at me, not to me, and sat down.

"Evening," he said to Power, "I wanted a chinwag with you."

Again he looked at us. He put us in brackets, in parenthesis, without a word. He elided us.

"Most inconvenient," Mr. Power remarked, taking a cigarette-case from his pocket, offering us cigarettes, lighting one himself, and then returning the case to his pocket. "Where the devil did you learn these manners, Sibbins—in the Blue?"

That positively did good. Mr. Sibbins closed his mouth, then grinned, and went as near as he could do to an apology.

"Didn't know you were busy."

"I'm not—that's the trouble! I get paid to work in business hours."

"I was in a hurry to see you."

"That's no excuse," Power said firmly, "none at all."

Now Sibbins blew up. "Dammit, you're my lawyer."

Mr. Power considered that. "Your lawyer? H'm. I was, I may be, but don't take it for granted. What do you want?"

"To talk to you—alone."

"N.G. If my friends, Mr. and Mrs. Mercer here, don't mind—Oh, by the way, Mr. Sibbins; Mr. and Mrs. Mercer."

We bowed and smiled at him. He bowed to us.

"You see," said his tormentor, looking the black-browed, insolent man in the face, "this is England. Moth-eaten with conventions. When you are introduced to a lady, you stand up."

Mr. Sibbins stood up. "I'm going!"

"Close the door quietly," said Power. "As I was saying, Mrs. Mercer—"

Mr. Sibbins looked angry, but did not go to the door. "I wanted to ask you about the case," he said.

Power nodded. "I had that impression. By the way, Mr. Sibbins, Mrs. Mercer."

Mr. Sibbins bowed to me, and I smiled again. He resumed his seat.

Power looked at us. "You don't mind Sibbins bursting in on us like this, Mrs. Mercer?"

"Not at all," I said.

"Too kind," said Power. "Carry on, Sibbins. Mr. and Mrs. Mercer know all about the case."

Mr. Sibbins filled a pipe. I feared that Power was going to suggest that he should ask my permission before he lit it. But he merely smiled, and watched our guest.

"The police want to know where I was," said the man.

"When?"

"When my uncle died."

"They would. And you said?"

"I told them to go to the devil."

"You would. And they said?"

"They had no power to force me to answer questions."

"Silly of you to be so sticky about it."

"Look here," cried Mr. Sibbins, "I won't stand that sort of thing from you."

"Then don't!" said Power. "Take yourself, and your business, to the place you recommended to the police! I really don't like the look of you, and my friends here are of the same mind, but far too polite to say so. Any deeds, papers, and documents, belonging to you go back to-morrow. Just give me an address."

To our surprise, Sibbins looked crestfallen. Power says that type is always appreciative of a poke in the eye.

"I'm a bit worried," he said, and sat down. "Any feller would be in my case."

"Right," said Power, "I am just reminding you tactfully that you are not addressing the Umfuzzle tribe of Bushmen on the iniquities of elephant poaching. If you can keep that in your mind I may reconsider my decision."

Mr. Sibbins swallowed something. It might have been a lump in his throat. "Well, I know my uncle left me most of his money, but that does not justify these police fellers calling me a murderer, or good as."

"There's no 'as good as' with the police," Power remarked; "if they think you are, they'll tell you so; a warning preceding of course."

"Why don't they get on to that woman then?" the man asked, "Mrs. Davey-Renny, or whatever they call her? Rose Davey-Renny."

"Great Scott!" said Vincie. "The language of flowers."

"What's that?" said Sibbins.

"Is she really called Rose?" I asked.

"She is," said Mr. Sibbins, "so they say."

"Ah," said Power, "a reminder of what?"

Mr. Sibbins gaped, then looked at him. "You mean she sent him a rose, the rose?"

"She did," Power agreed.

"And some josser told me it was poisoned."

"What josser?"

"I met a feller in the hotel-bar, called—oh, Withers."

"Tressy Withers," I murmured. "He said so?"

"The fact is that there were traces of cocaine on it," Power said.

"Smart woman!" said Sibbins with unwilling admiration. "Who ever would have thought of that? It wouldn't occur to anyone to examine the rose, you see."

"Only me," said Power, "but get on with your applecart, Sibbins. The police want to know where you were about the time your uncle died. Where were you?"

"Well, I'd left Africa, of course. The Yankee feller I was hunting for shot two elephants on a one-elephant licence, and the game warden gave him hell. He huffed up and left."

"Put that in your next book," said Power, "but let me hear what you did in old prosaic England the last week or two."

Mr. Sibbins pondered. "The fact is that I've been staying quite near here for ten days," he said, unwillingly, at last. "Dossed down in a pub in Plymly. 'Bout ten miles from here."

"See your uncle?" Power asked.

"No."

"Why not?"

"Well, other fish to fry."

"I see. What fish?"

Mr. Sibbins looked at me, then mumbled that he had met a pal or two on getting home, and heard rumours there was a woman vamping Nunky. Didn't quite know how they heard, but he'd come down to see.

"Bright boy," said Power. "But let's get this right. Speaking directly and frankly, as you would speak to the Umfuzzle tribe, you came down to snoop about near Fairlawn Cottage?"

Mr. Sibbins reddened unbecomingly. "I wouldn't call it snooping."

"Very likely not. That's what I'm calling it."

Perhaps our visitor thought I looked sympathetic. "I put it to you, Mrs.—er—Mercer," he said, "if you hadn't a bean, and you had a rich uncle, and you heard some snakey female was getting round him, wouldn't you go round and have a dekko?"

I laughed. "Perhaps I might."

"I certainly should," said Vincie.

Mr. Sibbins regarded us more interestedly. "Well, that's what I did. I found there was this Rose woman, who knew my uncle, though I didn't see the old chap come along there."

"Who did you see?" Power asked.

Mr. Sibbins wrinkled his brows. "I was taking snaps, nominally. Scenery, you know. Lemme see. Oh, yes, one Beaver, who looked a bit oiled when I saw him."

"Item, one artist," said Power.

"Oh, is he? Then there was a feller with a big dog. Dane, I should say."

"Feller or dog?" Vincie asked, imitating his voice marvellously.

"Dog. Great Dane."

"One bank manager, retired," Power murmured. "Mr. Jolson. Small man with big dog."

"Any more suitors?" I asked.

Mr. Sibbins was now more at his ease. "Is that what they were? Yes, there was another bloke. Fact is, I began to wonder where my uncle came in."

"Or if he came in at all."

"That's about the size of it. I was beginning to feel hopeful that my pals had been pulling my leg."

"But you remained Persevering Percy?" said Power.

"I went to mouch round, the evening before the old chap conked out. I saw a feller arrive in a car, pretty old vintage stuff. Light was bad for a snap, so I was looking in the hedge for birds' nests when he came along. He got out, carrying flowers."

"Ah," said Power, "when he comes back from his holiday the police will know you were in the vicinity, even if you don't tell 'em."

"You know him?"

"Inspector Kay, of the county C.I.D.," said I. "He'll be back in a day or two."

"A blas—a copper?" said Sibbins.

"Who has seen better days," said Power. "But what was the great idea behind all this scouting campaign of yours? It may have had a highly ethical intention, but that's not apparent on the face of it."

Our visitor looked rather shamefaced, and again he addressed himself to me. "I think it's pretty obvious. No harm in a bit of family pride, I say. There was my old uncle, set upon by a designing woman, so to speak, fallen for her, and no doubt as blind as these old fellers get when they do fall for the female of the species."

"Your campaign was in the nature of an eye-opener?" I suggested.

"I ask you!" said Mr. Sibbins. "If the young woman had been out of the top-drawer, warranted sound and free from vice, so to speak; well, that was where I got down. But it seemed to me if she wasn't, and so forth, it was up to me to save the old feller, what?"

"And the monetary residuum," Power said gently, if dryly. "Yes, I see your idea. Somewhat officious and damnably impertinent, but I see it."

Undoubtedly our friend knew how to handle this type. The more often the toe of his moral boot landed, the more anxious was Mr. Sibbins to have his legal support. It would certainly look odd to Voce, when the inspector said he recognised Sibbins as a man he must have seen hanging about near Fairlawn Cottage.

"I haven't a bean," the latter repeated, as if this was a full excuse for any course of conduct, however dubious, "so I couldn't afford to let this Rose person get away with it."

"That's obvious too," said Power. "Your intention was to visit your uncle, and give him a list of the visitors to the mystery house in the park."

"Well, he ought to have been told."

"A moot point, Mr. Sibbins. I think you had better tell Chief Inspector Voce all this before Inspector Kay *does* come home."

"Just a mo," said Sibbins, his eyes lighting up. "What about this ambitious Bobby, eh? Roses were what he had, come to think of it."

"Four white, eight red," said Power, "so he told Voce."

"Then you know about it?"

"He made no secret of the fact that he had brought roses to Mrs. Davey-Renny, my dear man."

"And you don't see any point in that?"

"Several. What's yours?"

"At a guess," said Sibbins, rather excitedly, "it might be their job, you know. Things aren't as bad as they might have been. I mean to say, uncle only left her a dollop out of the lot. But I bet seven thou, odd, will look lots to a village copper."

Power laughed. "I see, policeman and lovely lady want to get spliced. Like you, they haven't many beans, and decide to do in your testamentary uncle for what's coming to the lady. They decide to say it with flowers. Kay goes for the roses, he and she dope one with cocaine; knowing the uncle had an idiosyncrasy against it, hoping his old heart will go on strike at the first sniff. A pretty plot, methinks. But where does the copper collar the cocaine?"

Mr. Sibbins was not put down. "It sticks out a yard—how he could have got it, anyway. Antinarcotic business. Part of a policeman's job."

"Not here," said Vincie. "'Coke' in the country is unusual."

Power raised his hand. "Kay was in town first, exchanged here owing to asthma."

Sibbins gave a chortle. "Throat affection? I know a feller used to sing (professional, you know), had a throat spray given him at times. Or a raid."

"What raid?" I asked.

"Raided some dope den when in Town," said Sibbins. "Turned in most of the snow, but pouched a trifle, in case he could find a use for it."

Mr. Power got up. "Well, Mr. Sibbins, I think we must say good-bye for the present. See Voce and put your case before him. You can take it from me that what Voce doesn't know he soon will. He's an apple, that man; a simple apple, but you can't bite on him without losing a tooth. Also keep your eye on Sergeant Bohm. Bohm is sly."

Mr. Sibbins had had his lesson in politeness. He said good-bye to Vincie and me very nicely, and was shown out by Power. When our friend came back, he raised his hands in a gesture of surprise.

"Put him in your book, Mrs. Mercer," he said, "put him in your book! A thoroughly nasty piece of work."

Vincie nodded. "He was down here all the time. It looks as if the detective-story convention was coming true after all, Power."

"*That* commit murder?" Power was very scornful. "Have some sense! No guts, no brains, no nothing, but a supply of impudence."

"A big-game hunter would surely have the 'guts' to commit murder?" I said.

He screwed up his face. "No criterion. None at all, Mrs. M.— look at the southern Italians. Fond of knife-play in civil life, but pretty cheap stuff in the war. You can take it from me that if bongos went about with sub-machine guns Sibbins wouldn't collect many."

CHAPTER VIII

UNLESS he has to be on the golf-course, a lawyer generally spends a good deal of time in his office. I mean to say, he puts business before pleasure when he can't help it. Even Mr. Power had jobs of work to do, and he was gone in his car next morning before we got up.

We decided to map out our day. In the first place we would frequent the High Street, where Vincie says you generally see most of the residents, have a spot of coffee in some tea-rooms, and try to get a closer glimpse of some of the men in the case. In the afternoon, we would ask Voce or Bohm to tea, and trust to their good-nature to tell us what might helpfully, and not irregularly, be told.

Everyone knows that plans are made to be broken, by other people. It was so with us. Having stoked up, as Vincie puts it, on ham and eggs, finnan "haddy," toast and marmalade, with a little fruit, we sat in long chairs in the garden, and smoked ciga-rettes. Every day should be begun with some ritual like that. The only danger is that the long-chair-and-cigarette habit is an eater of time. You sit down for a few minutes at half-past nine, and at twelve the grasshopper is a burden. Though of course you may be asleep.

It was perhaps ten when the gate opened, and a nervous little man with a very big dog at his heels came in and, seeing us, walked across the lawn. He raised his hat, bowed in an odd nervous way, then turned to Vincie.

"Good morning, Mr. Power," he said, "I wanted a talk with you. I remember reading something about your conduct of a case a while back."

"I am not Mr. Power," Vincie told him, as he shook hands; "he has gone to town. But we are close friends of his."

Mr. Jolson seemed to me to be extremely confused and upset. He fidgeted when he stood and fidgeted when he sat down. The immense dog advanced on me, and put a monstrous paw on my lap.

"What a marvellous dog," I said.

"Yes, 'Elsinore' is the daughter of Champion Menelik," he said, and added in a rush: "But I must apologise for intruding on you. I am really very sorry." He half rose again, and removing his hat, mopped his brow.

"Sit down and smoke," said Vincie; "you might leave a message for Power."

"Novelists, you know," I added, "are really the most harmless creatures. Vain and pushful, perhaps, but really nothing worse. It's about the case, perhaps."

He jumped, commanded himself again, and said: "Yes, it is, I suppose. My name is Jolson, and I am, or rather was, the manager of a bank here."

"Delighted," I said. "Our own manager is a darling."

I might have been mistaken, but there seemed a distinct flavour, or scent, of sherry on the air as he leaned towards me. "Ah, in London."

The huge hound curled itself at my feet. Vincie smiled.

"We've heard of you already, Mr. Jolson," he said. "Power had the pleasure of calling on a local resident, Mrs. Davey-Renny, yesterday, and she mentioned your name."

"How extraordinary," he said, "I—that is to say it was a matter indirectly related to that which—"

"You wanted to see Power about?" Vincie and I saw that the little man's secret nervousness tended to make his speech long-winded and verbose.

"Yes, this tragedy here," said Mr. Jolson, looking distinctly nervous, "into which the local authorities have introduced two blundering police from—er—London."

"Did you know the dead man?" I asked ingenuously.

"I did, in a way. In fact," said Mr. Jolson, in a lowered voice, "I called on him on the morning of his death."

We creditably repressed starts, and cries, of surprise. "Why," I said, "how thrilling! You may have been the last person to see him alive."

He changed colour. "I trust not. I mean to say, it would be extremely unfortunate."

"Surely," said Vincie blandly, "there is no harm in a social call, even in the morning?"

"I—well, I did not think it necessary to mention it yesterday," he burbled.

"But why yesterday?" I asked.

"I had a call from these London boors," he said. "They were quite rude about my reticence."

"So uncalled for," Vincie murmured, "and unusual. I hope you told them so?"

Mr. Jolson coughed nervously. "The facts are these: I went to see Mr. Morgan that morning about eleven, just turned in off the lane as I was passing."

"No harm in that," I commented. "Did you find him alone?"

"Yes. He was sitting on a garden-seat, smelling a rose he had taken from his button-hole—at least, I think he was."

We sat up. If Mr. Morgan was smelling the rose, he must have inhaled the dope, or someone must have put dope on the rose after Mr. Jolson's arrival.

"So you see," he went on nervously, "if that was so, and it is correctly rumoured that some drug was on the rose, my position is a very awkward one."

"Just a moment," said Vincie. "As no one heard about your visit till yesterday, I assume that you reached the garden by—by the back way?"

"I have done so on one or two previous occasions."

"Quite. Still, Mr. Jolson, the fuss about it is more startling than the visit itself. Why should they suspect you of any ill-will to Morgan?"

Mr. Jolson started. "Do they? Incomprehensible."

"Did Mr. Morgan show the rose to you?" I asked.

"He did, in a sense. He got up, held it out in my direction, put it back in his button-hole, and said: 'A present for a good boy'."

"Was he usually facetious?" Vincie asked.

"No, not at all. It struck me as an offensive remark, and possibly intended to be such."

"The term 'good boy' used sarcastically?" I suggested.

"Oh, no, Mrs. Mercer. He was referring to himself. He added: 'Sweets to the sweet, Jolson. A rose from Rose. She sent it to me this morning'."

"And that struck you as offensive?" Vincie asked in his most puzzled tone.

"You see," poor Mr. Jolson had to explain himself now, "I resented his familiar reference to Mrs. Davey-Renny, and his obvious desire to exasperate me."

"So he was in the running too?" Vincie asked.

"I don't quite understand. The lady is one for whom I have a deep respect. In fact, I called to tell him that her name was being coupled in rumours with his own, and I hoped that he would give no further occasion for such a thing to happen."

"Quite right," I said warmly. "You showed a very nice and natural feeling there, Mr. Jolson."

"In fact," said Vincie, taking up our agreeable game of pat-ball, "the police probably fastened on your feeling for the lady, and the suggested rivalry between you and Mr. Morgan as an excuse to worry you about the visit."

He nodded. "Yes. I am anxious to see Mr. Power about that. He is said to be a man of great cleverness in criminal matters."

Vincie agreed. "He often talks his cases over with us, and gives us the advantage of his experience. I shall tell him what you have said, and you may be able to supplement your information now. We may take it, I suppose, that this insult, as you consider it, did not lead to blows?"

"I have neither the desire, nor the physique, to struggle with a man like Morgan, Mr. Mercer."

"Were you alone?"

"Except for 'Elsinore' here, I was."

"Ah, the dog. I see. Is she quiet?"

"As you see," Mr. Jolson pointed. "I trained her myself."

"I was wondering if she might not be a silent witness to your peaceable conduct in the garden," Vincie observed, and made as if to strike Mr. Jolson.

"Elsinore" jumped up and began to gambol about us, but, to our surprise, did not bark or exhibit any signs of anger. Mr. Jolson looked more nervous than ever and, after telling the dog to lie down, glanced very earnestly at my husband. "What was your idea, Mr. Mercer?"

"I was thinking that the dog would make a noise if there was a scrimmage—" Vincie told him, "she didn't."

"It was clever of you to think of it," said the little man, "but 'Elsinore,' while an affectionate pet, is not particularly intelligent. In any case, I can assure you that Mr. Morgan did not threaten me."

I nodded. "All police suspicions in cases like this are vague and spread over a wide area, Mr. Jolson. I expect even they merely think that someone may have hit Mr. Morgan in a fit of temper."

Mr. Jolson turned all colours, so that any policeman would have believed him guilty on the strength of his obvious embarrassment.

"Mr. Morgan was not a violent man," he said. "It is violence that begets violence."

"There was this rose now," Vincie said. "It was a white rose, I hear."

Mr. Jolson started again. He would have made a tremendous record on an oscillatorometer, if there is such a thing.

"Yes, yes, it was," he said, "white."

"I don't suppose you stayed long enough to ask where it came from?"

"A very short time indeed," Mr. Jolson replied to me.

"Say a quarter of an hour?" said Vincie.

"Only a few minutes," Jolson said. "I spoke to him about a little matter which I regarded as offensive. He made vulgar game of my protest. I left shortly after, and walked to a village, Plymly, which is about five miles away. I arrived at twelve precisely."

The public-houses opened at twelve, I believe.

"If I were you I should tell the police what Mr. Morgan said," Vincie observed; "that will show them that the matter was not very important. You told us that he was not violent?"

"No," said Jolson, "not at all. But offensive. He said if one was such a 'jealous little tick,' one should take care to bark up the right tree. He said further something to the effect that while in his office Rose was a nice little girl. Judging by my nasty mind, he took it that I had never been a nice little man, either in my office or elsewhere. And all this because I had simply called to check a rumour!"

"Rumours don't pay to check," I said. "But surely the police don't suspect you because he called you a—what was it?"

"A little tick," said Mr. Jolson. "An unpleasant observation."

"Perhaps he meant that you were on the watch," Vincie suggested gravely.

"Did he mention the chance that someone else was coming to see him later that morning?" I asked.

"No. I can't say that he did."

"It didn't occur to you that he might be unwell?" Vincie asked.

"Not at all. Probably he was. I mean to say—" He paused and added: "Of course I couldn't say. I was upset. I was naturally upset. I hurried away to walk it off."

"And you say you reached the village inn, five miles away, by twelve?"

Mr. Jolson admitted it. "Yes, about then."

"So, unless you are a champion walker, you can prove that you were not long with Mr. Morgan?"

"So I can. Much obliged to you for the suggestion. I shall be glad if you will tell Mr. Power and ask him to arrange to meet me. It was a fortunate chance that I called."

He rose, and the dog rose and butted him playfully in the back. We all shook hands and Vincie saw him to the gate. When he returned to me Vincie raised his eyebrows.

"Quite the little gentleman, if somewhat dry," he said. "But how odd that we should have the first intimation that Morgan had a visitor that morning. If one arrived privily, and retired in the same order, why not two?"

"Or three?" I agreed. "I expect Voce has statements from the servants showing how they passed their time that morning, and if any of them had a chance to see who came to the garden."

"But would they look?" my husband asked. "I mean to say, sweetheart, can there be any pleasure for them in looking at a man sitting in a grass plot, even if he is their master? Unless some strange visitors came by the front way, they would not expect to see anything interesting or exciting."

I had to admit that, though it is my experience that all maids do like to break the routine by an occasional glance out of the window, even if there is no drama being enacted on the lawn. "We may hear this afternoon," I said; "meantime, what about haunting the High Street?"

The High Street is a mixture, but not too incongruous a mixture, of new and old. A few bow-windowed shops jostle newer shops, which have attempted to imitate them in rawer materials; three-storied, parapeted houses, of the type occupied by country lawyers and doctors, are divided from each other by half-timbered cottages, or restored inns. Even the best tea-shop shows knowledge of the past by its sign: "The Old Tea-Shop."

"We do, at least, know how 'Ye' was pronounced," as Vincie said, when we went in.

We ordered coffee and looked about us. Evidently we had come a bit late, for there were only seven people there; two being elderly country-women, one a motorist whose car stood outside, two young girls who giggled at intervals, and two men. One of the two men I recognised as Mr. Tressy Withers, and he made an audible remark to his companion.

"Ye gods! The policewoman!"

I looked at his companion. He was tall and good-looking, and I had an idea that he was the dentist, Mr. Edwards. He stared at me for a moment, then dropped his eyes. Withers continued to stare at me.

"Who are those merchants in the corner?" Vincie asked me.

I told him and he turned to have a better look at them. He was turning away again when a newcomer entered the café. It was Chief Inspector Voce. He nodded to the men in the corner, then came towards us.

"Ah, good morning," he said, "I just turned in for a drop of tea."

"Join us," I said, and he did that willingly enough. "You said tea?"

"Thank you."

He smiled at me gently. "How's the book getting on, Mrs. Mercer?"

"Not so bad," I replied, "just getting the skeleton, you know."

"Ah, any more bones?"

"One or two small ones," I replied. "By the way, if you can spare the time this afternoon, come to tea. You won't regret it."

He pondered, and glanced at a note-book. Meanwhile I saw that the dentist had got up and gone out.

"If you can wait till half-past four, I'll be delighted," he said.

"We can just manage to make it," Vincie told him.

As our coffee was brought, and Voce gave the order for a large pot of tea, Mr. Withers reached for his hat, got his bill, and came across to our table.

"Morning, Chief Inspector," he said, in a fat unctuous voice, "any luck yet?"

"Not yet, sir," said Voce. "Oh, Mr. Withers, let me introduce you to my friends. Mr. Withers, Mrs. Mercer, a well-known novelist. Mr. Mercer is also a novelist."

We exchanged bows, and Mr. Withers remarked, flatteringly, that he knew my books well. That was, of course, a lie, since I do not write under my married name.

"What a jolly business too," he added. "Staying long?"

"For a week or two," I said. "What a charming place it is."

Mr. Withers smiled. "I wonder if you and your husband would honour me by coming to tea one day? It's always been my ambition to meet a novelist. A brace at once is a bag."

"Why not?" said Vincie. "You have no idea how much novelists love to be met. We're insatiable, you know."

"Ha, ha." Withers laughed just like that. It was the flattest sound I ever heard. "Do you know, Mrs. Mercer—and I'm sure you'll forgive me—I'd heard you were a policewoman in disguise."

"I heard you say so," I remarked demurely. "Now that would be exciting! Would your people take me in, Mr. Voce?"

Voce had now got his tea, and was stirring the pot vigorously. "I am sure they would," he said. "Jump at it."

Mr. Withers took a coin from his pocket. "At the Old Rectory, aren't you?" he said. "I'll drop you a card."

There were bows all round, and he went off to the cash-desk. Voce shook his head slowly when we were alone once more.

"That's a nice cup of tea!" he murmured, leaving us in no doubt that he spoke sarcastic. "You'll get something for your book, Mrs. Mercer, if you go."

"Why, is he—" I began.

"You saw him colloguing with the dentist," he replied cryptically, and applied himself with gusto to his tea. "You can mention it to Mr. Power."

CHAPTER IX

IT WAS quite obvious that Mr. Withers thought he could get some information from us, while Voce had decided that we might extract some information from Mr. Withers. Wooed thus by both sides, we thought we had a bargaining margin in dealing with the Chief Inspector when he came to tea.

"Do you think he suspects the dentist?" Vincie asked me, as we strolled back for luncheon.

"No, I don't, really," I said. "Withers may have been trying to pump the dentist, possibly about the dope."

"Voce will, of course, try to trace dope to any of the men who were rivals," he murmured. "None that I have seen so far look like addicts, unless the little artist draws his inspiration from two sources. Kay, on the other hand, being a policeman, would be an unlikely victim."

"I wonder what Mr. Withers does?" I said.

"Nominally independent, but with the air of a racing crook," Vincie suggested. "Terribly vulgar good-looks, but a fishy eye."

"I wonder if he is a bookmaker in retirement?" I asked. "I mean under an alias, not actually out of business?"

"We'll ask Power, my dear. He's a quick worker."

There was a short but violent thunderstorm after lunch, which kept us indoors. At half-past three, the sun shone out once more, and we decided that tea in the garden would be possible. Mrs. Jennifer made no objection, and we were assembled at the tea-table, on nicely dried turf, when Voce appeared.

"Drying weather," he remarked, as we got him a chair. "Half an hour ago I was mud to the heels." We did not ask him where, or how.

"Short grass and gravel soil," said Vincie. "By the way, why did you wish us on to Mr. Withers?"

"There was a mutual look in his eye," said the big man. "I knew he couldn't be anxious to see me, so I guessed the attraction."

"You think he imagined me to be a policewoman?" I asked.

"No, I don't. He may think you both know something he doesn't."

"Why should he worry?"

"Well, Mrs. Mercer," he said, as the maid came in sight with a tea-tray, "he seems the sort of fellow who wouldn't weep if someone, or something, butted in to remove a rival or two."

"Then you think his intentions are serious?"

"So I hear," Voce replied, as the table was set out. "When he falls, a big 'un comes down as heavily as a little 'un. That used to be the phrase when I played rugger."

"There is something rather unethical," Vincie objected, "in our going to tea, and pumping our host for your benefit, Voce."

"I don't mind a harmless swap now and then," Voce admitted.

"Then we'll waive the ethics," Vincie said. "You start first."

Voce took the cup of tea I handed him and doubled up two pieces of bread and butter. "The little bank gentleman came to see me," he said, took a bite, and a mouthful of tea, and added: "He went to see Mr. Morgan the morning he died."

I looked at him reproachfully. "You call that a swap? Why, we told him to tell you."

Voce took another bite. "So he said. But I had an idea he had been there."

That was news of a sort, and Vincie jumped in to ask when this brain-wave had smitten him.

"At breakfast," said Voce. "Between you and me, and Mr. Power, I had an interim report from our people."

"We beg your pardon," I said. "This is a generous swap after all. Try a cake."

Voce took a cake and passed his cup. "Analysed the surface sweepings we sent them," he remarked. "Dog's hairs among 'em."

Voce applied himself to the pastry with appreciation, and Vincie and I exchanged happy glances. He might look slow, but our Chief Inspector is ahead of his looks. Searching for traces of the lethal powder, he had seen the significance of the dog's hairs.

"Good," Vincie approved. "But you are sure they were dog's, not bits from, say, Mr. Bone's beard?"

"We have no proof that Mr. Bone took his beard there that day," said Voce. "The little man should have told us before," he added.

"Frightened of being mixed up in it," I said. "Is that all you have for us?"

He passed his cup for the third time, drank it off, wiped his mouth, and graciously accepted a plate of strawberries I passed him.

"First strawberries I've had this year," he told us. "I have some nice ones coming on, but they're late."

That was the end of that chapter we knew. We dropped Mr. Jolson, and Vincie turned back to Withers.

"Well, we'll have tea with our bookmaker, and try to repay you in kind," he said, watching Voce's lavish hand with the cream.

The Chief Inspector winked slowly at me. "The only man I know who can get away with that kind of question is Mr. Power."

Vincie was unrepentant. "I admit it was a try-on. Isn't he a bookmaker though?"

"I'll credit you with a good shot, Mr. Mercer. Bohm was of that opinion till he made inquiries. We don't want it known locally, of course, but the general impression so far is that he's connected with the stock market."

"A broker!" I asked excitedly.

"Not exactly. Something to do with futures and margins. No complaint so far, but you never know."

"Ah," said Vincie, "you never said a truer word. I take it that there was no business connection between him and the dear departed?"

Voce got up. "I'm not Moses, the Vicar of Wakefield's son, to swap it all for some green spectacles," he remarked. "In any case, I have to meet Bohm in ten minutes. I may say I enjoyed my tea."

"So glad," I said. "We enjoyed having you. Our love to Sergeant Bohm."

Vincie saw him to the gate and came back smiling. "You'll know a thing is not important if Voce tells you," he said, and added: "Quite a quarter of a pint of cream wasted choking that dog. But you must bait your ground for these heavy fishes."

This mixed metaphor was the measure of his disappointment.

When Mr. Power came back in the evening, we told him what Voce had said, and told him too what had happened when the little bank manager called.

"Dog's hairs?" he repeated. "I suppose Voce is thinking of the Great Dane."

"A monster, an elephant of a dog," I remarked. "I was thankful that Mr. Jolson could control it when Vincie tried to test its temper."

Vincie smiled. "You can take it from me that I thought the brute thoroughly tame. But it didn't strike me as moulting."

Mr. Power stopped in the lighting of a match for his cigarette. "That may mean nothing. There are always a certain number of loose hairs in a dog's coat. Stroke it, and out they come."

"I don't think Vincie was suggesting that Jolson set the dog on Mr. Morgan," I said. "The test showed that it might protect its master, but was easily calmed down. And dogs use their teeth when they attack."

Mr. Power bowed ceremoniously to me. "Do they? A great thought! So this canine elephant barked, but did not bite."

"Barked, bounced and butted," Vincie said.

"Butted!"

"In fun," said I. "You saw that, Vincie?"

My husband nodded. "Not the kind of playfulness I should encourage in a beast weighing a hundred pounds or so. You remember Thompson's big deerhound, Penny? Had a silly habit of placing its forepaws on your shoulder suddenly and pushing you over."

"What exactly did the G.D. do this time?" Power asked.

"When its master got up to go, it playfully butted him with its huge nut," Vincie informed him.

Power frowned. "Does Voce think he trained the brute specially, and went round early, in view of Morgan's reputation as a heavy-breakfast eater?"

"I suppose," said Vincie, to whom this great thought had not occurred, "a dog like that could butt you in the tummy, and knock you out—other things being equal?"

"Your constitution being unequal," said Power, "I think it could. But whatever Jolson knew, the dog wouldn't know Morgan's weak spot."

"That, however," I said, "might just happen to be about the level of a Great Dane's head."

"True, Mrs. M.," Power murmured, "having placed the doped rose in his button-hole, the intelligent beast had secured a red herring, and promptly butted Morgan in the midriff."

"You laugh," Vincie said genially, "but who put the idea in our heads? But is it possible? If a man after a heavy meal could be killed by the impact of a big dog's head on his middle, eh? Reminds you of Bret Harte: 'A chunk of old red sandstone struck him on the abdomen'."

"Morgan falls, Mr. Jolson finds that he is dead, and slinks away at top speed, to get a time-alibi in a village inn," I added.

"Surely he isn't another soaker like Bone?" said Power.

Vincie shook his head. "He started his private sherry party very early to-day, I think, but that might be to pull himself together."

Mr. Power admitted that. "Joking apart," he said, "the tentative suggestion of the pathologist's report is that Morgan may have died of an injury to the abdomen. I won't say that a dog might not have done it. If Jolson's dog is playful in that way he might have done it. There might have been a row between the men, and the dog, without taking actively vicious measures, might charge in, and literally bump off Mr. Morgan."

"Which still leaves the rose unaccounted for," I said. We were called in to dinner, and during the meal Mr. Power told us roughly what Bohm had ferreted out concerning the movements of the staff on the morning of Morgan's death.

"First the butler," he said. "He was busy cleaning some silver when Morgan went into the garden, and after Mrs. Davey-Renny's maid had called with the rose. In fact, he did not know of that fragrant gift at all. At half-past eleven, having been given permission the previous evening, he left the house by the front door, and went to see a niece, who had just arrived in Malpertuis to take a place in Captain Hollick's house."

"He did not go into the garden before he left?" Vincie asked.

"No, his last sight of his master alive was when he brought him *The Times* after breakfast. It was usually put in the study. Mr. Morgan was not one of those who cannot breakfast without first hearing how the world wags. Cook and the other maid washed up the breakfast things, and went about their routine work without either seeing Mr. Morgan in the house or garden. Both swear that they did not peep out of the windows, neither saw any visitor, or heard sounds of conversation much less rows. In other words, none of the staff is any help in tracing a murderous intruder."

"Very possible," I said, "Vincie and I once lived in a small block of country flats, and were often a day at a time without a glimpse of at least two other families who shared the house."

"Now what did you do in Town?" I added, when this illuminating remark had been received in silence. "Any discoveries?"

"Two," said Mr. Power. "One of my partners had failed to clear up my arrears of work at the office. That was the first. He didn't intend to. That was the second. So I had to! I am not like old Voce, who is paid to wander about doing what he likes best."

"There's one mystery solved," said Vincie. "Power isn't the big noise in his office he pretends to be! But to get back to business. We were saying that the mystery of the rose was still unaccounted for."

The maid brought in the joint, and we left Power to carve it. He does it with ease, grace, and the pleasure which comes of being master of his material.

"I am going to try an experiment with that," he said, as he sliced off a delicate bit of undercut, and put it on the plate intended for me; "I mean vicariously."

"We'll be vicar," said Vincie.

"That was my idea—a little fat, Mrs. Mercer?"

"No," I said, "not for me."

"Let's have full instructions, and we'll do our best," Vincie told him. "Shan't you be here?"

"I'm afraid not. I have to go to Birmingham."

He began to carve for Vincie, saw to his own plate, and then resumed:

"You can borrow a bike, and all you have to do is to reconstruct the scene. It will mean getting Mrs. Davey-Renny's co-operation, but I have arranged for that."

"Who's to act the *Rosenkavalier*?" I asked.

"It ought to be a woman, to make the plan complete," he said, "but Mercer is stronger. By the way, you must meet her. A charming woman."

"Delighted," I said. "By the way also, I wonder if she noticed Mr. Sibbins wandering about?"

"She did, and I was able to reassure her. If there is any point in this dope business, she isn't sitting pretty. She obviously sent the rose to Morgan, she comes in for a nice bit of money as a result of his death, and it might be argued by a fanciful policeman that Sibbins was not just hanging about for evidence to convict her as a vamp to his uncle."

Voce is not fanciful, but we saw the thing at once, and could not at once dismiss it from our minds. The *ipse dixits* of suspected persons in murder cases are not of great value in themselves. Sibbins gave his account of the matter but, as Power had explained, that might be an excuse to explain his hovering near Fairlawn Cottage.

"As we said before," Vincie argued, "if one came into the bower without being observed, why not two, or three?"

"Exactly. I think it is that which stirs my unpleasant client to anxious thought," Power replied. "He knows that he and the lady are the sharers of the fortune. It might be said that they were both anxious to hasten the happy event, fixed it up between them, and so forth. And," he added with a wry smile, "who can say that they did not?"

Now, why the wry smile? We had taken Power to be proof even against charming women. But it did look as if he were more concerned about her fate than was strictly necessary.

"I'll give you a note to her," he added. "Perhaps you could go over to-morrow about eleven."

"If you have spoken to her about it, we will," Vincie agreed. "But talking of a possible complicity, where does the dope come in?"

Power looked doubtful. "That worries me. It might be that whoever put it on the flower knew of Morgan's idiosyncrasy, expected that the sniff would put him out of action for the moment, and enable the murderer to hook a heavy one to the tummy. But there should have been easier ways of doing it than that."

"Alternatively," I said, "given knowledge of the idiosyncrasy, it might be an attempt to suggest that Morgan had died of cocaine as the result of a plot by Mrs. Davey-Renny."

"But there is no real proof that cocaine, especially in an adulterated form, has killed a man with one sniff," Vincie remarked.

Power shook his head. "My dear fellow, not one person in a thousand has the barest knowledge of toxicology. Take the commonest and one of the beastliest forms of poisoning, arsenic. How many of your acquaintances could name the minimum fatal dose?"

"I hope none of them has studied it," I said.

CHAPTER X

IF NO human being, male or female, can add a cubit to his stature, most women can add at least five years to any other woman's hypothetical age.

When we met Mrs. Davey-Renny in her charming bower next day, I saw at once that thirtyish meant at least thirty-five. But she was a man's thirty, and young looking at that, pretty, graceful, and frank. We both liked her, though we did not suggest that our liking is as good as a moral testimonial. It was a purely personal matter.

"Mr. Power has been so kind," she said. "He has promised to help me. But what is it exactly that he wishes to do now?"

"As I see it," Vincie told her, "I am to be your maid, complete with bike. I have it outside. Power has provided me with a little packet of powder. You give me a rose. I dust it, and you place it in tissue-paper. We must get that part right. I then mount my bike, and set off to ride to Mr. Morgan's house. Power telephoned this morning to Sergeant Bohm. He will be Mr. Morgan."

She smiled fascinatingly. "Such a pleasant policeman."

"Velvet pads all right," said Vincie. "Well, he takes over the rose, puts it in his button-hole and, thereafter, perpends upon it."

"The idea being," I said, "to decide if there would be any powder left after Mary (my husband) has jounced and jolted on her bike for a considerable distance."

"But surely," said Mrs. Davey-Renny in dismay, "no one imagines that I put poison on a rose, with the idea of killing poor Mr. Morgan?"

"You had motive, you see," said Vincie. "They may wonder why Mr. Morgan left you the money."

"According to Mr. Power," she objected, "everyone may wonder why he left Mr.—Mr. Sibbins the rest."

"I agree," said Vincie. "But there are some people who always leave money to relations, whether they deserve it or not—keeping it in the family is, I believe, the term used. Have you ever seen Mr. Sibbins?"

She replied at once. "I saw a man hanging about taking photographs. He looked disagreeable. Mr. Power said that was Mr. Sibbins."

"You ought to be off, Vincie," I said. "Ask prettily for your rose, and vanish."

"I hope you will stay with me till your husband comes back," our hostess remarked, as we all went into the garden to get a rose; "I am so anxious to hear the result."

There were no white roses in Mrs. Davey-Renny's garden, but it was the flower, not the colour, that mattered. She gave Vincie a rose, about the size and shape of the one she had sent to Morgan, and he powdered it, and carefully handed it to her, to wrap gently in tissue-paper. Finally we all paid a visit to Mary, who described how she had carried the rose, and then saw Vincie to the road.

"How kind of you to take all this trouble," our hostess said, when we returned to the cottage. "Oh, would you care to see over my little nook. Such a sweet place."

What woman does not want to look over someone else's house? We went over every room, and I admired the daintiness of it, and was struck by a Boston quilt, "cottonwick," she called it, which she had brought over years back from America. It seemed that she had once gone there for six weeks as Mr. Morgan's secretary.

"I suppose you have made quite a lot of friends," I said as we adjourned to the garden for a cup of tea and cigarettes.

"Not many women," she said, with an odd glint in her eye; "I think it must be these girl-typist novels that do it."

I did agree. "Goldsmith's poor female, unadorned and plain," I said, "is about the only one who would be safe from the tongue of scandal. Or it might be arranged that all dictation was done with the door open."

"And so silly!" Mrs. Davey-Renny cried. "Mr. Morgan was well-to-do, and polite, and he left me money. That damned me— not the money. They didn't know that till now. Just that I'm not an absolute horror and *that*."

She was allusive, but I thought I understood her. "Of course your years with him gave you a disillusionising close-up," I suggested.

"In little things," she agreed. "If it had come to being attracted, I mean. I liked him. I had a great respect for him. But, well—there is no harm in saying it now—when he dictated, he kept on tapping his front teeth with a pencil. The first month I nearly went mad."

"Most 'damnable iteration'," I quoted.

"Once or twice, or at long intervals," she said softly, "one could bear it. Of course I stood it for years. But for a long time it gave me a sympathetic jar in my teeth."

"I think you earned the money," I said frankly.

"It was like a monumental mason tapping a grave-stone," she said. "That may sound exaggerated, but I am sensitive, and it wasn't so much the noise as the anticipation of it, you know, It put me off."

"So natural," I agreed. "The trouble lies in explaining imponderables like that to the police."

"Quite," she smiled. "Sergeant Bohm, I imagine, wouldn't mind if one tapped a dentist's whole stock with a hammer."

"And even Voce, who is more sensitive than you would think," I said, "might ask if you expected to take down from dictation after you were married."

She looked at me reflectively. "Yes. It was really only what I might call a professional gesture. But that was not all."

Obviously she was referring to some social solecism. "Snoring, for example," I said, "is distressing."

She smiled suddenly. "How pleased the locals would be if I mentioned that! Of course I know nothing about it. What I was going to tell you was that he had a habit of scratching his knee. It was his bad knee, and a doctor would probably say there was a reason for it. But he did that even out of office hours."

"My husband shall tell Voce," I said. "Policemen of his rank have quite a good knowledge of human nature and its foibles. They aren't the dumb animals in uniform people think. Of course I see it. It's a gesture I have heard that even well-bred women in South America exhibit, but not from choice."

"Do they really?" said Mrs. Davey-Renny, with a shudder. "*They* never worry me, but, of course, in very hot countries you can't tell."

I felt that her shudder and her explanation of Mr. Morgan's unattractiveness as a man, were both genuine. Irritating gestures and good hearts are often found in common. And only the super-suspicious decide that men must leave money to unattached women from dubious motives.

Intuition is often no more than good guessing helped by observation. I don't put mine forward as any great shakes. But I felt at once that Mrs. Davey-Renny had simply been Morgan's invaluable secretary-typist and her possible motive for murdering him could only be greed.

But she did not look greedy. If she proved to be guilty, I knew I should be surprised. Even the theory of collaboration with Mr. Sibbins began to look thin. A woman who couldn't fall in love with a man because he scratched his (arthritic) knee, would not be attracted to one who would scratch her soul every minute of the day. A glance was sufficient to show anyone that Sibbins was a bully, and probably a nagging one.

"I loved your simile about the dentist's stock," I said after a pause. "Of course your talk of sympathetic jarring was more a spiritual metaphor. I can see you have lovely teeth."

Mrs. Davey-Renny shook her head. "Alas, my dear Mrs. Mercer, if I am to believe the experts, they are only whited sepulchres!"

"Very whited," I said. "But do tell me! Has your expert ever studied pyorrhoea?"

She laughed. "How *do* you know?"

"When they specialise in that," I said, "I never visit them. You have no aches, no pains; your friends congratulate you, your enemies say that you smile twice as often as you need. But you can't escape the man who has made a study of Py. 'Out damned spots, out I say,' is his cry."

"I shall tell Mr. Edwards," she said. "He went specially to some clinic to study it. I won't let him touch mine."

It did strike me at the time that a lover must be very much in love with his work if he introduced dentistry into his wooing. "What big teeth you have, Grannie" is only right for Red Riding Hood. But possibly Mr. Edwards was merely anxious to make her smile.

"He was pointed out to me the other day," I remarked, thinking that pyorrhoea had served its purpose. "A handsome fellow."

Her smile came into play now. "Who knows it better?"

"Then you agree with me?"

"I was speaking of Mr. Edwards." She lay back in her chair, and gave a little laugh. "Even if you have been here such a short time, I expect you have heard *ad nauseam* of my knights?"

I nodded. "It seemed unavoidable. And I can understand it."

"Sweet of you." She offered her cigarette-case, and added: "I could do without them."

"What, *all* of them?" I asked.

She laughed again. "Now how much do you know, Mrs. Mercer? Mr. Power said you were a novelist, 'Henrietta Clandon.' Am I to be potted?"

"You are already being prepared for potting," I said. "Yes."

"Filleted sole; or is that too bad a pun?" she asked, with unexpected quickness.

"They're all too bad," I answered, "my husband is taking to them. But I'm taking him in hand. As for your suitors, I have an idea that the absent one is most in the running."

"Poor Inspector Kay," she murmured. "They can't quite swallow a policeman taking me in charge."

"Then there is Mr. Jolson," I said. "We met him. Rather overwhelmed by his dog."

"The dog has become a habit," she said. "He was brought up to be overwhelmed by something, or someone, bigger than himself. While his mother was alive, he was kept in his place. Now she was gone, he adopted the dog. Just like the little comedians in the old musical comedies, who always played opposite a huge solid woman."

"I remember," I replied. "He's out then. Next, on my gossip roster, is Mr. Paul Bone. Anything unkind to say about him?"

"Nothing," said my hostess. "My experience of artists is that they are either neck or nothing."

"But persistent?" I asked.

"That certainly. He told me he would cut out the drink if I accepted him. Now I don't drink, and I hate drunk men. But Paul sober is more sloppy than any man I ever knew. And a temper when not."

"Jealous?" I asked.

"My dear! A perfect little bantam-cock. It's as much as I can do to persuade Frankie—Inspector Kay, not to take him up and lock him up."

"Last, but not least, Mr. Tressy Withers?" I said, "he has asked us to tea one day,"

"Why?"

"He wants to know something," I said, "but before I make any more comments, and if it isn't too cheeky of me, what are your reactions?"

"I like your cheek," she said, and added, with a dimple, "and I mean that quite nicely too. Let me see: Oh, bold, importunate, unpleasant, and a bounder of parts. It just shows you how little

I really knew about Mr. Morgan when I say that I could never understand how he made a friend of that man."

"We agree," I said. "He makes me think of a prosperous book-maker, Vincie has an idea he's a crook. Join the mathematical talents and insolent good humour of a bookie to the instincts of a crook, and what do you get?"

She reflected, then shook her head. "Dark horse, by Sinister out of Jollity—unnamed. Frankly I don't know the answer."

"Keeper of a bucket-shop," I said, "or super share-pusher."

"Might be," she admitted. "Mr. Morgan was in stocks—outside."

"And Withers should be inside," I said. "He's oily and good-looking. But I think we shall go to tea. It will be all hands to the pumps then, whatever he may think."

Mrs. Davey-Renny glanced at me thoughtfully. "Is that how you make up books? I often wondered."

"Well, there are different methods," I said. "But really I want to help Mr. Power, and he wants to help you."

"I see. Well, fair do's, Mrs. Mercer—don't you think my explanation of the rose a natural and respectable one?"

"Yes," I said, "if Mr. Morgan really invented that rose."

"He did," she said. "If anything could have turned me against roses, Mr. Morgan's passion for growing them would have done it. In his spare time he talked of little else. I know nothing about them. He killed any desire I might have had. You see, he never talked of their beauty. It was all the technique of growing, grafting and so on. It was a tremendous compliment when he named the 'Rennavy Rose' after me and my husband. We had to see it at the Chelsea, of course, but neither of us thought it very pretty. I don't suppose that matters with those connoisseurs, any more than it does with dog-fanciers."

"Look at our Airedales, for example," I said.

"Or Sealyhams! All noses, both of them, and most melan-choly-looking beasts. Show points! But our nice dogs have gone."

"How did you recognise the Rennavy?" I asked.

"How could I not? Common vanity won't let you forget anything that has been named after you. Besides, it's a curly sort of rose, and—oh, at any rate I know it at sight."

"What puzzled us," I said, looking hard at a chaffinch which was doing the same for me from the lawn, "was why he stopped growing."

"Vanity," said Mrs. Davey-Renny. "He wasn't a vain man, but that was what happened. You see the Rennavy was what had been said to be the ideal of a white rose, of some silly species. He went at it for years, and then it came. But the judges belonged to a rival school or something. I mean to say, it's like women's hats, our hats. One day you are all hat, and the next all forehead."

"I hate most foreheads, don't you?" I asked.

"I loathe them. Talk about the old knobbly knees, for bumps I think the human forehead has it every time. And the new fashion gives you such a strange look—as if you were trying to look up into your own hair, which had gone back on you."

"I think we're fools," I said, "we don't dress, or hat, to personal style, but in mass. Square faces, long faces, ovals and oblongs, all under damnable hats. We used to laugh at men's bowlers. Why, they're things of joy beside the ridiculous top-hamper we have now."

"Something like that had happened to the rose while Mr. Morgan was thinking out his," she agreed. "His rose got a third prize. Imagine a great artist doing his magnum opus, and then finding they'd stuck some surrealistes on the jury."

"He lost interest?" I asked.

"Flopped, my dear. One of the gossip writers at the time— there were fewer then, thank heaven—said he took a specimen from his buttonhole, and trampled on it. Of course that was silly; he was more likely to trample on one of the others, or assault one of the judges."

"So he gave up roses and retired to the country," I remarked. "But surely it was rather backhanded sending him one?"

"He would know," she said. "It was meant to say that, after all the abuse, the Rennavy *had* become known, and was actually being sold with the famous Matilde Perot. Those were the red ones, you know."

"I see," I said, "the crux of the matter, I think, is that some-one must have known you were sending a white rose that day."

"No one could have, but Frank and Mary, my maid."

"Inspector Kay will be back in a day or two?" I said.

"Yes. I am not worrying about him. He only gave me the roses. He didn't know I was to find an old acquaintance among them and send it to Mr. Morgan."

"Would he mind?" I asked.

"He might have, soon after I came," she murmured. "I hate a man not to be able to be jealous. It makes one so cheap. There's too much of that nowadays. That's why so many men marry third-hand girls. I'd hate it. But I'm old-fashioned. Let them have it in them, but don't give 'em cause for it, is my motto. I told Frank all about Morgan, and my job with him, and my first marriage."

"But how candid!"

"I'm not like the people who love to have something up their sleeve," she smiled. "It isn't often liked, if it accidentally comes out."

"I am sure you married for love, not merely to get away from the tapping pencil," I told her.

"Yes, I did—in a way. I think there's half love and whole love, you know. There may be something that just keeps you back from the first. It's as irritating as being stung by a midge you can't see. Even if you could only see it *after* it stung you, there would be some satisfaction in having a smack at it."

"But you were happy?"

"Very. Half-happiness is a thing you're not so conscious of, until you have bagged the lot. Then you *know*."

CHAPTER XI

AT THAT moment someone rang a cycle-bell violently from the lane. It was Vincie coming back. A minute later he came to us, beaming.

"You're cleared!" he said, "and I'll need a clothes-brush."

"Tell us about it," said Mrs. Davey-Renny gratefully, as he sat down and accepted one of her cigarettes.

"There isn't much to tell," he said, mopping his hot face. "I cycled along, trying to feel and ride happy and carefree, thinking of a postman. Don't tell me that Mary, good girl as she seems to be, had her mind fixed on your rose! Besides, she wouldn't know it was powdered."

"If it was," said our hostess.

"Well, I got to the garden-gate to find old Bohm on the look-out. I handed him the rose, and then went inside after him. He undid the paper, and some of the powder made me sneeze, and some went into the turn-up of his nice slacks. I hope Power simply supplied me with boric powder, or I may be in danger of becoming an addict."

"Was none left on the rose?" I asked.

He nodded. "Hardly enough to asphyxiate an aphis, my dear. But taking Bohm to be Morgan, his jacket was simply coked up. In other words, that powder's clinging."

"I am most grateful," said Mrs. Davey-Renny, "but I did think that they said this traffic in cocaine and dope was really done with."

Vincie smiled. "There is relatively little done in this country," he said, "and I believe detective-story writers are almost forbidden to mention it. But, of course, the stuff is sold here and there, and big profits made out of small quantities. The idea of huge rings with clogged warehouses operating in England is bunkum."

"You sometimes read of cases in the papers," she said.

"And half the cases aren't found out," I said, "but a few individuals, as I think even Voce would tell you, can make a nice bit out of the traffic. And there must be as many more who think there is a fortune in it, and hope to work up a connection."

She nodded. "Then I suppose some individual, of one kind or another, is, or has been here, with some of the stuff."

Vincie agreed. "Obviously, or the analyst is a donkey. The agents here are closely watched, but it could be got more easily abroad, I think."

She smiled. "Twenty years ago that would have made it more difficult," she remarked. "But now, when it's more distinguished not to have travelled abroad, it will be harder to find the individual."

"Much harder," he agreed.

"Take Mary," she said. "Last year Mary took her holiday, where?"

"Paris?" I suggested.

"Spain," said Mrs. Davey-Renny. "She saved up for two years, and went with a party. She was a bore about bulls for months. At last I had to tell her frankly that a corrida wasn't a corridor, and I hated cattle anyway. The North Pole jaunt is the only exclusive one now."

"On the other hand," I suggested, "dope is too dear and too exotic a taste for the multitude. ''Tis no sport for peasants,' as I think Byron said somewhere. Let's try to narrow it down. First, Mr. Bone; I know his Bohemianism stops at his beard, but a man who is so often tight, and must have explored all the doubtful pleasures of drunkenness, might experiment."

"And he goes every year to Paris," said Mrs. Davey-Renny, "and picks up the vogue of the year before. Last year he was, or so he said, a disciple of Picasso. I suppose in so-called artistic circles in Paris you could get dope?"

"Of course," said Vincie. "Let us put Bone down as having opportunity. Only to get dope, so far. What about Withers?"

Our hostess nodded. "If that man saw any money in anything, he would run at it. He goes abroad, he's often away from home, supposed to be up in London. And I think his conscience isn't one of the gorse-bush ones which give more pricks than ha'pence."

"We'll put him down," I said. "Opportunity and no inhibitions."

"Inspector Kay?" Vincie asked.

"Yes, let's be fair," she said hastily. "But I don't see how he could have got it, and I know he had gone that evening before I picked out the rose."

"On your own statement," he replied, "but we can't—I mean legally and theoretically—depend on that. I am sorry, but there it is. He was in the London C.I.D. He may have seized samples."

"I never thought of that" she remarked. "Just mark him Opportunity to Procure."

"Then there is Morgan himself," I said quickly. "He ate more Turkish Delight than is good for any man, or seemed to."

"That's perfectly true," said Mrs. Davey-Renny. "He used to have a box in his office. In fact, the juniors were rude enough to nickname him Fatima. But I have eaten some that he gave me. It was delicious. The ordinary stuff you buy tastes like scented chewing-gum in comparison. And I am sure I never had any dope dreams after it."

"It might be a stunt to smuggle in dope," I said. "There would be no need to pack the finest Turkish Delight. But that's only a suggestion. Now we come to Mr. Everard Jolson."

"Everard as a dope fiend strikes me as unlikely," she said. "His mother would have spanked him if she had caught him at it. And he's on velvet since his old client died and left him her money."

"But there," said Vincie, "you have a break in his life, which is apt to upset people who have led sheltered lives. For years he has been mothered. His mother dies. Everard is like a baby rabbit left alone in the bosom of a stoat family. He is bewildered, afraid. He develops an inferiority complex. His temper is a sign of that. The little man pugnacious, you know. 'What can I do to be different, to show 'em that I am a perfect devil, not the tame bank manager they think me?'"

"When she died, he went for a Mediterranean cruise," Mrs. Davey-Renny murmured. "He got as far as Smyrna."

"Smyrna?" I echoed. "That must be in the thick of the traffic. They push it over to Egypt, I've heard."

Mrs. Davey-Renny looked hard at me. "Is it? But I could never suspect Everard."

"I could," Vincie said. "Seriously, murders aren't committed by people as a habit. That's the rarest kind of homicide, and always, I should say, professional. People, other than gangsters or bandits, who kill others in numbers are maniacs."

"I admit that, Mr. Mercer, but I don't see the point."

Neither did I, but no wise wife will admit that her husband cannot be easily understood by her, even in his most cryptic moments.

"Vincent always hopes he can get away with it," I informed her. "Mr. Voce told him so frankly the other day."

"You're quite wrong," he replied. "I was going to say that it is habits which form our characters."

"I thought it was the other way about," Mrs Davey-Renny murmured.

"I'm not intolerant," Vincie remarked. "But my view is that it is as I have said. That being so, murder to a man who does not regularly commit one is an accidental. It does not alter his character, his expression, or his normal appearance. And those are the things which dispose us to suspect a man of murder."

"When the postman only knocks once, he doesn't leave many finger-prints on the knocker," I suggested.

"Roughly, no. Murder as a habit, I contend, must out. It will show somewhere. Before the first of the series, if I may put it that way, the serial homicide will give you the impression that he cannot be trusted with a knife, or a tin of weed-killer. If you are continually smiling, or frowning, you show it in time."

"There may be something in that," she admitted. "Everard, say, goes through life, to a point, with no desire to kill; not even a thought of murder in his mind."

"Crime leaves no wrinkles on his azure brow," I suggested.

Vincie ignored me. "From what we know of Jolson, only temper of a jealous kind, and that quite lately, could have disturbed the amiable and rather weak face he wears. One killing, and that unpremeditated, say, leaves no mark of Cain there."

"But surely Cain only committed one murder?" I asked.

"Cain," Vincie said, "is the archetypal murderer. We are supposed to regard him as another Habakkuk."

"Never mind, Mrs. Davey-Renny," I said, "I think myself that Mr. Jolson would hardly buy commercial cocaine, and carry a packet with him when he went to interview Morgan. He might do one thing, but not both."

"I am not saying that he killed Morgan," Vincie said, "merely that he is as much suspect as any of you. He was in the garden that morning, he had a cause of quarrel with Morgan, he admits that he is physically, or was physically, no match for the man. A little anaesthesia must be valuable as a prior aid to assault."

"I think this is very unprofitable speculation," I remarked. "As Mr. Morgan is not proved to have had any tender interest in Mrs. Davey-Renny here, while she has told us that he neither had any charms for her, nor attempted to exert them, Mr. Jolson's quarrel must have fallen very flat."

"I see what you mean," she said. "Mr. Morgan would have simply laughed, patted him on the back, and said: 'Go in and win, little man if you can! That woman means less than nothing to me.'"

"You forget the impulse, and especially the idle man's impulse, to tease," Vincie observed. "He had every provocation, the big man's good-humoured contempt for the little man, the fact that Jolson's charge was untrue and insolent, and so on. If some little bantam-cock squared up to me, and accused me of wife-enticement; being happily married, I should not endeavour to excuse myself. I should pull his leg with the greatest vigour."

"But pulling legs is your amusement," I said, "Mr. Morgan may have been more dignified. What do you say Mrs. Davey-Renny?"

"He had a queer sense of humour," she admitted, "and he may have chaffed Everard. He said to me once that the name was so like the man. But I think it only sounds feeble and silly because it is unusual."

"All the same," I remarked, "Vincie is right in the main. Nine out of ten of the British murderers during my life-time were not regarded by their friends as at all likely to take life. And their faces were no better and no worse than those of their friends. As for motive, what is adequate for one man would appear inadequate to another. Just as a jibe that is received by one man with a superior grin, drives another to unaccountable fury."

"Yes," said Vincie, "we're all mad in some way. Take myself. My wife would tell you that I have an equable temperament. A very slight jab from the point of a barber's scissors, when I am having my hair cut, causes me no serious physical inconvenience. But I can quite truthfully say that, when I have had such a careless jab, I have been nearer a perfectly absurd homicide than at any other time."

"That's what should be called hysteria," I said.

"Absolutely," he admitted. "But a jealous little man is as likely to become hysterical as anyone. The will to do ill deeds while you are unprovided with the physical means produces an ineffectual frenzy."

"I suppose both of you often talk cases over like this?" said our hostess, with a slight look of wonder.

"Not unless we have someone to show off before," I said. "Mr. Voce has a look which freezes speculation in your veins; Mr. Power likes to show off himself, which is death to our exhibitionism; and trying out wordy theories on Sergeant Bohm would be like pelting the Rock of Gibraltar with peas."

"In other words," said Vincie, as he rose, "Penny and I are very grateful to you for listening. You do that admirably. It won't last. We know that from sad experience with our friends; but it was lovely in its life. And you may also rely on Penny putting it into her book."

"But I thought it was to be a crime-story," she said. "That is, if it's to be about poor Mr. Morgan's mysterious death."

"You forget," I said candidly, "that we can't speed up the police in their work. Conversation like this is the same as *legato* to a singer, it links up one note with another, and makes the book run smoothly."

"I think it must be most thrilling to write books," she said, as she shook hands with us.

"Only to amateurs," said Vincie, "I suppose they do get a kick out of it."

CHAPTER XII

WE TOLD Power all about the experiment, and our visit to Mrs. Davey-Renny, and were glad to see that he was inclined to be impressed by our conclusions.

"She's too much at ease to be a murderess," he agreed, "at times when the murder is not under discussion. Most people can act when the occasion calls for it, but not one in a million can drop the subject and discuss another one light-heartedly. There must be an emotional *entr'acte*."

"Yes," I said, "people don't always go back physically to the scene of their crime, but very few criminals slip smoothly up a topical by-pass. Do you think that is because they imagine anyone who shows them one has a purpose behind it?"

"I think I do," said Mr. Power. "It's like an embarrassing incident, or a social solecism you discover. Your anxiety to lead the talk away from it doubles the offender's consciousness of it."

"Penny and I tried that idea out to-day," Vincie told him, "and the good woman frolicked after us, without a glance behind."

"And now," I said, "what did you do in Brum?"

"I was making inquiries," said Power. "The fact is that a good part of Mr. Tressy Withers' correspondence comes from there. Bulky, but quite harmless and unofficial looking on the outside."

"You haven't been rude enough to look inside?"

He smiled at Vincie. "Never had the chance, my dear fellow. But, acting on information received, as the police say, I looked round a few offices in that city, and more or less traced a connection between Mr. Tressy and the 'Natural Treasure Finance Co.'."

"It sounds like a dud gold-mine," I said.

"Brazen, but not gold," he replied, "I gather that it is prepared to sell shares in every part of England, Wales and Scotland, outside a fifty miles radius from Birmingham—longer journeys preferred."

"Then it is share-pushing?" I cried rather excitedly.

"Largely. There is some financing of a usurious kind too. I think the present big do is a company to extract radium from pitchblende."

"And where is the pitchblende?" Vincie asked.

"Some say one thing, and some say another," Power murmured. "In Wales it is mooted that Africa has it. In England, with its fondness for that country, Canada is the repository. In Scotland they hear that it is in Siberia. But the company is only in its early stages, and people are being let in daily on the ground-floor."

"At how much?" I asked.

"Like a doctor's fee it varies with the income of the patient," he replied. "The humble widow in the depths of the country is five shillings; unless very credulous, when she goes to ten bob. The shares, if they had a market, would be said to have a very wide market. I've heard of as low as three-and-six and as high as one pound five."

"And you think Tressy is at the head of it?" Vincie asked.

"I am sure he is the man who originated the ramp," Power remarked, "He never shows up at the office, but I had a description of the manager, who has visited his house on several occasions."

"Coming from Birmingham?" I asked.

"No. Bohm says Withers' cook said the gentleman came from Surrey, where he has a country-house. But that is merely what she heard from her employer."

"There may be a mistake," Vincie suggested.

"I thought there might be. But the manager of the company is the dead spit of the man who came here, and both have a lisp."

"Natural or national?"

"Natural. Of course my quest led me nowhere really. I cannot imagine Morgan dealing with a show of that sort."

"Withers, of course, wouldn't try to do him down," I said.

"It doesn't follow," was Power's reply. "There's a hook even for knowing fish, and they're the sort that doesn't expect to have it blatantly dangled before them. 'Pyorrhoea? Not me!' as the advertisement says. If you ever saw a leading batsman taken in by a silly slow, you'll know what I mean."

Vincie nodded agreement, but looked argumentative. "That's all very well. But look at it from another side. Suppose Morgan and Withers put their heads together in their country retirement, and started this show together?"

"Voce rather suspects that, but I am not so sure," said Power. "It may be so. In that case, the only motive for murder would be Morgan's discovery that profits were being concealed by his partner. Withers could not be anxious for a showdown."

"When is Inspector Kay expected back?" I asked, after a pause.

"To-morrow morning. As a matter of courtesy. Voce is to consult him about the case. So he says. I wonder what he screws out of him."

"Is there anything in the idea that Kay could have got dope?" I asked.

He nodded. "Yes, there is, it seems now. Kay was in two London cases, some years back, where seizures were made. That's not conclusive in itself."

"No," Vincie observed, "not in the least. Detectives don't imitate the crimes they investigate. If Voce gave me change for a pound, I wouldn't bite every coin, simply because he was the big noise in the Camber Coining case."

"Now you're being elementary," said Power, "I shall have to see Kay again, and I think I'll introduce him to you two, but there's too much arithmetic in his case for me to consider him guilty. He bought a dozen roses, he had four Rennavy roses among them, how was he to know that the woman would recognise it and send one to Morgan, and if so, which one? Would an officer who had worked with an anti-narcotic squad imagine that you could kill a man with a spot like that and so on. Finally, if he is in love with Mrs. Davey-Renny, would he put her in jeopardy by making her the medium of the gift?"

"No," I said decidedly, "but is there no possibility that a rival wished him to be thought the inspirer?"

"Granted three things. That the rival knew he had bought Rennavy roses, and given them to his inamorata; that he knew she would send one to Morgan; or that he intercepted Mary on the way and borrowed the flower for a few moments, which seems unlikely."

"Further, of course," Vincie said, "since Morgan gave up rose-growing before he came here, who would connect him with that particular rose? If it had been called 'Morgan's Fancy' there might have been a chance."

We went into dinner.

After dinner we had a surprise visitor. It was Inspector Kay, who asked for Mr. Power, and was shown into the room where we all sat. He had come home earlier than expected.

Introductions effected, I had time to study the man. I liked the look of him. He was somewhat nervous, and the appearance of a nervous policeman had a peculiar charm about it, that of rarity perhaps. His original public school accent had been some-what blunted by consorting with plain officers in the country, but it still proclaimed him a member of the middle-class.

I use that term roughly. To ourselves, if we are middle-class, we are all upper-middle class. To the aristocrat there does not seem much difference between the fifty classes which make up the middle-class, unless one has an immense amount of money. You will find plenty of wealthy middle-middle-class people frolicking in the highest circles; even lower-class people, if they are film-stars of note. In fact, you will sometimes see these latter taken up by the aristocracy, when the middle-classes would turn up their noses at them. Which may be the reason why many of the middle-classes consider one-half of the aristocracy to have vulgar tastes.

"Well, Inspector," said Power, when coffee had been brought in, "I am thoroughly up the pole in this nice case here. So are Mr. and Mrs. Mercer, who take a great interest in criminology. They know damn-all about it, but that's the case with most so-called criminologists."

Kay smiled nicely at me. "I know even less, Mr. Power. I didn't even know that I had bought Rennavy roses. I bumped down the money and left it to the girl. Who knew of it, or stuck dope on one, I have no idea."

"Right," said Power, "we start even there. But you'll admit that you have to have the stuff before you use it. Short of a faked doctor's prescription, is it easy?"

"It can be had, if you know where to look for it."

"That's no help. Ever had what is vulgarly known as 'coke' in your possession?"

"Once," said Kay, rather uneasily.

"Only once?"

"Yes. It was morphine and heroin the last time. More fashionable now, you know."

"I do. Long ago?"

"I copped a fellow in '32," said Kay, "I took a quarter of a pound off him. That's a lot. Not pure, of course."

"Adulterated?"

"Yes, same as the stuff they analysed here."

"You turned it all in?"

Kay smiled now. "Of course I should say so, even if I hadn't. Of course I did."

"Alone when you made the cop?"

"Absolutely."

"There was no hint from Mrs. Davey-Renny that evening that she was going to send a flower to Morgan?"

"No, it seems to be—to have been—a brain-wave after I had gone."

"She recognised the rose as one Morgan had first produced."

"So I hear now. She did not say so at the time. What happened was this: I handed her the bunch and she said they were lovely, only would I mind putting them in water for her. I went to the kitchen, fished up an empty milk-jug, stuck 'em in, and joined her again."

"So that's your story. Do you think anyone knew of it, and wanted to involve you?"

Kay shook his head. "No. That's a rank impossibility. How could they know?"

"Is there anyone who might do you a nasty turn?"

"You can't be a policeman and not have a few wishing you dead?" he replied. "But you can't make omelettes without eggs. I've thought and thought over it since I've been away. I don't see who could have had the egg to make my omelette with."

"But there are people with whom you have never come into conflict officially. Take Bone!"

"The little blighter hasn't the venom."

"Mr. Jolson?"

Kay grinned. "Can't see Jolson with the poison phial, Mr. Power."

"Mr. Edwards?"

"I thought of him, because he may be able to get 'coke,' for all I know. But I never felt him a real enemy, except when he started drilling. Even then I was the offended, not he. Besides, who could have had his experience with local anaesthetics, and used one in such a silly way?"

"Mr. Tressy Withers is now my only hope," Power murmured.

"A perfect bounder," Kay agreed. "But I don't see that he had any motive for killing Morgan."

"Not jealousy, Inspector?" I asked.

He turned to look at me. "He had no reason to be jealous about Morgan, Mrs. Mercer."

"Well, about you?" I said daringly.

He coloured up, as Power had said he did. "I—well—" he broke off.

Power was amused. "Mr. and Mrs. Mercer paid a visit to Mrs. Davey-Renny, Inspector. Probably it wasn't an intentional leakage, but just slipped out."

Poor Kay looked embarrassed. "Oh, I see. Yes, that is possible. Has anyone discovered that Withers saw Morgan that morning?"

"Unless Voce has kept it dark, I think not," Power replied.

I gave Kay a cigarette to make it up, and he thanked me, and added in a dubious tone: "I have my own suspicions."

Power started. "Why, my dear fellow, you've been obstructing the police! Suppressing information, you know. But who is it?"

Kay frowned. "There was a fellow with a camera spying about at times. He may have seen me take in the roses—a stranger, I may say."

"And what motive would a stranger have for impheating you or Mrs. Davey-Renny?"

"That I don't know. I intended to make some inquiries about him, and then poor Morgan died and I was given my week."

"That's all right," Power told him. "That was my client, Mr. Sibbins, old Morgan's nephew."

Kay slapped his thigh. "The nephew, the fellow who comes in for the money. Then he had a motive!"

"Which we are keeping dark for the moment, Kay. You see, hanging about where he was, in the neighbourhood of a fellow beneficiary, it would look awkward for Mrs. Davey-Renny."

"But she doesn't even know him."

"We have to take her word for it," said Power, "and that's most unprofessional, as you ought to know. Don't get excited. I am not hinting at a dark past, merely reminding you of the good old rules on which police inquiries are conducted. If you came into court in another case, you wouldn't be such a goof as to remark that a thing was so *because* the accused told you so."

"No," Kay agreed, "of course not. It's jolly difficult to suspect one's friends of criminality though."

"Admitted," Power said. "But to our muttons again. You're outside the case, but you know the facts roughly. There's a presumption, not only that Morgan died of a blow in the abdomen, but that he and Mr. Jolson had a quarrel."

"That little chap wouldn't fight with Morgan, Mr. Power. Morgan had a gammy knee, but he would have eaten him. I don't suppose he even knows how to use his hands. A bit of a mammy's boy, in spite of his years."

"I said a quarrel. Now, Jolson had his dog with him."

Kay smiled. "They say down here 'the dog had Jolson with him'."

"I proved that the dog, though he did not bite, resented what looked like a mild attack on his master."

"It would."

"Well, it's a playful beast too, and heavy. Jolson was seen by my friends here. As he left, the dog, in a playful moment, butted him astern, so to speak."

Kay smiled. "It is a bouncing beast. It knocked over the curate once."

"Then what about this? Jolson and Morgan have a row. The dog resents it and rams Morgan amidships. Whether Morgan has a delicacy in that quarter, or was in the collision too soon after a heavy breakfast, Morgan conks out. Is that possible?"

"Short of making an experiment on a man with a bit of a tummy, you couldn't prove it," said Kay after a little thought. "If a dog of a hundred pounds or more took a run, I should say his head would be about equal to a bang with a seven-pound hammer. It's a thoroughly nice idea, all the same, but do you think Morgan was trying to cocaine the dog, and got the surplus thrown over his buttonhole?"

"Frankly, no," said Power. "All we can decide is that the stuff must have been put there after Morgan was dead."

"To what end?"

"To involve a third party; you, perhaps, or Mrs. Davey-Renny."

"But how did Morgan sniff it, if he was dead?"

Power laughed. "If I was found dead with the stuff in the nasal passage, does it follow that I sniffed it?"

"I suppose it could be blown there, the way an insufflator blows powder on objects, when you want to take finger-prints."

"I assume that it could. I'd guarantee to do it, if you provided me with a corpse."

"That presupposes Jolson to be in possession of: (1) cocaine, (2) a sort of insufflator."

"Or someone who came into the garden after Jolson had gone. As far as we can see, a visitor might have arrived and left again unobserved, that morning."

"True," said Kay, "but it's unusual to pay a visit carrying an insufflator and a charge of cocaine."

"You're spoiling the whole thing!" said Power, getting up. "You people full of common-sense are the death of all imagination! We were getting on very nicely till you came."

CHAPTER XIII

OF COURSE, Voce was wilfully keeping away from us. That might mean that he had something he did not want to disclose, or us to discover. But I gathered from Mr. Power before we all retired that night that the Chief Inspector had secured partial or limited alibis for Mr. Bone, Mr. Withers and Mr. Sibbins, and a whole alibi (crowning a tooth, which was a long job) for Mr. Edwards.

When I say a limited alibi, I mean that between half-past ten and the moment when Mr. Morgan was found dead, the three men were able to mention witnesses who were with them, or had seen them during part of the period. Mr. Bone had admitted getting a present of three bottles of *Bols* the day before, and seemed to have sampled them at intervals, so it was possible that the gap in his alibi was occupied by filling his glass, and the growing black-out later. But neither of the two was able to prove that he could not have paid a hasty visit to Morgan that morning.

To our surprise, Mr. Power did not go to town next day. He turned up at breakfast, and said that he positively had to worry Voce, who was pretending not to know him.

"And he seems to have taken a liking to Sibbins," he added. "Wants to know all about him, and is very busy about it."

"Does he think Sibbins filled in the hole in his alibi with a call on his uncle?" I asked, as I handed him a cup of tea.

"I shouldn't put it past him," was the reply, "Neither of them."

"Well, when are you going on Voce's track?" Vincie asked.

"I start at eleven," said Power. "By the way, I like Mrs. Jennifer's bacon. It has just the right curl at the tip."

Mr. Power was mistaken about the time of starting. At a quarter to ten, when we were all resting, and smoking in the garden, Sergeant Bohm came in.

We never expect him to look startled, impressed, or grieved. He was quite calm now, though not smiling, when he remarked that Mr. Jolson was dead.

Vincie and I jumped up. Power merely raised his eyebrows. "Little Jolson? Poor little devil! What was it?"

"We don't know yet, sir, but Mr. Voce said you ought to hear. He's over there now."

"At the house?" I said, feeling quite shocked.

"No, at the gravel-pit," said Bohm.

Power got up. "Any harm in our going over?"

"I don't think so, sir."

"Where is it, and what happened?" I asked.

"The gentleman broke his neck," said Bohm quietly. "It seems there is a fine view from the top."

"And how far to the bottom?" Vincie demanded.

"Nearly sixty feet, sir," said the sergeant. "The edge is grassed over and not so easy to see unless you keep an eye on your feet."

"Where's the dog?" Vincie asked. "They were supposed to be inseparable, weren't they?"

"The dog's dead, sir. It was shot."

"You're extremely tiresome," Power said. "Drawing you is like extracting an impacted wisdom-tooth. What happened, and why? Was Jolson shot as well as broken-necked?"

"No, sir. The dog seems to have gone over too, and a local farmer got his gun and shot it."

"Have you any idea yet when Jolson died?"

Bohm prepared to go. "Sometime last evening, the doctor thinks. But I must be getting back."

"Wait ten seconds and we'll tootle you over," said Vincie. "In that way we won't look so like a rubber-neck waggon full of morbid sightseers."

But Bohm was incorruptible. He hurried off alone and we set off five minutes later to the gravel-pit, following directions he had given us.

Fortunately, the gravel-pit was in a private field, and the barbed wire round it, supplemented by two policemen (one on the gate) had kept about a hundred and fifty locals from entering it. They were draped on and against the fence, and looked envious when we were admitted by the constable guarding the only entrance. Bohm had generously mentioned our projected visit.

The field lay up the slope of a hill. At the top was a clump of trees. A little way down, a portion of the hill had been scooped out, leaving a yellow scar, a rough and wide ledge below, an almost sheer drop down the face between.

From the top there was undoubtedly a wonderful view of the valley, fields, a stream, coppices, the park of a country-house, and distant woods fading and merging into a purple haze on the horizon. We left the car in the field below and climbed up.

Two local police, one the Superintendent, were at the top of the pit, and we saw Voce on the edge of the base, talking to someone who turned out to be Captain Hollick.

I admit that I was not anxious to see the poor broken body of the little bank manager, so I was not disappointed when I discovered that he had already been removed in the ambulance.

Voce received us gravely. "You know, Mr. Power, Captain Hollick," he said. "This is Mr. and Mrs. Mercer, who are staying with him here."

Captain Hollick bowed, but did not look very satisfied. "How d'ye do?" he said, but added to Voce: "They are not concerned in the case, are they, Chief Inspector?"

Mr. Voce nodded. "In a way, sir. It seems Mr. Jolson called to see them, and made an admission. I thought you might care to hear what he had to say."

Captain Hollick's face cleared. Military men, even when retired, do not like to see civilians on the parade ground. "Oh, good. I am just going up to see my superintendent, Mr. Mercer. Come along and tell me as you go."

Power walked down to where some men were examining the bottom of the gravel-pit, Voce looked at me.

"It was as much as I could do not to ask if Mr. Power had brought the whole circus," he said, rather bitterly, "they don't do these things in the Army!"

"As one of the performers, I thank you for your restraint," I said, "I never leave my husband, you know."

"As a matter of fact," remarked Voce, with a sudden appearance of his "Cat" smile, "I am glad you came. We can't be sure if it was accident, suicide, or something else."

"So we are excused because you can find some use for us. I knew that when Sergeant Bohm came," I said. "What exactly happened here?"

He led me to what had been the base of operations in the days when the gravel-pit was commercially worked. "He was lying just by that heap of sand," he said, and I could see that a tarpaulin had been laid on the ground to cover something. "Now look up at the lip of the pit."

I looked up and saw where the friable earth and gravel had given way. There was a slight overhang there all along, and one would have thought that local residents who came there for a view would know enough to keep a little back from it.

"That is the only sign showing where a body went over," Voce remarked.

"Well," I said, very dull for once, "there was just one body."

"Human body," said Voce.

"Oh, and the poor dog," I said. "I see. Where did he land?"

"There," he pointed, "a little further out from the base."

"But he might jump after his master."

"If he jumped, I think he would have jumped further."

I saw that. "I have no experience in these matters," I told him, "but don't you think a suicide, about to fling himself down from a height, would jump off, rather than simply slither down?"

He nodded approvingly. "I do. It's an instinct. They may have a feeling that a jump down hastens the speed. I don't think it would. I think once they're over, it's the gravitational pull does it."

Voce's approval is flattery to an amateur. I "swole" perceptibly. "I may be wrong," I said, with that excess of false modesty which characterises me when I have a brain-wave, "but don't you think it's clear that the dog was behind him?"

Voce permitted himself a dry smile. "If he was on the very edge of the face, there was no room for the dog *before* him."

"You are unkind!" I said, "I meant that there was no other visible sign of a second body breaking away the overhang."

"As a dog might jump over the edge from ten feet away, there might not be," Voce observed. "But let us look at the alternative. Mr. Jolson was attached to his dog. Suppose the dog made a dash at a rabbit, and went -over. Mr. Jolson might lose his head and run forward to see what had happened."

"Suppose the dog had made a dash at Mr. Jolson?" I said.

Voce considered that seriously. "That's one of our problems, Mrs. Mercer. Did he fall, or was he pushed? as the old phrase has it. It would be much more convenient for us if he jumped."

"You would take suicide to be confirmatory of guilt?" I asked.

"It would tend that way, no doubt. As you know, over here, in spite of loose talk, we have no third degree. At the same time a nervous man, suspected of murder, and stringently examined, might temporarily go off his rocker. I've known innocent people get into an awful sweat, and a fit of hysterics, after half an hour's questions. But that sort of thing is not common."

"What sort of an ordeal had he?" I asked.

"Mild as cream," said Voce; "in fact he came in himself, spurred by you and Mr. Mercer, and told his tale. He hasn't been worried. I can assure you of that."

I looked up the face of the quarry again. Mr. Power was now up there talking to the superintendent. "I don't know if we told you, Mr. Voce, but when Mr. Jolson called on us, the dog butted him as he was leaving. It was in a sort of elephantine gambol."

"I heard from someone that the dog was given to horse-play," Voce replied, "and I don't suppose it is a very reasoning animal. It wouldn't tell itself, for example, that its master was on the edge of a quarry, so that a rough display of affection might be fatal."

I agreed. "That is what Vincie and I felt when we heard the dog had gone over. If it was a yard or two behind Jolson, and bounded on to him, it could hardly save itself."

"It will have to be taken into account," he replied gravely. "Not that it's by any means proved."

"There are three alternatives," I said. "Jolson committed suicide, and his dog jumped over after him. Jolson fell over when he went forward to see what had happened to his dog. The dog butted its master over and couldn't stop. If it did, I do feel it is quite possible that the dog also butted Mr. Morgan in the tummy. It once knocked down a curate. There's nerve for you."

"Also upset a child on a fairy-cycle, overturned the last surviving piano-organ with a monkey on it, and was warned vicariously about its future conduct by the super here," said Voce. "Yes, it could do it. But why did Mr. Jolson not say so?"

"As they were alone, it would be hard to prove," I suggested. "Then Mr. Jolson had gone over to have a row. Lastly he had not mentioned his visit to the police till we hinted that he ought to. People have got the wind up over much less."

"We'll join the others above," said Voce, nodding. "I'll just pass on what you saw to Captain Hollick. He seems to have a feeling that people don't commit suicide in Malpertuis. Not good form, you know. So he may be glad to get this angle on the dog."

We climbed up by a circuitous route, and told Captain Hollick. He seemed pleased at the idea. "Dear old Jolson would not commit suicide," he said. "Quite a character, Mrs. Mercer, but one of the best."

There was nothing particularly logical about that remark, but one doesn't expect close reasoning from Chief Constables. I noticed too that Vincie was making signs to me that he was ready to go, and joined him when I had said good-bye to Voce and Hollick. Power had already disappeared.

"What's your verdict, darling?" I said, when we were going back to the car.

"Well, I had a good look at the ground up there, and I think the dog did it," he replied. "If Jolson was in the habit of going up there to look at the view, I am sure it was so."

"If not, it looks odd," I suggested.

"Yes. Voce, I imagine, is in favour of suicide. Hollick gave me that impression."

"What does Power think?"

"Power only knows!" said Vincie. "He was as dumb as a fish, and went off to Malpertuis. Personally I feel that we've clicked first. That rumbustious brute felt excessively happy and wanted to communicate its *joie de vivre* to poor Jolson."

Power was on the lawn—and only ten minutes to luncheon—when we returned. A policeman had given him a pillion-ride.

"What hastened you?" Vincie asked, as we approached him. "Some hot scent you struck, and felt greedy about?"

"A commonplace query," he replied. "Did he, or did he not, frequent the gravel-pit view? He did. At least, he went there once a week."

"Was yesterday his day?" I asked.

"No," said Power, "but this week has been different. He hung about expecting to be questioned, or something. At any rate, he often went to the scene, and this time he died."

"Killed by the dog?" Vincie said.

"Or else suicide," he agreed. "You or I would be deceived by the grass growing on the verge. I dashed near walked over myself when I was scouting about, but Jolson would know better."

"Any signs to show exactly where he was standing when he went over?" I asked.

"From the signs I should say that he stood about eighteen inches from the actual edge. In fact, if he had been on the real edge, he would have gone over without crashing such a bit of the overhang."

"I see," said Vincie. "There would only be the damage done by his feet slipping."

"Yes. As it was, my idea is that he fell forward in a sitting position, and the impact of part of his body carried away the edge of the turf and tufts of rough grass."

"There will be an inquest, of course?" I said.

"There will," said Mr. Power. "I think Hollick means to rope you two in. For evidence, you know."

"We know nothing about him."

"Very likely not, but local ideas of decency seem to demand that he shall not be a suicide. You may be asked about the dog butting Jolson, and so forth. If there is no evidence to point the other way, the jury will be glad to bring in 'Accidental Death'."

"By the way," Vincie said, "does Sibbins's partial alibi cover an absence from Malpertuis on the day of Morgan's death? He never said he had been there."

"That's what Voce dislikes about him," was the reply. "He never told me, but when it came to an official Stand-and-Deliver, he admitted—only for the purposes of his alibi, mind you—that he had thought of calling on his uncle."

"Did he say why?" I asked.

"With the delightful idea he sketched for us of saving uncle from himself, or rather from Mrs. Davey-Renny. At the last moment he faltered. Had an idea, it seems, that uncle mightn't quite like the thought of having a sneak for an heir."

"I'd love to hear how he put that into words," Vincie remarked. "Bit of a twister for a conceited and insolent ass like Sibbins to admit."

"I believe he said his uncle was old-fashioned," Power told us. "Decency is apparently purely Victorian."

"Do you think the case is any nearer solution?" I asked.

"I do not," said Power. "Now I have to go away for two days on business, and that's time wasted. What beats me is this: is there a chance that both tragedies were murder? That was in my mind when I went to the gravel-pit to-day. But there wasn't any trace of 'coke' about poor Jolson."

"Why should there be?" said Vincie.

"My dear fellow, if Morgan was murdered; that rose was doctored *afterwards*. If Jolson wasn't the murderer (and no one would murder him if he wasn't), it may be assumed that the actual killer either saw him come away, or knew he had been in Morgan's garden. If so, then he wanted to put the blame on Jolson. But the absence all along of any source of the cocaine would lead the man who pushed Jolson over to put some of the stuff in his pockets, or leave a burst packet where he went down."

"I see," Vincie said, "that would put it on Jolson all right."

"There's the gong for luncheon," Power said. "You have forty-eight hours from to-morrow to investigate that nasty little business of the dope. Where did it come from? Who had it? Is there a retailer here in Malpertuis?"

CHAPTER XIV

WE WERE asked out to tea. As a rule, being gregarious, and fond of tea, we accept without a qualm. This time we had several qualms, but accepted.

The invitation, of course, was from Mr. Tressy Withers. He added in his note that he had also asked Mr. Bone to tea. He underlined *tea*. Power was certain that Mr. Withers wanted to know how things were going. He took it that we, being boon companions of Mr. Power, and obviously in the pockets of the "Cat and the Kitten," had, what our friend called, the "low-down" on the case.

"What is it that he is afraid will come out?" Power asked next morning.

"And what does he hope to extract from Bone?" I demanded.

"The marrow of the mystery," said Vincie.

We regarded him with contempt. Power shook his head. "Mr. Bone may have seen something at some time, babbled under the influence, and now forgotten what it was, or muddled it in his alcoholic mind. But I do feel sure, from looking at Mr. Tressy, that he does nothing without an object. And that object is never an altruistic, or generous one."

We were both with him, though it was logically absurd to regard a man as a blackguard on the strength of an oily, curly, impudent, and self-confident appearance. But people do, and always will, judge others in that way, and intelligent ones come out fifty-fifty at worst.

"In fact," Vincie remarked, "we all agree that dope is not prevalent. We all feel that, if it is here, Mr. Withers would be a willing and eager retailer. So we'll go easy on the dope while

we're there. We don't want him to think we attach much importance to it."

"Work the dog for all you're worth," said Power, whose anxiety
to give me a story, as I knew, was partly accounted for by the fact
that we could carry on his good work while he was absent.

"Mr. Sibbins is also quite capable of handling the stuff," I
said.

"And coming from Africa, via Port Sudan, Aden, and the
Canal, may know how to get it," Power agreed. "But I'll sort him
for myself when I get back."

Voce, as we knew later, had already invoked the services of
the narcotic department at Scotland Yard. They were investi-
gating not only the odyssey of Mr. Sibbins, but the commercial
ventures of the Greek merchant who supplied Morgan with his
Turkish Delight.

As we set off to walk into Malpertuis, we met several people
who appeared to regard us as "in the know," and apologising for
stopping us, asked what really had happened at the gravel-pit.

To all of them we replied that Mr. Jolson had fallen over.
Captain Hollick was the best man to give them further information.

"Let him hold the baby," Vincie said to me. "I don't like this
growing feeling that we belong to a private inquiry agency."

"But we do, darling," I said, "very private. We're both feeling
thoroughly nosey, bad as it sounds."

It isn't really an excuse, but your novelist simply has to know
things. And he can't get them without being inquisitive.

Mr. Tressy Withers received us with great politeness, and
was on his best behaviour. When a man is, who usually isn't,
you know what to expect. *Timeo Danaos.*

Mr. Bone was very sober. He was also rather nervous, as
people are who don't make a habit of it, and are unused to the
reactions. I began to wonder if self-questioning, gossip, and
possibly the innuendoes of others, had made him wonder if he
too had strayed into Morgan's garden and forgotten all about it.

Mr. Withers's tea was like himself, lush and luxuriant, a great deal of it, and most expensive looking. And he had it laid out on a dining-table.

After a few remarks on the fine weather, our opinion of Malpertuis, and Mrs. Jennifer, we settled down to tea and talk.

"Pity," said Mr. Withers, looking at me, "that Malpertuis should have gone all gory just when you come to it."

"I hope you don't think we brought the germ with us?" said Vincie.

Mr. Bone said, "Ha, ha!" in the most flat laugh I ever heard.

"We don't usually die in our boots here," Mr. Withers went on, "Poor old Jolson! Fancy him dying in his?"

"The dog did it," said Mr. Bone, with an owlish look.

Mr. Withers grinned at him. "You seem to know a lot about it, Bone."

"I know the damn dog once bumped into me," said Bone.

"Sheer affection," said Withers. "What do you think, Mr. Mercer? Do you believe the faithful hound caught Jolson bending?"

"It looks like it, I admit," said Vincie, "Mr. Jolson did not look to me like a man who was tired of life."

Withers considered. "No, on the whole, I should say not. But lately I had an idea he was making experiments. Trying to ginger up an existence made monotonous by the absence of his mother."

"He was much attached to her?" I said, rather irritated by his way of talking.

"My dear lady," (now Withers was the kind of man who said that sort of thing, believe it or not), "poor old Jolson had never ceased looking round for the familiar apron-string."

"Mother-fixation!" murmured Mr. Bone.

"Away with you and your nasty Freud!" Mr. Withers was jocular, "I liked the old lady, and so did everyone. Jolson was one of your habitual leaners. Anyone would have served. He got used to having everything done for him, outside his business, and when he had to fend for himself life got dull."

"Surely that, and the new interests connected with it, would make his life more full and exciting?" I suggested. I was rather surprised at the man's shrewdness and insight, until I remembered that you can't run a successful bucket-shop on an empty brain.

He made me a little bow. "It works that way, as a rule, but it didn't with him, Mrs. Mercer. I don't suppose either of you saw much of him. He was really sensitive about his height, his weediness, and lack of impressiveness."

"That seems possible," I agreed.

"He never had done anything exciting," Mr. Withers went on, looking at me steadily. "A sort of flabby, decent, John Citizen sort of bloke."

"That was my reading of him too," said Vincie. Neither of us was going to give Mr. Withers a lead in the matter of Jolson's "gingering methods." He glanced at the artist.

"What do you think, Bone?"

"Dull little ass!" said Mr. Bone.

"Mr. Bone," said Withers, "is not what I should call a psychologist. I'm not an expert either, but I seem to have heard that fellows like Jolson either fade away, out of sheer boredom, or try to impress their neighbours with some daring deed, what?"

"If they impress themselves, it's good enough," I suggested.

When you heard Withers talk, you realised how share-pushers succeeded. He has a pretty good insight into human weaknesses and foibles.

"Right," he said. "Jolly true that. If they impress themselves. You are nearer the mark than I was there."

Mr. Bone turned the same owlish gaze on him.

"I think you're talking through your hat," he said.

"Well, it gives a focus," said the other, "ever see Jolson a bit odd and star-gazy lately, Bone?"

Mr. Bone shook his head. "I don't know what you mean. And it's all talk this. The dog pushed him over, and there's an end of it."

He passed his cup and cut a large slice out of a very sweet cake.

"You're perfectly right, Mrs. Mercer," Withers resumed, as she filled the cup, "what people think of him is bad enough for a man like that, but it's his own doubts about himself that hit hardest. He sort of asks himself isn't he even capable of being what he never has been—run right off the rails so to speak."

"Couldn't he out-Herod Herod?" Vincie suggested.

"You said it! One of the signs lately was going to Paris, and visiting Montmartre."

"Dog's hole now, Montmartre!" said Mr. Bone. "Out of date."

"Not to Jolson, Bone. You're out there. Chelsea's moved to Bloomsbury, Montmartre's shifted, but Jolson, bless you, wouldn't know that. Shouldn't be surprised if he still had illusions about the Moulin Rouge."

"Oh, that place," said Bone, with an air of contempt, and cut more cake.

"You see," Withers went on, now ignoring Bone, "Jolson didn't know that Paris was now one of the most depressing places in Europe. To him, going there was an adventure. He would take every artisan in a blouse for an artist, and every midinette for Mimi."

"You seem to be a good judge of character, Mr. Withers," Vincie observed dryly.

"Well, I get about a bit, and I know a bit."

"But you will talk rot?" said Mr. Bone.

Withers smiled and waited till Mr. Bone was attacking his tea once more. Then he took an invisible pinch of snuff between finger and thumb, and went through a little pantomime for our benefit.

"Frankly, that's what I think."

"You do?" I said.

"I do."

"There would have been signs of it," said Vincie.

Withers shook his head. "It doesn't always act as quick as that, especially if you only try it as an experiment. Once or twice, you know, to say to yourself: 'What a devil am I!'"

This was so near our own guess previously that Vincie and I exchanged glances. It might be a case of parallel cerebration, as someone calls it, or due to the fact that Withers had studied the man with a view to touching him financially. Even bank managers are not secure from the attacks of that kind of sharp.

"Our own theory," said Vincie, remembering what Power had told us, "is the dog one. In fact that might cover both cases."

"How do you mean both?" he asked.

"Well, it's pretty well established that the actual cause of death in Morgan's case was a blow in the abdomen," Vincie remarked.

"Oh, was it?" said Mr. Bone, looking up sharply, and I thought, in a relieved way.

"But how did the dog get into the garden?" Withers asked.

"The dog—" I hesitated, for we saw now that Jolson's statement was not common property. "How stupid of me," I added hastily, "unless, of course, the dog strayed in there."

Withers laughed. "Strayed? My dear lady, the dog was very friendly with Morgan in any case."

"But playful," said Vincie, and turned to me. "My dear, we're letting our ingenious theories run away with our common sense."

"I don't suppose Inspector Voce would think much of it," said Withers, "or does he?"

Yes, he was trying to fish. I shook my head. "Inspector Voce is a regular oyster."

"Then what about your friend Power?"

Vincie smiled. "Mr. Power is like a dog running after its own tail. He makes a very pretty circle, but that's all."

Mr. Bone had relapsed into gloom. He got up now, suddenly remembered an imaginary appointment, and said good-bye. When he had gone, Withers asked us if we would have any more tea and when we refused, took us into his drawing-room and offered cigarettes.

"To hark back to the dope business," he said, when we had lit up and sat down, "I think I am right about Jolson. Now he's gone, poor fellow, there is no harm in saying that I really believe he experimented once or twice."

"With what they call 'snow'?" said Vincie.

"I don't know what it was, but some sort of dope. What you said about the dog may be more true than you think. Who can say that Jolson didn't call that morning?"

Vincie looked puzzled. "But I don't see the point, unless Morgan was experimenting too. You're not hinting that a man like Jolson would try to start someone else on the same vice?"

Withers considered. "Don't be too sure. He may have thought Morgan a rival of his and wanted to impress him. That was Jolson all over. If he thought you looked down on him, he was anxious to let you see that he was equal to anything."

"There may be a psychological point in that, Mr. Withers," I conceded, "but to fill the bill in the present case, Jolson would have had to persuade Morgan to try a pinch."

"Morgan might have done, for a joke."

"But why put it on a rose?" Vincie asked. "Or do you mean that Jolson asked him to let him look at the rose and spilled some 'snow' on it?"

"Well, Mr. Mercer, that might have been done. I mean to say, people have put gin in a teetotaller's lemonade before now, and that's much the same." Whatever else he was up to, it was clear to us that Mr. Tressy Withers was anxious to write Jolson down a (possibly intermittent) drug addict; to father on him the responsibility for the dope found on the rose Mrs. Davey-Renny had sent to Morgan. Why? Well, there was one unpleasant explanation of that, and we both felt that Withers was the type of man who might be an illicit trafficker in drugs.

"Even then," said Vincie obliquely, "you have no proof whatever that Jolson was in the garden that morning."

"That's true," said our host, "but suppose he did, then your theory doesn't sound so ridiculous as you think. If that dog rammed Morgan amidships, there you are! Of course that involves Morgan being in a physical shape to conk out over it. But apparently, and according to you, the medical theory is that he was."

"I admit that," said Vincie, "but what we can be more sure about (since both Jolson and the dog were obviously at the top of the gravel-pit on the day of Jolson's death), is that the Great

Dane bumped playfully into his master and sent him over. It wouldn't require a great deal of a push to do that."

"Yes," said Withers, "but that still leaves the dope unaccounted for. If, as I think, Jolson had some, it seems to connect him with Morgan's death."

CHAPTER XV

JUDGES very often decide as much by the demeanour of witnesses as by what they say. And that has its possible defects as a system, since a judge may be an authority on law, but a poor judge of faces, or vocal inflexions.

We were both judging Withers on his demeanour that afternoon, but also on the opinion we had formed of his character, mixed with a general prejudice against the man himself. Impartiality is a gift of the gods, and they are more sparing with it than anything else.

"I wouldn't trust that man as far as I could throw a bull by the tail," Vincie confided to me as we walked home. "He's a thorough twister, and he may have asked us there to get the dope idea passed on to Power."

"It seemed so to me," I said, "but why rope Bone in?"

"Heaven knows. I thought Bone pricked up his ears when you said the blow to the tummy did it. He was relieved too. Perhaps he—" Here Vincie broke off and shook his head. "At all events, if Withers is trying to put it on Jolson, the presumption is that he finds his account in it. But how can that be, unless he did the little man in?"

If Voce does not know what you are doing at any given moment, Bohm does. Voce came round that evening, having had a busy day exploring every avenue, as the politicians say, and failing to see the wood for the trees.

He made himself very comfortable, did not refuse coffee, and frankly expressed his pleasure when we produced a big cream-jug.

"Well, how did you find Mr. Withers?" he asked, when he had lit his pipe. "Your first visit, wasn't it?"

"That's right," Vincie replied. "A very nice tea."

"And conversation?" said Voce.

I laughed. "Well, we weren't quite dumb," I told him. "We had you in mind, you know, and did our best."

"Anything come of it, Mrs. Mercer?"

I nodded. "Mr. Withers evidently thought it would," I said. "It's quite plain that he hopes fragments of his talk will be passed on."

"To be frank," said Vincie, "Withers is anxious that you should know his opinion on a recently acquired habit of the late Mr. Jolson."

Voce sat up. "A habit?"

"If we are to believe Mr. Withers, Jolson was anxious to swamp his inferiority complex by some deed of derring-do," I said. "Drink may be a mocker, but it's too common to impress anyone."

"You had some idea like that yourselves," Voce murmured. "So Withers thinks he doped?"

Vincie corrected him. "We can't say that. We can say that Withers hints that he doped."

"I think the habit would soon tell."

"Well, we're beginning to disbelieve in our own theory since Mr. Withers backed it up," I said. "I expect you've often had witnesses you wouldn't believe on oath, Mr. Voce."

"Not under all conditions," he said with a smile. "No. Noses, 'narks' as they used to be called, are very useful, but rarely men with any moral sense. By the way, did Withers ask you if we knew anything about Mr. Morgan? Of course he knows I know you."

"About Mr. Morgan," Vincie repeated, "is there anything to be known?"

We fully expected Voce to close up like an oyster, and turn the subject another way. To our surprise, he regarded us with his most amiable expression, and deliberated for a few moments before he spoke.

"Yes," he said, "yes; there is. And Withers is no doubt wondering why I haven't been at him about it. Of course, Bohm and I went through all the dead man's papers, but we haven't let it out."

"Aren't you going to?" I asked.

"I may, and I mayn't. If I do, perhaps you and Mr. Mercer would let it out for me, when I give the word."

"I wondered why you were so forthcoming," Vincie remarked cynically. "Right. We'll be mum about it, till you give the word. After that, we'll be indiscreet if you wish it."

"Thank you, sir. The fact is that Withers has got the wind up, and I always find it pays to let the wind do its work."

"Very right," Vincie agreed, "practical and alliterative. I seem to see a connection between Withers and the dead man which, nicely exposed to the light of day, will produce a gale."

"Something in that," Voce murmured, putting his empty cup down, and knocking out his pipe.

"I'll draw a bow at a venture, and shoot an arrow into the air," said Vincie. "Watch his face, Penny, for signs to show that I have hit the gold."

"Hopeless," I said.

"Now"—Vincie bent forward—"was Morgan behind Withers in the Birmingham bucket-shop?"

Mr. Voce raised his eyebrows and said nothing. I remarked that we might take his silence for consent, and indeed I am sure that he meant us to. There was a reason for that, of course. Our friend sells nothing for nothing, and very little for nine-pence.

"But how unlike a respectable broker, outside or inside, to do a thing like that," I remarked.

"I once knew of a very reputable linen spinner, who acted as a money-lender on the side," Voce told us. "He had had losses in his regular business, and pulled up with the aid of the second string."

"Ah, so he *had* losses?" Vincie asked.

Mr. Voce did not explain if he were speaking of the linen spinner, or the late Mr. Morgan. Vagueness is a virtue in a practising policeman. He can always say that he didn't mean what you mean.

"Yes, considerable ones. After all, a year or two ago, that was general. The man who broke even was lucky."

"That must have been after Mrs. Davey-Renny left him," I said, "or she is less candid than I imagined."

You could see by the look in the inspector's eye that he had been waiting for that, leading up to it, perhaps. He knew that we could jump a little ahead of him if he gave us half a chance.

"Ah, that lady," he murmured. "I was beginning to forget that she had been his secretary. You liked her, I think Mr. Power told me."

"We did," I said. "In fact, I am going to ask her to have tea with us here one day. Would that suit you?"

Voce laughed. He thinks we are an impudent couple. "Now, Mrs. Mercer, I don't expect you to act as 'noses'."

"No," I agreed. "say narks! It's older-fashioned and not so unpleasant. Let's be frank. I am writing a novel about this, and a novelist is as savage as a journalist about copy. You want to scrounge some information about Mrs. Davey-Renny—"

"*From*—about Mr. Morgan," he corrected.

"Anyway, some evidence. If we thought Mrs. Davey-Renny was concerned in this we wouldn't go narking for you. But we are sure she isn't, so a-narking we will go!"

"And that stands for me too," said Vincie, "I think she's a nice woman, and I know she's in love."

"With one of your fraternity," I added.

Voce nodded. "Yes, I heard that. I'm going to rope him in to help. The local bigwig seems to have a bee in his bonnet, which I hope to remove. The idea of suspecting a man because he bought a bouquet for the lady is too funny."

Vincie agreed. "Does Power know what you know?"

"Part of it," said Voce. "It was he got on to the bucket-shop."

"So Morgan wasn't really honest?" I said.

Voce did not look very certain. "It was financed by him, and after all these places vary. It depends on how the bucket is used, and if any water is ever drawn up in it."

"You mean that it wasn't necessarily plain stealing?"

"We're going into that. An absolutely honest man, of course, would take precautions to see that the business was honestly conducted by the man he financed. A thoroughly dishonest man wouldn't care. I take it that Morgan was between the two."

"He didn't watch too closely in case the—"

Voce stopped Vincie, and finished for him.

"I only say that as long as the divs came in he stayed 'retired,' and didn't make sure."

"Do you think Withers roped in any locals?" I asked. "You see, he was supposed to be independent too. If he did and they discovered Morgan's hand backing him—"

"There might be a motive, I admit," said Voce, "but that's as far as I can go."

"Was Jolson a dupe?" I asked.

Voce's face remained impassive.

"Or Bone?" said Vincie.

Voce laughed at us. "Fair play!" he said.

"You know there are some things I mustn't tell you, and Mr. Power won't—not that he can know what you ask."

"I wouldn't swear to that," I said. "Mr. Power is a good guesser."

"Well," Vincie observed, "we'll ask Mrs. Davey-Renny to tea to-morrow and do our good deed for you. Meantime, what about the inquest. Shall we be asked?"

"You'll be notified to-morrow," he replied, "Captain Hollick is very pleased with your dog theory. It's up to you, he thinks, to come forward to say that you saw the dog in this garden butt his master playfully. A word to the rural jury, who have heard of the dog's pretty ways, will set things in train for a nice verdict."

"But surely they will require something more than that?" Vincie asked.

"They won't need it, for juries don't like returning verdicts of suicide," Voce said, "but they'll get it."

We stared at him and then at each other. "What do you mean?" I gasped.

He smiled. "Once the dog came into the question, we adopted the Morgan technique," he told us, "I mean that dog's hairs do come off, and if they moulted from that brute when it simply sat down, what would happen when it tried ramming with its head."

"That I can't say," said Vincie, "though I have an idea the hair on a dog's back is longer, and looser, than on its head."

"True," said Voce, "what happened was this. As you know, things that you don't see at a glance come out in the wash, and more still when you beat the clothes and have them examined under a microscope."

"Then they got something?" I asked.

He nodded. "If a man is standing with his back to a dog, and is butted over a pit, you'll pay particular attention to the point of impact. Mr. Jolson's bags (if you'll allow me to mention them, Mrs. Mercer) gave up two dog's hairs to the examiner. They were compared carefully with those from the dog's head. I just read the report before I came here."

"Then it really is definite?" I said, relieved, for I did not think that little Jolson had killed Morgan, and suicide was unthinkable unless he had. "I am glad."

Voce gave a judicial pronouncement. "Even from my point of view, Mrs. Mercer, I shouldn't say it was scientifically proved. And, of course, the expert on the job surrounds his conclusion with a good many qualifications, and doubts."

"For example?" said Vincie.

"First, hairs are clinging things. The Great Dane was a pet dog, allowed some liberties, which must have been tiresome at times, and even painful. A hundred or so pounds of dog bumping into you can't always be a delight. Anyone who knows the ways of pet dogs knows that they occupy chairs in the house, and especially when their owner is single, and has chairs to spare. The dog sat on chairs; Mr. Jolson sat on chairs: result, hairs."

"Voce is getting quite poetic," Vincie said and added to Voce, "I can tell you, without owning a dog, that dogs don't stand on their heads on chairs!"

"They sometimes rest their muzzles on chairs," I said.

Vincie laughed at me. "This dog's muzzle would come a bit higher than the seat of an easy-chair."

Voce looked at him, his eyes narrowed, then he pulled out a note-book and made a note, afterwards returning the book to his pocket. "I am glad of that illumination. Our experts, who can take sections of a hair and compare it with another hair, should be able to say if there is any difference between the hairs on top and those under the muzzle of a dog's head. As a matter of fact they have examined the dog's body. We'll telephone the Yard at once about that, and have it seen to."

Vincie told him where the telephone was to be found, and he went out to have a talk with headquarters.

"That was evidently quite a point, darling," I said. "But there is substance in what Voce said too. Undisciplined pets make hairy chairs. And when you talked about the dog's muzzle being so high, it only applied when the brute was standing up."

"Solomon come to judgment!" he murmured. "Yes, I see that. If it were lying on the floor and saw a convenient chair to rest its muzzle on, it might do it. We must just hope that the local jury refuses to be bull-dozed by scientific objections and assumes that poor old Jolson regularly brushed his bags."

"I should not be so sure about that, dear," I said rather acidly. "I know when I turn down the ends of your bags I find quite a lot of grass-seed, dust, and other things. Yet you assure me that you brush them."

"Ah," said Vincie, with the injured air of a small boy charged with failing to wash behind his ears, "that's justifiable. No one sees it."

"My dear boy," I replied. "You know the definition of a gentleman: one who uses the butter-knife even when he is alone."

"A prig!" said Vincie, "but here comes Voce again."

Mr. Voce sat down. "That shall be done," he said, "but to return to the practical side of things, as it concerns us here: Captain Hollick is quite satisfied that the hairs prove that the dog butted Jolson over the edge. The scientific objections may be of use to me, that is all."

Vincie nodded. "You still think Mr. Jolson may have done the first job?"

"That would be unscientific too. I do know that he is the only man we know visited Morgan that morning. Don't forget that in real life, Mr. Mercer, the obvious murderer is generally the one who did it. It's all very nice for the purposes of your stories to have a lot of suspects. In our cases suspects are likely to come in single spies, not in battalions, like troubles."

"What a learned man Mr. Voce is," said Vincie, as our visitor got up. "He needs no police college to give *him* culture."

Voce grinned at us. "I've been swotting it up against the new competition," he said; "my only handicap is the lack of an old school tie."

"Did you never go to school, Voce?" my husband asked.

"Yes, sir. I left it at the age of fourteen to go on the stage."

"You've been an actor?" I cried.

He laughed. "Assistant scene-shifter," he replied. "I left that, when I let down the drop-curtain too suddenly in a 'fit-up' in Gloucester. The star fell, and I ran!"

CHAPTER XVI

BEFORE we went to bed that night, I wrote and posted a note to Mrs. Davey-Renny, asking her to come to tea with us next day. Mr. Power did not turn up, so I spent the next morning writing, and mapped out a few possible incidents for the future.

At eleven Mrs. Davey-Renny's maid came with a note of acceptance. So I sent Vincie out to get special cakes, asked Mrs. Jennifer for strawberries, and arranged that cream should be supplied in bulk.

I was smoking a cigarette on the lawn, after two hours' hard work, when Vincie deposited his purchases in the house and joined me.

"I have been thinking things over, Penny," he said; "Bone is on my mind. Withers and he don't look friends by type, and Withers seemed to treat him rather contemptuously. I wonder if he has invested his patrimony in some wild-cats bred by our oily friend."

"I wondered, too, why he was there at tea," said I. "Grumpy, and a bit ratty about something."

Vincie lit up. "I saw Edwards on my way back," he said, "and I was rather daring too. I asked him if he could tell me anything about the effects of cocaine on a novice."

"Did he bite you?"

"Nary a bite. He was at pains to explain to me that he had never used cocaine in powder form, always some improvement, and could not state exactly what effect it had—snuffed."

"Was that all?"

"No, my dear, there's more. I said that I expected he was tired of being asked about it. He said he was. Not only the police had worried him, but Withers had been trying to pump him about it. The day, he added, when we came into the café, and Inspector Voce joined us."

I started. "So that was what Withers was up to?"

"Apparently. He wanted to know if a sniff of 'snow' would affect a man who had never used it before. Also if there were not some people who had an intolerance of the drug."

"Did Edwards tell him?"

"He said that he had agreed that was so, and mentioned Mr. Morgan as a case in point."

For a moment I felt delighted, then deflated. "But, of course, all this took place after the event," I said. "If Withers wanted to do Morgan in that way, he would have questioned first and acted after." Vincie was not so sure. "Look here, Penny," he remarked, "if I had killed a man, say, with the old, old, threadbare 'curare-and-poisoned-arrow' wheeze, would you take it as proof of my innocence that I buzzed off to a friend who was a toxicologist, and asked him what curare was, and how it would affect a victim?"

Even the most bigoted wife must admit that her husband is sometimes right. "Yes," I said, "you have me there. I spoke far too quick. Of course it would be a good bluff, if I had an idea that my questions would be mentioned to someone else later on. I see. And we both feel that Mr. Withers is a better candidate for the Hangman Stakes than anyone here."

"After what Voce told us, tacitly, I should not be surprised if Mr. Morgan had also been done in the eye by Mr. Withers," he said. "I saw Mr. Brown, his Baston lawyer, hurrying along to his office, and he wore a very worried air."

"That is no proof," I observed. "Lawyers must be worried at times, if they are married and have families, as he has."

"I am going by what Edwards said, my dear, I was with him and he remarked on it. He said Brown was never known to frown or scowl, and he was doing both at the time he passed us. He has a wife with money, who dotes on him, and a model son and daughter on whom he dotes. All I say is that if I put any finance in Mr. Withers's hands, I would go and have a look at it, and count it over, every second day."

We dropped the subject for the moment, and I told Vincie the lines my work had taken.

"Provisionally," I said, "I have taken it as a theory that, after Mr. Jolson left Morgan in a hurry, the dog having playfully committed assault and battery, someone else came in, found Morgan dead, and had to do something about it."

"Quite. What he had to do about it was to send for a doctor and the police."

"Correctly speaking, Vincie, you are right. But suppose someone entered who had come there with a grudge; or Mr. Bone, with a grudge and a skinful of *Bols* as well."

"I had forgotten the gin," said Vincie. "You mean that the fresh visitor, having sneaked in, and conscious of a personal vendetta, was afraid he would be blamed for the deed. He is a 'coke' addict, and decides to fake a death through snuffing a drug to which the victim is physically intolerant. Possible, I grant, if the man was in a muddled state of mind. But *would* Withers be muddled, or, say, Sibbins? Of course Sibbins might get the wind up, since he was the heir and had not announced his coming. He would know he had a motive. On the other hand, Bone would be the most likely donkey if he was, as he admits, mopping up the present of gin all the morning."

"In that case, Bone must be at least an occasional doper," I said.

Vincie agreed. "Yes. But I did not see any signs of it. His eyes were a bit blood-shot and bleary, but the pupils didn't show any narrowing."

"Look here, my dear," I remarked, "he wouldn't touch the stuff so soon after the tragedy, in case someone noticed it. There is another thing. In the country, and in town for the matter of that, we don't meet many dopers. We don't look for them."

"That's true. Only for the mention of 'coke' in this case, I should never have looked at the little waster's eyes."

"Then again," I went on, "if Bone was a quiet, sober, healthy-living, little man, and suddenly became an addict, people might notice a change in him. But as he is always boozing (and moons about half the time with a hang-over), whatever he looked like would be put down locally to the drink. Don't you agree?"

"Yes," said Vincie, "I do now. Bone might even have gone in, in a boozy temper, seen Morgan lying back on the seat, spoken to him, and, receiving no answer, given him a knock, or a push. Morgan falls off, Bone tries to get him up, sees that he's dead and thinks he must have done it. Then what?"

I thought it over. "As the stuff was undoubtedly there, he must have had a drunken notion of leaving a false clue," I suggested at last. "If he doped himself, he might have an over-stimulated imagination, and decided to put some of the powder on the rose, and make Morgan take—"

"Just a moment," Vincie said grinning, "a man's not dead till the breath's out of his body. Agreed?"

"Absolutely," I said, rather crestfallen.

"That being so, Penny, and 'snow' not being a liquid one could pour, how did he make a dead man inhale? Unless you go even farther, and suggest that Bone accidentally had an old-fashioned ear-syringe with him and puffed the stuff in."

"I dismiss that idea," I said, "I grant you that a man could do it, if the business was pre-meditated, and he provided himself with the doings in advance, though. As it is, I pass the question back to you.”

“I pass too,” said Vincie, “and I had better wash my hands before luncheon. I have an idea Bone may be in it. I think the ‘snow’ was a red-herring of sorts; but the breathing dead man is too much of a paradox even for me.”

“We’ll put it to Power,” I said, “when he comes back. Meantime, I could do with a wash too. My typewriter ribbon had to be renewed, and you know what filthy things they are.”

We felt, too, that washing our hands was symbolical. Our hope was that Voce or Power would get to work a bit quicker, and let us have some results.

Mrs. Davey-Renny came punctually at four. She was wearing a very smart little suit in black and white, of some very thin material, and looked very cool and handsome.

We gave her a seat under the trees, provided her with a cigarette, and listened with approval to her gently sympathetic comments on the latest tragedy. Under a mild and natural contempt for the little man, she had an understanding feeling for his case. Ineffective, and rather silly, he had something decent in him. His occasional moods and tempers, she gave us to understand, were the result of his discovery that when he left the bank he left the sphere in which his word was law, and his position (at least to those about him in it) unimpressive.

“It is rather humiliating, you know,” she said softly, “to be only a big man in your office. Finding your level in the ordinary way is bad enough, but you do have a sneaking idea of it, don’t you?”

Vincie laughed. “In your moments of humility you can ‘place’ yourself fairly well.”

She nodded. “And when it came to that, you see, poor Mr. Jolson wasn’t anywhere.”

“Like one of those unhappy notes *so* far below the stave,” I said, “I do think you must be right. He would say to himself at first: ‘Let me be modest and assume that, outside the bank, I shall just be second-rate. I needn’t put it higher than that!’”

"Quite," she said. "And then it was a question of other people putting it lower—much lower. 'Such a decent little man, after all,' people said. 'Decent,' you know, and 'after all'."

"That's always a nasty one," Vincie murmured. "When I go, I hope no one will 'after-all' me."

"I warned him against that dog several times,' she remarked. "In fact, I hated the beast. It may seem unkind to say so, but over-kind and friendly people, and over-affectionate dogs are definitely dislikeable."

"At any rate, there was no question of murder," I said. "That is a good thing. Poor Mr. Morgan they still seem doubtful about."

"Yes," she said, "they do."

The tea was brought out and I began my duties, while Vincie looked thoughtfully at our visitor and asked her if she had seen Morgan's lawyer yet.

"I had a note from Mr. Brown, asking me to call to-morrow," she said, a tiny frown crossing her brow. "It struck me as rather oddly phrased."

"I hear he is looking very worried," I remarked, as I passed her cup, "I suppose there is no hitch?"

"That I can't say, Mrs. Mercer. But I had that impression. Why, I don't know, for the figures were given in the will."

"Some years ago, if you remember," Vincie observed, "a peer died and left a lot of money. When it came to the reckoning up; well, he seemed to have been terribly optimistic."

"You mean that he may have thought he had more than he really had? But he wouldn't, and couldn't, retire here on nothing."

"Not when he retired," said Vincie. "But he's had time since to speculate. I suppose outside-brokers can? I mean to say, there is an idea members of the House are not allowed to."

If she had anticipated Morgan's legacy with any eagerness, she spoke more calmly than one would have expected.

"I suppose it is possible. He was an odd mixture in some ways: as we all are, of course. I have known him to play his fancy on the markets now and then, and it wasn't a very sound fancy. But even stockbrokers are human, and do break out sometimes."

"I wonder how one would set about touching a broker?" I said. "You would start handicapped by the idea that he would know too much for you."

She laughed. "Oh, I don't know. It's like racing. You know a man who goes racing intelligently and now and then he meets someone who gives him a silly tip. He turns down a tip a day as a rule, but every now and again, it strikes his fancy, and he bets on it."

"And then wonders why?"

"Yes. Well, of course, Mr. Morgan knew some very big men in finance. I needn't tell you that some big men in finance are due for a bust before long. But as long as they are reputed big, their word goes."

"I see," said Vincie, as he passed her the cakes, "Mr. Morgan might buy stock if recommended to him by some important man—buying on the name of the recommender, rather than on anything he knew of the stock."

"Yes. Of course it does come off sometimes. There it's like racing again. It's the odd chances that come off that stop you from being put off by the more frequent duds, Mr. Mercer."

"At all events," I said, "you admit that Mr. Morgan might be tempted to risk his money on a stumer, in spite of his business experience?"

"Oh, yes. And, of course, the more business experience you have," she added wisely, "the less easy it is for you to imagine that you can be fooled."

"I can see," said Vincie, "that Mr. Morgan had reasons for being sorry when you left. But, tell me, did Mr. Withers ever try to induce you to invest in anything?"

"Mr. Withers? Well, he's independent, you know."

"Oh, is he?" said Vincie, "no vulgar connection with business or trade, of course."

"Surely even those who are not professionals offer market tips?" I asked, and signalled to Vincie to hand the strawberries and cream. "I am right, aren't I?"

She laughed. "Oh, they do; more than professionals, who like to keep a good thing to themselves. Thank you, Mr. Mercer, what delicious strawberries. Mine are wretched this year."

"Better than handing you a lemon," he remarked, with a twinkle.

"You're quite right. Oh, yes; Mr. Withers did once or twice."

"And you took a bite?"

She shook her head. "No. He said Mr. Morgan had put him on to them, in confidence, and he had bought a lot."

"Can the secret be let out?" I asked.

"I see no harm in it. They were 'North Queenie Reps.', also 'Dumber Factors'."

"Surely, if Mr. Morgan recommended them, they were good enough?"

Mrs. Davey-Renny smiled even more pronouncedly. "They sounded like one of Mr. Morgan's morning-after sore heads," she said, "I never heard of them before."

"Wise woman!" Vincie murmured. "How many of us would be richer and better to-day if we had avoided things we had never heard of before."

Vincie had forgotten the cigarettes and now went into the house for them. He was some time away, and I heard from him afterwards that he had rung up Voce on the telephone, and was lucky enough to find him at the police-station.

He had given Voce the names of the shares Withers had been trying to work off on Mrs. Davey-Renny, and suggested that it might be worth while inquiring if the late Mr. Morgan had held any.

"Or Mr. Jolson, *or* Mr. Bone," he added, "I leave it to you."

We dropped the subject after that, and thought we could do no harm by gently hinting to our guest that Voce was going to employ Inspector Kaye on the inquiry. She coloured charmingly, and remarked that she wondered why he had not been asked before.

"I think," I told her, "that it wasn't thought judicious; since he had given you the roses."

CHAPTER XVII

MR. POWER seemed very pleased when he returned late that evening and heard our story of what had happened since he went away. He had tried to get hold of Voce or Bohm on the telephone, and failed, it seemed.

"That's the trouble with the blighter, and not so much his own fault," he told us. "He knows something he won't give away, so I have to outguess him. He's after Jolson all the time, as far as I can see."

"It will be a long chase then," Vincie commented, grinning, "but what do you think?"

"I have an idea that your discovery lets out Withers, at least in the major case," he replied. "If he really asked Edwards's opinion after the death of Mr. Morgan, I assume that he was snooping about to get a line on the murderer."

"But why?" I asked, for I could see no point in it.

"Well, I have had a clerk checking things, and it's clear to me that Withers did run that show, in conjunction with Morgan. I mean Morgan was financially at the back of it. He took no active interest. Then what you heard from Mrs. Davey-Renny suggests that Withers was fishing here for markets for his stuff. The two shares you telephoned Voce about, Mercer, are dud companies run by a Yankee in Seattle."

"Very likely," said Vincie, "but how does that prove Withers was trying to get a line on the murderer?"

Power lit a cigarette and considered. "Do you think Mr. Morgan, who had left his former secretary money in his will, would be a party to working off dud shares on her?"

"I don't," said Vincie. "Anyway, she didn't bite."

"Very well, then. If not, Withers was working for his own hand, independent of Morgan, and the chances are that he was doing him down as well."

"In case he was likely to be found out, that would give him a motive for killing Morgan," I said. "He might be afraid too that Mrs. Davey-Renny would tell Morgan of the offer of shares."

"May be so," Power returned, "but it is my idea that Withers was preparing to make a clean-up when the murder happened. I think he had been catching other local clients as well."

"For example?" said Vincie.

"Bone," Power replied, "Bone would be easily touched, and Jolson."

I started. "Surely Voce will be going into Jolson's papers?"

He nodded. "Bohm has been in the house all day, I hear. My point is this: Withers is one of the suspects, and Voce may demand to get information about his financial doings at any time. If he does, and Withers turns out to have swindled his backer, and the other two as well, he's for it. On the strength of an exposure of that kind a jury might take your view and think he had a motive for killing Morgan."

"I see that," I said slowly, "but I am still in the dark about the value of Withers's snooping about for traces of a doper."

"I have an idea what Power means," said Vincie.

"You can both hear it now," our friend remarked. "Say Withers (who has no alibi for fifteen minutes on the morning of Morgan's death) is proved to have swindled the dead man, or put him on to worthless shares. If I were defending him, my line would be that Morgan had been a stockbroker, and was a man of experience. Was there anything to prove that he did not buy the shares of his own free will?"

"Mrs. Davey-Renny said he might be done down now and again," I said.

"Who can't?" he observed. "If he was done down, then he was offered the dud shares at a low price. You may cheat a business man, but you must have a likely bait for it. I would go on to suggest that Morgan, who was already partially discredited as an honest man, by financing a bucket-shop on the side, intended no doubt to unload those shares on mugs, here and elsewhere. At the worst, I would say, this court is not a court of morals, and we are not trying a financial issue, but one of murder. Mr. Withers may have been running a bucket-shop, but so was Morgan; and whatever Morgan did was his own free choice."

"All that is very nice," I said, "but you're still shirking the issue raised by Withers's question to Mr. Edwards about the effects of cocaine."

He laughed. "Now the great brain's a bit under par, Mrs. Mercer!" he chaffed me; "I was leading up to that. As Withers and Morgan were partners, even if one was only sleeping, it could be held that both knew all about the dud shares. If Morgan had taken them up willingly, away goes Withers's motive for killing him, which would arise from his having done something unknown to Morgan, and being afraid it was coming out."

"Carry on," said Vincie.

"But say there was another local mug—Jolson perhaps. Or Bone. Say one or the other of them was getting wise to the nature of the stuff he had bought, and making things nasty for Withers. Up to date, there has been no real official inquisition into Withers's doings in the bucket-shop. If he could discover a hint that Jolson, Bone, or whoever it was worried him, was even an occasional user of 'snow,' you see what he could do with the knowledge."

I did see that and said so. "Use it as a gag, Mr. Power?"

"Exactly. If he learned, or could apparently prove, that the late Mr. Jolson used that dope, most people would assume that Mr. Jolson had killed Morgan and tried the muddle-headed way of sprinkling dope on the rose, as a red herring. Withers would be able to slide out of the case, for Voce and Bohm would concentrate on the real charge, murder. They were not sent down here to discover signs of share-pushing."

"That does look like it," Vincie admitted. "Withers gave us to understand that he was sure Jolson took dope occasionally."

"Quite so," I agreed. "But, my dear, who would believe a fellow like Withers? The very fact that he put forward that theory makes me suspect it."

"There the Court is inclined to be with you," said Power; "I must say that Withers, as a witness, fills me with dismay."

"And you do believe that Mr. Jolson's death was the result of an accident, don't you?" I said. "Not a short way out of a nasty situation?"

"It looks like that to me. Have you been warned about the inquest yet?"

"Just before dinner," Vincie told him, "and we are going all out for the dog story. I can't think the two cases have a connection."

"Unless," said Vincie with a smile, "you assume that Jolson put some aniseed on the seat of his slacks, and the dog ran hastily at him to sample that canine delicacy among aromas. Dog-stealers use it."

"Vincie's thinking of Miss Ella, you remember, who got twelve months for her poison-pen letters," I said. "If he meant to kill himself, he only had to jump, without troubling the dog."

"At any rate they found no dope on him," Vincie said. "That does not prove, of course, that he never had any, but it helps."

"Wait till Voce gets to work, or Voce's expert in town, on the dead man's clothes," Power said. "It isn't easy to carry 'snow' about with you in a packet without losing a few spots. All these finely precipitated powders 'creep' most miraculously."

"The difficulty is that Voce won't tell us," I said. "He is quite right, of course, but it does keep us in the dark."

Power assented. "I am in the dark. Voce treats me as he treats you. If he can sell you, or me, a ha'p'orth of information for a bob's worth that we collect, he'll be very matey. But he doesn't give anything away."

"There's one thing," I said, quite irrelevantly, the idea having stolen into my head. "Was the rose Morgan wore a big one, or a little one?"

Power stared. "A large specimen; why?"

"It just struck me," I said, "that very few men will put a big rose in their button-hole."

"Trust a woman to notice a point like that," Power observed, "but it was a tribute from his former secretary; a message, so to speak."

"But not sentimental. They both kept away from that," said Vincie.

Mr. Power considered it worth a short silence. "Yes, I see. And you only fly a tribute before other people. While we can assume that Morgan didn't expect a visit from Jolson."

"Good man, Penny!" Vincie approved me. "I shouldn't be surprised if the visitor, whoever it was, stuck it in the lapel afterwards."

"But Mr. Jolson admitted seeing it there after all. I forgot that," I said, trying to be fair.

"That's a snag," Power hinted. "All the same, the idea of that big full-blown thing does stick in the gullet. If it had been a bud, it would have been a different matter."

Vincie frowned. "Short of wearing it, what would the receiver do with a flower sent him by the maid?"

"Carry it in his hand, look at it, remembering it was his own creation, and perhaps put it down on the seat beside him, I think," Power suggested.

It was at this point that our talk was rudely broken into. The maid came in to say that Mr. Sibbins wanted to see Mr. Power at once. She had the startled look of one who has come in contact with an angry visitor, but received no explanation as to the cause of it.

"Show him in here, please," said Power, and pursed up his lips in a low whistle when the girl went out. "What is it now? Voce on his heels; or the abnormal anxiety of Mr. Brown?" he said.

Mr. Sibbins was no longer a figure symbolical of insolence of the silent variety, but might have stood for a statue of baffled rage. He bounced in, stared at Power, forgot to bow to us, and then bellowed a question.

"What's this about the money?"

"There are so many money questions that you must define before I can explain," Power said. "Take a pew, and expound."

Mr. Sibbins snatched, rather than took, a chair. His hot and red face seemed to swell as he stuttered. "My uncle's money, of course."

"Have a cigarette," said Mr. Power, extending his case. "No? Well, that's all I can offer you. I don't know the answer to your riddle. I take it, as an outsider, that the money is invested."

"Invested?" said Mr. Sibbins, breathlessly. "Invested!"

It was just like that: first a question mark, and then a dash that was invested with the full weight of the commination service.

Vincie leaned to me and whispered. "Two duds that beat as one."

"I haven't had a heart-to-heart talk with Brown," Mr. Power said, "but I gather that you have. Let us hear about it."

"Brown says it's nearly all invested in—" and here followed the names of two companies run by a Yankee in Seattle. "He made inquiries for the probate valuation."

"And the result?" said Power.

"No market," said Sibbins, as if the words choked him. "The damned old fool!"

This obviously referred to the late Mr. Morgan. Mr. Power nodded very gently. "You mean to say they're worthless?"

Mr. Sibbins was promptly called to order by Vincie, who has old-fashioned ideas about the language women ought not to hear. Mr. Sibbins just risked apoplexy in an unexpectedly gallant attempt to choke down a further selection of blasphemous obscenities. He gurgled a little, his eyes bolted, and Mr. Power took up the tale.

"Your uncle should have known better," he said mildly, "but though you may try to get at the man behind the deal, or steal, I am afraid you can't make a market for a dud share by cursing it."

Mr. Sibbins gave us an expurgated account of what he intended to do to the man who had unloaded all this perilous stuff on his uncle. Mr. Power did not mention our suspicions about it. He gave some cautious advice instead.

"Go round to see Voce," he told our visitor, "the information may be useful to him, and he's the police, after all. I shall, of course, go into the matter to-morrow. You might bring a civil action—"

I laughed without meaning to. The idea of Mr. Sibbins in his present state being associated with any *civil* action was ludicrous.

"Or the police might proceed against him in the criminal courts," Vincie remarked, to cover my impolite mirth. "Other share-pushers have got it in the neck before now."

Mr. Sibbins ignored us both. "Don't you realise that I mayn't get a penny?"

"That's obvious," said Power, "equally obvious that it's growing late, and none of us will get a sleep if we don't go to bed."

The rise of a rocket, and its further tumultuous flight, was nothing to the way in which Sibbins left us. Even the hissing and crackling noise was there, as he seemed in one continuous movement to go from his seat to the door, to fling it open, and vanish in a rumble of sulphurous exclamations.

"That was Sibbins, that was!" Power murmured, as the door banged.

Vincie and I exchanged glances. "That lets Sibbins out," we exclaimed almost simultaneously.

"I'm afraid so," said our friend calmly, "it looses him on friend Voce. I bet Withers is wishing he could cut and run, and hating the knowledge that he daren't run for fear of being roped in for the murder. Just for lack of a quarter of an hour's alibi, too. He has a friend who can swear to meeting him at a certain hour, but, between that and fifteen minutes later, Voce has only his word for it that he stood in his garage in that lane behind Morgan's, fixing up oil-cans, and putting tools on a new shelf and a row of hooks. And was not seen, *or heard*."

"I am sorry for poor Mrs. Davey-Renny," I said.

"Don't worry!" said Power, "I hear she's quite comfortably off. And I don't think she even spends all her income down here."

Vincie nodded. "Anyway, Sibbins will put Voce on the right track. It will be quite clear to him that Mr. Tressy Withers did his backer down; a tribute to his slickness, but no proof that he murdered him."

"I think I'll try to get on to Bohm, if he is available," Power rose and went out to telephone.

When he came back he looked pleased. "Voce is talking to Sibbins. I managed to hook Bohm and told him. I had to, if I wanted him to open up."

"Did he?" I said.

"As good as," Power replied. "He didn't ask me what the two companies were when I asked him. And he was going through Jolson's effects before. He knew."

I got up. "To bed," I said, "we've all had a busy-body day. I bet someone will wonder now if Jolson discovered where he stood and committed suicide."

"You mustn't be imaginative!" said Mr. Power.

CHAPTER XVIII

THERE is nothing more uninformative than a properly conducted inquest. The one we attended was arranged with such strict regard to the rules that Truth was never even asked to come from her well. It was enough to peep down the shaft to where, doubtless, she was hiding in the murk at the bottom.

There was identification, address to the jury, evidence of finding, medical details of the injuries received, subsidiary report on the injuries received by the dog, and the examination of a few witnesses.

The only sensation was caused by a report from a pathologist who, as somebody said afterwards, very successfully split hairs.

It was not news to the crowd in the Parish Hall (turned Court) that the rumbustious beast was over-handy with its head. A farmer had once remarked that it should have been a bulldog, so fond was it of charging head-on. But it was news to most of them that it was possible to decide where a hair came from; and the expert's reasoned judgment, to the effect that certain hairs found sticking to Mr. Jolson's trousers had come from between the eyes of the Great Dane, made a stir.

He had, it seemed, cut sections of hairs, and compared them under the microscope.

Certain other sections of hairs were put in as evidence, and it was proved that these came from under the dog's muzzle. They corresponded with some gathered from the middle and outer edge of an easy chair often occupied by Mr. Jolson. It was demonstrated how a large dog might lie at its master's feet, and affectionately lay its head on the seat there.

Since general truth was not desired, but only a side-light, and confirmation of the theory of accidental canicide (or does that mean murder of a dog?), our evidence was briefly asked, and briefly given. We both stated that, on the occasion of Mr. Jolson's visit to us shortly before his death, the dog had charged into its master from behind.

"There was no question of this being done in a fit of temper?" the coroner asked Vincie.

"No," said Vincie, "high spirits. I should say that the dog was an exceptionally good-tempered one."

"A puppy-like gambol?" said the coroner.

"Exactly," said Vincie; "he was going away; the dog ran at him, and bumped into him."

"If Mr. Jolson had been standing on the edge of a quarry, where the foothold was uncertain, and he was gazing before him, not thinking of the dog," said the coroner, "a similar movement on the part of his pet would have sent him over?"

"I am afraid that is too much of a hypothetical question for me to answer off-hand," Vincie said gravely. "It is possible."

"Thank you, Mr. Mercer," said the coroner. "You can only speak to the best of your knowledge and belief."

Finally, evidence was given as to the state of Mr. Jolson's health, mind, and financial position.

As to the latter, it was elicited (somewhat to our surprise) that Mr. Jolson's affairs were in good order, and his small fortune invested in sound securities. His debts were negligible, and his bank balance quite adequate.

The coroner was naturally terrified at the idea of being pilloried in the newspapers if he referred to anything not immediately germane to the cause of death. He summed up briefly, did not even make a passing reference to the reason for Mr. Jolson's visit to Mr. Morgan, or to us, and turned the thing over to the jury.

The verdict was, of course, that Jolson had met his death as the result of injuries inflicted by falling into a gravel-pit. The fall was assumed to be in its turn the result of the dumbness of the dog. Unable to express in words what it thought of its master, it had (though it was not expressed in that way in the verdict), shall we say? patted him on the back.

We went home to luncheon. Power had stayed for the inquest, and now remarked that Jolson had proved less vulnerable than Mr. Morgan to Withers's wiles.

"I heard it from Bohm, too, just before the inquest opened," he told us. "He said there was no question of Jolson having any grudge against Withers, or his sleeping partner, Morgan, on financial grounds. There was no evidence among his papers that Jolson had been speculating. In fact, there was evidence the other way. In the back of a drawer Bohm found a letter from the bucket-shop, dated six months back. Jolson had scribbled across it: 'Ramp'."

I think Mrs. Jennifer was really beginning to thaw, or had discovered that authors, unlike actors and film stars, are not really disreputable people. We had a most delicious luncheon; cold salmon; a ham that must have come from more celestial regions than York; salad that reminded one of accounts of salad prepared on the Continent (district vague); a tart that almost floated on air, and would have suited a dyspeptic; and the best coffee our landlady (hostess?) had yet given us.

"Ah," said Power, sighing with delicate reminiscence as he lit a cigarette, "ancient monarchs ennobled their *chefs* for much less than that. I feel a better and brighter man."

"That being so," said Vincie, giving me a light for my cigarette, "tell us why Withers tried to make Jolson out an occasional dope-taker. It was the idea that the little man had invested not wisely or too well that—"

"Excuse me," Power interrupted, "novelists' ideas about facts are born with a haze about them; trailing clouds of imaginative glory, don't you know! If Mr. Withers wanted to stop someone's mouth, as he undoubtedly has cause to wish, he might buy their silence by promising to find a scapegoat."

"The goat being only valuable if it was dead," I said, thinking I saw light.

"Yes," said Power. "And there is also the fact that a goat can't be a scapegoat for itself. The function of the S.-G. is to direct attention away from the guilty animal."

Vincie nodded. "Undoubtedly. But if you are thinking of Mr. Bone, does it not suggest that the boozy little wretch must also have strayed into Morgan's garden that morning, as we suspected before?"

"It does. And it suggests that this took place somewhere about the time when Mr. Withers was fixing his garage, and putting things on the new shelf," I said hurriedly.

Power grinned. "Correct. Now Voce did not tell me, but I know that Mr. Bone was witness for part of Withers's alibi; and, naturally, Withers to Bone's."

"The assumption being," said Vincie, "that Mr. Bone came away hurriedly by the lane, and was seen by Withers who was in the garage."

"That is what I think."

"Then you believe Mr. Bone may have been the unwary speculator?" I asked.

"If Withers took in a sober stockbroker," Power murmured, "a gin-soaked little artist would be easy meat."

"It does look," I said quickly, "as if we were getting on the trail. Let me see how it runs: Mr. Bone visits Morgan, but keeps it dark; he is spoken to by Withers on his flight, via the lane—"

"It may be flight, but that is uncertain," said Power.

"Going away, at any rate," I went on. "Now Mr. Bone may have discovered that Withers had swindled him over the shares he had bought—"

"After Morgan's death, of course," Power interrupted; "not before, or at the time."

"Well," I said, rather put out by these interventions, "Withers either suspects that Bone killed Morgan, or can be mixed up in it with a little thought, and more or less lets Bone know that the less he talks about dud shares, the less Mr. Withers will talk of little artists making suspicious morning calls."

"That, finally, is my idea," said Power. "Only an idea, of course, but fits so far. You see, I can't believe it of Withers; and

Sibbins, if he murdered his uncle, is more like a lunatic than anything else."

"Yes, he hung about secretly so long, spying on Mrs. Davey-Renny," Vincie said, "that when it came out, it was a perfect advertisement of bad motives. Then he has openly proclaimed his disappointment at finding Morgan's legacy is worth about tuppence. Any murderer, with a chance to plead sanity, would have kept quiet."

"In fact, he has a moral alibi on account of his immoral eagerness," Power agreed. "But let's get back to Bone. You dear people had a better view of him at Withers's tea-party than I have ever had. I admit that a tippler when sober is not himself. But he appears to have made some rather significant comments."

"Brief and rude," Vincie said.

"Yes; so they sounded, as retailed by you. But significant by their very brevity and rudeness. Does it not occur to you that a man or woman tells the truth more often when he is rude, than when he is civil and polite?"

"Any truths about my work have had that flavour," I admitted. "After all, politeness is as much the enemy of truth as oil is of friction. Both wine and temper have the effect of their effervescence, and bubble over annoyingly."

"Well, Bone is sober, but the effect on him is to make him a poor ally in Withers's campaign to prove Jolson took dope. He said Withers was talking through his hat. He scoffed at all these charming psychological theories of the little man anxious to impress. He left without doing or saying a single thing to exculpate himself, and inculpate Jolson."

"Could you not see Bone, and put the fear of death in him?" Vincie asked. "Voce daren't bluff, and we know he is a stickler for the rules for taking evidence. But that shouldn't worry you?"

"It wouldn't, if it were opportune," Power informed us, with his well-known grin. "But it isn't. I don't want the Law Society on my tail, you know, and even Voce has limits to his indulgence. If he thought I was messing up his case, he would take steps. That is really what I like about old Voce. He's thoroughly sound and conscientious."

"Well, if you want to hand Bone over to him, he'll try his best," I said.

"I thought"—Power paused, twinkled, and resumed—"that you two had done so well over Mrs. Davey-Renny and Mr. Withers, that you might like to try some of the detective work you are always writing about."

"We have our pride and *amour-propre*, if no Law Society to sting us," I suggested. "Nosey is as nosey does. But we have no desire really to be known as the curious couple."

"Think hard, and you'll find some excuse for it," he said. "I find that the best way, when I practice to deceive. You may even clear Bone himself, and that will be something."

"We might tackle it on those lines," Vincie informed him. "*Pro bono publico* is a good horse, and flattering to the self-esteem."

"Thank you," Power said gratefully, "I shall be in town all day to-morrow, and that would be a good time."

I assented. "If we can manage an interview, we will. But you must coach us a bit. We can't simply breeze in, and ask Bone what he was doing playing about in Morgan's garden on the day of the murder."

"No," he replied. "Excuse me a moment, while I telephone."

He came back very soon, and remarked that he had asked Mrs. Davey-Renny if she minded Withers's tip to her being mentioned. "I assured her that it was rather important, and would do good. She agreed readily. By the way, she says Inspector Kay has been asked by Captain Hollick to trace my friend Sibbins's movements! What fun."

"Very well," Vincie said, "we can mention the two dud companies to Bone. Just slip it in, eh?"

"Work it in as quietly as you can."

"And wait to see if Bone knows of them?" I asked.

"Yes. You might say, too, that you heard one or two local people had been stuck with those stumers, and see how he takes that."

"Can we make it personal?" said Vincie.

"Well, I don't know how Bone will take your remarks. If you can, do. He thinks that you, and Mrs. M., and I, are all in Voce's full confidence."

"There's another thing," I suggested; "I think we can touch on the alibis, and wonder why Withers was in the garage, and did he see anyone pass down the lane?"

Power nodded energetically. "That's the ticket! Ten to one, Bone will mention his alibi, and that will give you a chance to suggest that Withers may be wondering what Bone was doing there."

"But did he say he saw Bone in the lane?"

"No, at the mouth of it, which, as you know, debouches in a quiet street. I think the impression Withers gave Voce was that Bone was coming down the street when he himself emerged from the lane. He would, of course, if he was shielding Bone in payment for his silence about the wild-cat shares he wished on him."

"Very well," said Vincie, "we'll think over the best way of cornering Bone. I don't think we shall ask him to tea. But I might call."

"Do your best," said Power, rising. "There is just the chance, of course, that Withers thinks Bone was the guilty man. He never mentioned seeing Jolson go up, so we may take it that the late Mr. J. had gone before he got to the garage."

CHAPTER XIX

It was really rather extraordinary the way people invited Mr. Bone out to tea. Wise and safe, no doubt, but about as apt as offering a pike a mouthful of lettuce.

Next morning, when Power had gone, and Vincie was trying to write some of his new novel in the garden, Mrs. Davey-Renny's maid came with a note. It was an invitation to tea, an appeal for help, and an opportunity to do our good deed, all in one.

"Dear Mrs. Mercer [she wrote],

"I should be delighted if you and your husband could come to tea with me this afternoon. The summer seems to have forgotten itself, and to be going on, and I have asked Mr. Bone to come.

"Tea for three is rather trying, but a foursome will be quite nice, don't you think? The little man really wrote to me, and asked if he could come, but he is rather excited, I hear, and there are other reasons. All these horrid doings lately seem to have made him nervy and odd.

"He added something about business in his letter, and it is rather funny to hear that we were talking a little on the same lines the other day.

"At any rate, do come to help me with him.
"Yours sincerely,
"Rose Davey-Renny."

I told the maid we would come, and went out to Vincie. He was very angry with his hero (who had wantonly stepped out of the plot, and was heading for an anti-climax) but brightened up when I told him about the invitation.

"Splendid," he said, "I bet Bone has something on his mind. We'll lift it. Apropos of nothing, Penny, here's Willie hankering after the flesh-pots of Egypt, and making a mess of my plot. I don't know how he ran away like that."

"I do," I said. "It's your rotten habit of making a plot in advance. If you don't make a plot first no one can step out of it. You just push them along the way they want to go."

"So you say," he grumbled. "Well, if you have any work of your own to do, go and do it! Even Willie's wandering isn't going to make me change my methods of work at my time of life."

We have been married too long now for me to argue with Vincie. I went away, and began my work again. I had only got as far as the moment when Bohm came to tell us that Jolson was dead.

At luncheon, Vincie was quite happy. He had headed Willie off the flesh-pots, and done a good six pages.

"I've been thinking of Bone since," he told me. "That little man is capable of some kind of loyalty."

"What kind?" I asked.

"Well, if we are right, it was to his advantage to back up Withers in his dope story. But he didn't. And you could hear from what he said that he had a kind of sympathy for Jolson, even if he did think him a fool."

"You may be right," I said, "but do you think Mrs. Davey-Renny means that he mentioned the dud shares to her?"

"What else, my dear? He may want to know if she was let in too by that crook Withers. I really have a nicer opinion of Bone than I had. I may be wrong, of course, for a tippler is a sort of chameleon. He never stays steady long enough for you to study him."

"I thought chameleons were more famous for change of colour than movement," I said.

"Well, it involves movement, you juggins!" he returned. "He changes colour when he moves to a different background. You see, Bone may be a wise man, bemused; or just a plain fool, drunk or sober. You can't say which is character and which beer."

"Gin," I corrected.

"As you like. And sobriety may give a new twist to his character. He was sober when we went to tea with Withers."

"You think, Vincie, that he may have known Jolson did dope now and then, but kept quiet about it because the poor fellow was dead?"

"Yes. But I am partly banking on the fact that Mrs. Davey-Renny tolerated if she did not encourage him. She's a clever woman, and I think she would have turned him down long ago on account of his habits if she hadn't known there was something fundamentally decent about him. What do you think?"

"I agree," I said, "but you can't bank on anyone's infallibility in judging character. I make mistakes myself."

"I never heard you say so before," Vincie observed. "Well, if I can get Bone to myself, I'll see what I can get out of him."

Bone was certainly strange that afternoon when we met; intermittently excited and subdued. He and his hostess had been talking about the shares, and we were roped into the discussion soon after we arrived.

"Mrs. Davey-Renny has just been saying that she was once asked to invest in some shares," Bone began.

"That often happens to me," said Vincie. "The world's full of philanthropists."

Mrs. Davey-Renny seemed surprised that the subject had been launched so soon. "I was telling him that Mr. Morgan had held a lot," she said. "Extraordinary, really, for they have no value."

"But how odd!" I said. "Still, Mr. Bone, if you haven't any yourself, you needn't worry."

"I have," said Bone. "I only bought them because I was told Morgan had."

Vincie shook his head. "That's rotten! Very hard luck. I hope you were the only one who got let in. I mean to say, poor Jolson was much more likely to be fooled than a man of the world like you."

Bone did cheer up a little. There is hardly a creature living who does not look brighter after being told he is a man of the world.

"Jolson," said Mr. Bone, "wasn't an artist."

Whether this made sense, or emanated from his perennial hangover, it was impossible to say. But Vincie had a shot at interpretation.

"You mean that the artist, with his love of colours, is more likely to be attracted by a bright picture?" he asked.

"I mean," said Mr. Bone, more sensibly than before, "that Jolson never did anything; only threatened to do it."

Tea was now brought out, and while we perpended over this cryptic statement, Mrs. Davey-Renny gave me my cup, and turned to Bone.

"Threatened to buy shares?"

Mr. Bone seemed at a loss to explain. "No; not shares; everything. You must have noticed. Being the kind of man he was, and anxious to show you he wasn't, so to speak."

"Oh, quite," said our hostess vaguely, as she poured out his cup and Vincie's.

"But, threatening? Is that the right word?" Vincie said.

Mr. Bone sipped his tea with distaste. "Well, talking. He had to talk. That was all he could do. His investments had been settled for him. He had to feel safe. It's only people with a superiority complex who live adventurously."

"Now that is very interesting," I murmured. "He wanted to feel a big, competent man; impressive, perhaps. But he was ineffective, and knew it really. He daren't sell out safe stuff, even if he wished to make a daring gesture, but—talked, you said?"

Mr. Bone waggled his head uncertainly. "Not about shares. I don't know if he ever bought any. I think not. But talk he did."

"Look here, Bone," Vincie said daringly, "there is no truth in the rumours about dope, is there?"

Mr. Bone laughed shortly. "Pack of lies!"

"You should know," I said. "We're strangers, of course."

"Jolson never took dope in his life," said Bone. "Never! He was all of a piece—*talk*!"

"The dope is ruled out," said Mrs. Davey-Renny. "In the first place, I don't believe the poor little man could have got it."

"Most unlikely," said Vincie, and glanced at Bone.

It is always most difficult to keep in something you know, when those about you are telling each other that it simply couldn't happen. I was watching Bone's face, and saw that he did know something and was inwardly wrestling.

"Quite impossible," I said, "in the circles Mr. Jolson would frequent."

"Oh, I shouldn't say that," Mr. Bone murmured.

"Why not?" asked Vincie. "Why not? There's a lot of nonsense talked, and more written in books, about walking into a café, say a foreign café (it might be Paris, or Berlin), and being offered a packet of dope."

Mr. Bone was now nearly down and out, and I saw it.

"And these peddlers must have some rough knowledge of psychology," I said. "Ability to judge a ready buyer. After all, Mr. Jolson didn't look to me like the type they would select."

"Well, I know he was!" said Bone, with uncalled-for pugnacity.

Vincie started. "What? But you said just now—"

"Wait a moment," Mr. Bone interrupted, and looked rather sulky. "I know what I said, and what I'm saying. I am saying that he was offered some, in Paris. He told me so himself."

Now that it was out, Vincie frowned at me, and made his voice sound as indifferent as possible.

"Bit of nerve, wasn't it, offering dope to a stranger?" he said. "I mean to say, if I'd been the blighter, I'd have chosen someone who looked thoroughly dissipated."

"I don't think Mr. Jolson ever did look dissipated, even in Paris," Mrs. Davey-Renny remarked.

Everything depended now on our not forcing the pace, or letting Bone think he was giving evidence. I smiled at him rather sceptically.

"Mightn't that have been talk, too, Mr. Bone?"

I inquired. "Perhaps he wanted to impress you with a dangerous adventure in a French café. That would fit in with your impression of him."

Mr. Bone shook his head. "Not a bit of it. He—"

"What?" cried Vincie, as Bone paused.

I felt dismayed. It isn't often that Vincie rushes in like that and gives the show away.

"Gave you details you could believe?" said Mrs. Davey-Renny.

"Why, he actually—" began Bone, then hastily passed his cup for more tea. It was still half full, and I saw Vincie glance at it. This was bad stall work on our part. Twice he had been on the point of making a revelation, and twice we had balked him somehow.

"I suppose he said it was in a small pill-box?" said Vincie at last. "That would be the sort of thing a romancer would think of first. You can generally pip them on details."

"He—he said it was a white packet," Bone replied.

We noted the slight hesitation after "said."

"What sort of packet?" I asked. "Do tell us all about—all he said."

Mrs. Davey-Renny was filling Bone's cup. Vincie looked up a tree at a bird which had begun to sing, as if his whole heart lay in that. Mr. Bone was perhaps lulled into a sense of security.

"Well, he was a bit vague," he remarked.

"Thank you, Mrs. Davey-Renny."

"I mean to say, he didn't seem to know exactly where the place was; some mean street on the left bank, you know—that's the way he put it."

"Probably called it the *rive gauche*," Vincie murmured. "That always sounds so much more romantic."

"I believe he did." Bone sipped his tea, and resumed. "He was sitting in a café there, drinking a bock, and noticed a dark-complexioned fellow, like a southern Frenchman, sneaking about, and talking to one or two women at other tables."

"Sounds just like a magazine story," I said.

"That's the way he made it," Bone replied. "Anyway, this man came up to him presently and offered him a white packet—held it just out of view under the edge of the table, you know. Jolson wasn't strong on French, but he thought the fellow said *cinquante francs*."

"Not more?" I asked.

"Not so dusty either," Vincie suggested. "That's over ten bob."

"I wonder Mr. Jolson knew what it was," Mrs. Davey-Renny remarked.

"Well," said Bone, "if you were asked fifty francs for a headache powder, you would think it a dear headache."

"How aptly put!" I smiled at Mr. Bone, and added: "What a cunning idea."

Bone raised his eyebrows. "Oh, I don't know. Anyway, Jolson guessed it must be some dope. He had *nous* enough for that. And, of course, he went abroad expecting to find the place living with crooks, dope fiends, apaches; all that sort of wildfowl."

"He got a kick out of his ideas," said Vincie.

"Yes, he got thoroughly bucked on the strength of it," said Bone. "I don't suppose he was ever in the least danger, and the people in the café were probably just common-or-garden artisan-class folk, but he would feel a perfect adventurer there. Knife-in-your-back, and into-the-Seine-with-you any moment. *You* know."

We simply daren't ask him to cut the cackle now. He might dry up, or begin to suspect. Vincie hid a yawn.

"Absolutely, Bone. You should be a darned good portrait-painter, you know. You have the gift of seeing character."

Mr. Bone looked pleased. "Oh, it was pretty obvious. Anyway, he looked at the packet, and it had a label *'Cachet Nez'* on it, and—well, that's all."

"But how disappointing!" I said. "I thought you were going to say that he bargained with the man, and blued thirty francs on it, then went back to his hotel, and made a beast of himself with it."

"I tell you he never took that sort of stuff in his life," Bone said hastily. "A good judge at that."

We saw that he wanted the subject dropped, and we thought we knew why. After all, Jolson had convinced the little painter on the matter; that is to say, convinced a man who (when away from the gin) was intelligent enough, that he had actually been offered a packet of dope. A man, too, who had always seen through him, and knew that he bolstered up his ineffective little soul with imaginary adventures and high deeds. And all this with a yarn that sounded spurious from the start. You don't peddle dope to French artisans in cafés, or waste your time in mean streets trying to sell the stuff at fifty francs a time. And Bone, who knew Paris, would know that much.

It was on the cards that he was making an artistic attempt to get back to the shelter of Withers's story, but somehow one felt there was more in it than that.

"Well, the poor chap's made an end to his adventures now." Vincie yawned again. "So it doesn't much matter. Talking of painting, Bone, are you doing anything at present?"

Mrs. Davey-Renny smilingly remarked that Mr. Bone wanted to go on with his portrait of her.

"I may be able to give you a sitting or two this week, Mr. Bone," she added, "if you aren't too busy."

Of course we had to see the picture, which was stacked on an easel in the house. It betrayed signs of Bone's several attempts to get going; in different moods, and under the influence of several schools of painting. It might have been really good, if he could have made up his mind to be representational, subjective, or psychic, but he never had.

He did not go back with us, when we left, and we walked silently along the road for quite half a mile before Vincie spoke.

"Well, Penny," he said at last, "there was a hole in the ballad, wasn't there?"

"Was it just to get his breath again?" I suggested.

"I don't think so. It was my fault. I rushed him once. And I do not believe Jolson took him in with that story."

"You think he made it up?" I asked.

"No, I don't, but I think Bone believed him because he had the goods on him, my dear."

"You mean that Jolson bought the stuff?"

"Yes," he said earnestly. "I think Bone was going on to say that he was shown a packet of it. For instance, I don't think he invented the odd name on the label. But he decided it was dangerous to say that Jolson had shown it. He invented the bit about it being merely described to him. I felt sure he substituted the word 'said' for another word; 'showed' very likely."

That had been my own impression, but would anyone buy a single packet of dope, and pay fifty francs for it, without trying it?

"If Jolson didn't use it," I said, "what was the great idea?"

"Evidently a trophy, Penny."

"That would square with what we heard," I remarked thoughtfully. "I suppose it was equivalent to the buffalo-horns brought home by the man who's been in Africa. If you can't swear he shot the beast, you can't swear he didn't."

"I look at it this way," said Vincie. "Jolson meets Bone, and, I expect, feels what a pull a painter daring enough to get drunk has over him. He puts up this yarn about the Paris café, gives Bone the impression that he plunged into vice headlong, gets laughed at for his pains, and pulls out this packet. 'Have a sniff, Bone?'—you can hear him saying it—'Got this in Paris. Hot stuff!'"

"We'll put the case to Power," I replied. "I am sure you are right. But even if he made a habit of carrying the old packet about with him, I can't imagine how he was such an ass as to sprinkle it on the rose. The whole thing is probably a wretched coincidence."

"We can't tell," said Vincie. "But this is the only yarn admitting the possession of dope that we have come on yet."

CHAPTER XX

"ARE you working on the case, or are we?" I asked Mr. Power when he came back that evening from town.

"Well, I suppose you two are," he returned, with his most irritating grin. "Joking apart, my occupation is gone; in that case, at least. Voce has informed me that Sibbins is definitely out of the case. Kay has gone into his movements, and they support Sibbins's own rotten confession. Now the only reason, beyond pure pleasure, that brings me down here, is the fact that my client wants me to investigate his uncle's losses."

"Sibbins does?"

"Yes. Up to date, he does not know that Morgan financed Withers in a bucket-shop. And when he went to see Voce, on my advice, it's obvious that Voce did not tell him. So Voce does attach some importance to the point. But I am not a detective; merely Mr. Sibbins's lawyer. So I have to put any knowledge at the disposal of my client."

"You should see Voce about it first," Vincie suggested.

"I must. As far as I can learn, Voce has intimated to Withers that he is to remain here till he gets permission to go. Now at this moment, when the whole story threatens to break loose, Withers must be most anxious to get away. He was just working up for the final coup when Morgan died. To run would have meant suspicion. Now that Voce's fiat has immobilised him, with his booty, he must be furious."

"Then Voce does suspect him?" I suggested.

"I am not so sure about that. In spite of everything, our one-idead cop suspected, and suspects, Jolson. But, for some strategical reason, he is holding up Withers. Now for your news. Did you get anything out of Bone at your tea-party?"

We beamed. Here at least we had some information which would show we had not been wasting our time.

"You tell him, Vincie," I said, "I want to watch his face."

Vincie at once began to tell him what had happened at Mrs. Davey-Renny's tea-party, and as he went on, I saw Power becoming more and more impressed. When Vincie had finished, he clapped his hands appreciatively.

"Good work. Very good work, you two! The story, boiled down, is that Jolson once bought a packet of 'snow' in Paris, and hoped to feel a big man on the strength of it for months to come. Every time his inferiority complex pinched him, he took out the packet and said: 'What a Bad Boy Am I!' And once, when he thought Bone had the bulge on him, as a very superior drunkard, he put the artist in his proper place by exhibiting evidence of his rarer vice."

"Well, that was what Bone gave us to believe," I said. "The only weak thing about it was the story. I mean to say, the café bit."

"But there is the stamp of truth about the main yarn, in the fact that the packet, as far as Bone knew, remained intact."

"I don't suppose Jolson actually opened it to show," Vincie said.

"Now, look here, Mercer," Power observed indulgently, "that's implicit in the character of the little man, and everyone of his kind, type, and upbringing. I mean the failure to go the whole hog."

"You think he didn't?" I asked.

He addressed me even more indulgently. "There are two things you must ask in a case like this: Does a man do a thing he needn't, if the results may be dangerous, or unpleasant? Carrying a packet of dope in his waistcoat pocket was just as good to Jolson as taking a sniff, and telling someone he had."

"Without being able to prove it," I agreed.

"Well, how could he prove it? Ask Bone to have a good look at his eyes? The second question is this: would any timid, little man, with no knowledge of drugs or their effects, start sniffing the contents of a dubious packet he got from a sneaking rascal, in a foreign town? For all he knew, it might be a deadly poison."

"That's true," Vincie admitted. "So you think Jolson had a packet of dope to carry about with him as a stiffener of morale? It reminds me of that story of Conrad's, *The Secret Agent*. Wasn't it in that that the little anarchist was always telling the police inspector, when he met him, of the bomb he had, ready to poop off?"

"And the copper almost drove him mad because he only smiled at him," Power remarked. "Yes. That was a good one. It didn't occur to you, I suppose, to ask Bone what the packet looked like?"

"He gave us the impression that it was a paper one, such as you find headache powders in," I said.

"That's right," Vincie said. "Sedlitz powders used to be packed the same way."

"You're barking up the wrong tree," Power smiled, "I mean to say, if the packet was dirty."

"Power's right. We ought to have asked that," my husband said, "but it never occurred to me. Waistcoat pockets are always full of dust and stuff; as my wife would tell you, Power."

"Perfect ash-bins!" I said heartily.

"And if Jolson carried it about with him, the packet would soon be soiled," Vincie added.

"But did he?" I said.

"I think he must have done," Power remarked. "That is, if the contents of his packet found their way into Morgan's garden. There wasn't any packet on him when he was found dead, and none among his effects."

"I'll ring up Mr. Bone," I said, and went away at once to do it.

He was not at home, so I tried Mrs. Davey-Renny's. Yes; she had asked him to stay to dinner, and he would be at the telephone in a moment.

When I heard the little man's voice, I plunged at once into the question: "You remember a certain white paper packet you told us about, Mr. Bone?"

"Yes," he said, in a rather dubious voice, "of course."

"I wonder if you could tell me what it looked like?"

"Like? Well, like a packet, not very big. In fact, small."

"I mean was it clean, or not?"

I could almost hear him pause and think, then he replied: "Rather soiled. But he carried it in his pocket, you know."

I thanked him and rang off, before he had time to ask me why I wanted to know.

"You were right," I said to Mr. Power, when I returned. "It was soiled. And Mr. Bone suggested the same reason for that."

Power looked pleased. "Good. Now Mr. Jolson was in Morgan's garden that morning, and he had the doings, if he wanted to use them. That's affirmative for guilt. But not even a lunatic would think that the stuff could be administered to a man in Morgan's condition. If the dog assaulted the man in fun, and killed him; why the dope? If Jolson assaulted him in anger and, possibly to his own surprise, found that he had conked out; why the dope? In fact, the only explanation for it being used is that it was used to make the victim incapable of defending himself."

"And if Morgan wouldn't take it, that's washed out," I said.

"Absolutely," said Mr. Power sadly. "In fact, you have just added a new complication to the case. And so unpleasantly like the real thing that one can't dismiss it off-hand."

"So that it remains misleading?"

"Very much so. We wanted traces of dope, and here they are, but in the wrong hands. I wish I had never discovered the damn' stuff. It just comes of my habit of prying into what doesn't concern me."

"We all do it," I said. "But we don't often confess."

After dinner Mr. Power said he was going round to see Mr. Withers. "I may have to make a frontal assault," he said. "Much as I dislike my client I think I have to make Withers cough up at least some of the proceeds. Now that I have handed the main case over to you, I advise you to ring up Voce, ask him to come round, and unburden your souls about the tea-party."

"We are rather afraid he may think Bone made it up to save himself," I said.

Power shook his head. "You ought to know Voce better than that, Mrs. Mercer. He's about as good a detective as Scotland Yard boasts. But if you fail to let him know about this, he may have other suspicions. You get him, and see."

We rang up Voce, finding him at last at Captain Hollick's house. I told him that we had some information for him, and he replied quite dispassionately that he would like to hear it.

"If I may come in about a quarter to ten," he added.

"When you like," I said, and rang off.

He came in punctually and sat down. "Captain Hollick didn't quite approve," he told us. "I think he's in favour of having you both court martialled for interrupting his drill."

Vincie laughed. "Well, we don't get paid for this, you know. It's all to help on the cause of law and order. We went out to tea this afternoon, and met Mr. Bone there."

"The artist?"

"Yes. Now I'll explain all that took place."

When he had finished, Voce looked interested. "I see. It's funny, sir, how anxious you were to hear all about Jolson's character, but I expect that was for Mrs. Mercer's book."

"Characterisation," I said. "Quite."

"The point is this," Vincie remarked: "Does it sound sense to you?"

"It does," said Mr. Voce. "It sounds true. I once had a sergeant, who wasn't very well educated, but wished he was. He carried a school Virgil about with him. It gave him a feeling of access to the fount of learning, if I may say so."

"The curious thing to me, Mr. Voce," I said, "is that Mr. Bone seems to have been swindled by Withers into buying shares, and doesn't know that Withers makes a business of it."

"I must tell him," Voce replied thoughtfully. "I didn't for reasons of my own. I can do no harm if I say that I have no reason to believe Withers had anything to do with the death of

Mr. Morgan. But he had something to do with someone who may have killed Morgan, and that is what I want to find out."

Vincie put in. "I agree with you. Now, our theory was that Withers saw Bone come out of the lane, and hearing of Morgan's death, imagined Bone might be responsible. What do you think of that?"

"I'd like to hear more of it, sir, before I tell you."

"And even then you mayn't!" I said.

Voce favoured me with a bow. "Too true, madam. I hate keeping things to myself, but that's the worst of being an official."

"To go on," said Vincie. "We assumed at first that Bone had learned that Withers had not only tipped him about the shares (mentioning Morgan as another buyer, to gain his confidence) but had also got to know that Withers was the actual share-peddler."

Voce considered the implication of that. "I see your drift, sir. Bone walked into Withers about it, and Withers remarked that he had seen Bone coming from the lane behind Morgan's, and what about it?"

"That was our line, at first," I said. "Withers to Bone: 'It will look nasty for you if I give you away.' Bone to Withers: 'I like that! You let me in for a swindle, and then you threaten to involve me in a crime I never committed.' Withers to Bone: 'I'll do what I can for you about the shares, and you must shut up about them. In return I'll try to put the murder on Jolson'.'"

"And then," Vincie took up the tale, "we see Bone, hear him talking about being done over the shares, discover that he doesn't know Withers did him down, and find our theory has gone west. But, if it has gone west, why is Withers bothering at all?"

Voce gave us that information quite readily. "I make mistakes like other people, Mr. Mercer, but isn't it quite likely that Mr. Withers had gathered together all he could, just before Morgan died, and was prepared to get out with it? He doesn't want it known that he did Bone. He is afraid investigation of Morgan's papers will disclose his Birmingham business; but that will only be to the police, and the lawyers. If Bone, on the other hand, gets wind of it, and makes a charge against him, or brings a case for the recovery of the money, that will be an open affair. People will ask if Withers had a motive for killing Morgan."

"You are suggesting," I said, "that if Withers has not already tried to hush up Bone, he was getting evidence which might shut his mouth later?"

"That's on the cards," said Voce.

"If Bone was really coming from Morgan's garden when Withers saw him," I observed, "we may take it that he had been in to see Morgan."

"Quite possible, Mrs. Mercer."

"Went in to have a row with him, possibly," said Vincie.

"The fact is," Voce replied, "that some of the men here were jealous as tom-cats over the lady at the cottage. Withers is an insolent devil, and I hear he used to amuse himself by making remarks which suggested that he was the favourite horse in that stable. You may think Bone a stupid little tippler—"

"He's not so stupid when sober," I said.

"Or Jolson a silly little man," Voce resumed, without comment. "But they were both in love with the lady. I interviewed Mr. Edwards to-day, and he admitted that Withers made little jokes. There was a recent jest of his to the effect that the batch of lovers must keep their eye on Morgan—'Morgan the Mormon,' I think he said. That sort of thing would get under Bone's skin, and having a skinful of gin as well, he may have gone round that morning to check the scandal. Drunken men are incalculable."

"Well, either Bone saw Morgan before Jolson did, or Bone has not been frank," said Vincie.

Voce was frank again. "We have no doubt about the times. Withers's alibi for Bone shows that he must have seen Morgan—if he did see him—after Jolson did. But we have no witness to prove that Bone *did* see Morgan. The lane is sometimes used as a short cut."

CHAPTER XXI

"There remains the question of the packet," I said, when Voce begged permission to fill a pipe. "If that were found, it would throw some light on the business."

I wanted to know if Voce admitted the packet, and for once he did not catch me out. "Yes," he agreed, "but Mr. Jolson was not suspected at first, and he had a long time in which to dispose of the paper packet."

He did not add: "If your theory is right that he had one, and Bone knew it." So we could presume that he had other information he had kept back from us.

We agreed, after he had gone, that the examination of Jolson's clothes by the Home Office analyst must have disclosed some specks of the cocaine; perhaps in the dust from the lining of his waistcoat pocket; chemical powder may be discovered by high-power microscopes, even if it is not visible among dust to the naked eye.

"Which is awkward for the memory of Mr. Jolson," Vincie said.

Voce lit his pipe. "Don't be let in by the *post-hoc* fallacy too soon, Mr. Mercer. We should have to prove the administration by some logical or practical means. Also the point to be gained by its administration. And that would be a job, especially the last. I say frankly that Jolson is the obvious suspect here, but if I had a solution of the point we have been discussing, the business would be cleared up pretty soon. As it is—"

He rose, rammed down the tobacco in his pipe, and was interrupted in his preparations for departure by the entrance of our friend Mr. Power.

"Going, Voce?" the latter asked; "why, the night's young yet! Sit down, and let me hear what you three have decided."

"Nothing," said Voce, still on his feet in spite of the invitation, "unless it is that we know very little."

"So little; when we ought to have known more," Power murmured. "Sit down like a good fellow! You fidget me, standing about."

Voce had a good look at him, evidently decided that he meant something, and resumed his seat.

"What more, Mr. Power?"

Power lit a cigarette. "Most things, Voce. Every case I come into shows me how little I know about the common things of life. From this time on, I intend to develop my general knowledge."

"And then?" said Voce calmly.

"As I came home here," Power went on, "I passed a garden from which came a most delightful scent. All I know about gardening could be put on a sixpence. I was curious enough to ask a passer-by what the scent was. Tobacco plant, which gives off its scent at night."

"Oh, does it?" said Voce, with a bored air. "I never knew that. But what's the idea; that Morgan was poisoned with nicotine, and the pathologist didn't know it?"

"You're too hasty, my good man. What happened was that the scent of the tobacco plant made me think of scents, and put me on the scent of something else."

"It would," Voce grumbled; "I never knew such a man for seeing one thing, and thinking of another."

"Well, it occurred to me," resumed Power, who loved to irritate Voce by dallying down verbal by-paths, "that in colour and form our world grows more wonderful every day, but our taste in scents; the very scents themselves that we use and enjoy tend to become more synthetic."

"A sad thought, sir," Voce remarked, "but I daresay you'll come to the point in time to let me get home before my pub closes."

"So I intend to look up some information on a subject on which I am very ignorant," said Power, rising and going to a bookcase. "I noticed the other day that Mrs. Jennifer has a gardening encyclopaedia; new and extensive. To my shame, this is the first time I thought of consulting it. Here goes!"

Voce did light up a little bit now, as he watched Power go to the shelf, remove and open a book.

There was a silence for at least two minutes; then Power laid the open book on his knee and looked very pleased with himself.

"Yes, this is a good book, and a new book. It has forty pages on roses and rose-growing. It even mentions Mr. Morgan."

"Mr. Morgan?" I cried excitedly.

"As the originator of the Rennavy rose," Power said. "And it gives the points of this, now much advertised, flower."

"What about it?" said Voce, very earnestly.

"Something which confirms my remark that we don't expect or look for natural scents nowadays," said Power. "Thirty years ago anyone given a rose smelled it. Now we simply don't."

"Great Scott!" said Voce, in a tone of disgust. "So the beastly thing is scentless? Why the devil—"

"Probably because you thought nothing of it," Power interrupted. "In my case, because there was 'coke' on it, and I should have hesitated to disturb evidence. Actually," he smiled, "I overlooked it."

We were surprised that Power had thought of it even now, but Voce was much impressed.

"The pathologist never mentioned it. No, that would be the analyst," he murmured. "Mrs. Davey-Renny never mentioned it. Do you think it occurred to her?"

"No," I said, "if she smelled the flowers at all, it would be out of compliment to the giver, Inspector Kay, when he handed them to her."

"You say 'them'? Oh, I see"—Voce looked at me, and nodded approval—"I suppose the others were scented roses?"

"You'd better ask her," said Vincie. "Now where are we? The inference Power draws from all this is that most roses are lacking in perfume, so the ordinary man or woman doesn't smell at 'em. Not having done so, the point about the scentlessness does not occur to him."

"Which allows us to discriminate, sir," said Voce. "A chemist does not need to taste all his wares, to say if they are poisonous or not. Especially when he sees a jar labelled scientifically."

"Exactly," Power remarked, and went to put the book back on the shelf. "Still less if he manufactured, or invented the stuff."

Voce nodded a wise head. "I can always look to you for what jazz musicians call the twiddley bits, Mr. Power," he said warmly. "Mr. Morgan was about the only expert in roses among the people here, and he didn't apply his nose to a scentless rose of his own discovering."

"That leaves us still in the air," I ventured to say. "Obviously he didn't put his nose to it—*who* did?"

There was a short silence. Then Power shook his head. "Good old spoil-sport you are, Mrs. M.! What about it, Voce?"

Mr. Voce rose. "At this time of night it's too much for me," he said, "I'm for bed. But I will say that you've given me something to cause insomnia, Mr. Power; and not for the first time. Come and see me to-morrow, if you can manage it."

When he had gone we remembered that Power had not attempted to tell him about his visit to Withers.

"You knocked old Voce that time," Vincie said. "I suppose you thought he had had enough shocks without describing what you got out of Mr. Tressy Withers."

"There was another reason," he replied. "I rather overstepped the limits with Withers. He got a bit fresh, and I felt I had to call him down. Though he did not say so, his nerves are not what they were last week. I should say he was in a funk, and not only over the chance of his share-pushing coming out."

"Why then?" I asked.

"Well, Voce's warning to him not to leave the town seems to have made him wonder if our inspector really believed he *was* busy in the garage all the time. I believe Voce does; and I am sure Withers has mistaken the meaning of the warning. He had time, of course, to slip from the garage to Morgan's garden and back, but he wouldn't rig up an alibi so near the place where Morgan was killed; giving him opportunity as well as motive, the two things your detective looks for."

"Did you suggest that he had?" Vincie asked.

"I said that I knew Morgan had been sold a pup by him, and that he wouldn't want details of that dog-deal to come out into the papers," Power replied. "An unwise suggestion; but I made it, and he curled up at once. Thoroughly yellow, that blighter."

"But surely he didn't admit it?" I said.

"No, not specifically. He asked me what I wanted. I said that my client, Mr. Sibbins, had been Morgan's heir. He wanted his money back, or as much of it as he could get. Then Mrs. Davey-Renny came in for some thousands. What about that?"

"Rather like compounding, or offering to compound, a felony," Vincie observed doubtfully.

"Oh, no," said Power, "near the wind, but not that. As far as I knew, which is not so far, Morgan had not complained of his investments. Mr. Bone has not laid any charge. In any case, Bone can file his claim. But I am hoping that Withers still has the boodle intact."

"Anything else?" Vincie asked.

"Well, I had a stab at exonerating Bone. I asked Withers if he suspected that Bone had seen Morgan that morning. He said he didn't. I asked him if he suspected Jolson. He said he did. I asked him point-blank if he had any other ground for suspecting that Jolson used dope than a mere idea that the man had occasionally looked what the Yankees call 'dopey'."

"But, of course, Bone may have told him about the packet," I said.

"Well, he hadn't, it seems. Withers was so dashed anxious to prove that he had been usefully occupied in the garage (not busy slaying Morgan), that he invented the theory the moment he heard of the cocaine on the flower."

"He actually told you that?" Vincie looked amazed.

Power laughed. "My dear fellow, he is yellow, and his nerves have suddenly given way, but he is not such an ass as to admit that he faked evidence to involve Mr. Jolson. But he hummed and ha'ed, and finally said no. Mr. Jolson's looks at times had given him that impression, and that was all."

"Another blow to our theory," I said. "Mr. Bone hasn't charged Withers with swindling him, so Mr. Withers hasn't any reason to buy his silence. And he wasn't trying to involve Jolson so as to let Bone out."

"Which just shows you," said Power, "that not all evidence is tainted that comes from what you consider a tainted source. It's a common fallacy that it is; and one often applied to religion. Someone sees a rank bad parson, and concludes that what he preaches is bad too."

"That's true," said Vincie. "It leaked out that Jolson had visited Morgan, and Withers heard of the 'coke' as well, and made up a nice yarn. But is he sufficiently frightened now to cough up what he got from his dupes?"

Power looked thoughtful. "I had a delicate business there. I couldn't promise to hush it up, in case Voce took further steps. What I did suggest was this, that Withers should see Brown, the lawyer, to-morrow, and say that he had made some bad investments for the firm. He now realised it and decided that none of his clients, or his late partner's estate, should suffer from his own folly. Needless to say, it was not as crude as that, but Withers could see what I meant."

"What was his reply?"

Power chuckled. "It was distinctly funny. 'What! Out of my private fortune, do you mean?' Those were his exact words. 'Which is partly Mr. Morgan's fortune, and Mrs. Davey-Renny's bit, and some more,' I told him. 'What you say to Brown is not my affair'."

"He wouldn't like that," Vincie remarked.

"He didn't. But he thought it over. His next question was on the mark. If he did not see his way to do this, what would I do about it?"

I had difficulty in visualising Withers with his tail between his legs, but then I had last seen him while his nerves were in good order.

"What did you say?" I asked.

"I said that I would consider initiating a prosecution against him on a charge of share-pushing. I explained that I knew all about the bucket-shop he worked under cover, and had a clerk making inquiries about it. That had nothing to do with Voce or his investigations, but it was on the cards that Voce would be interested when he heard of it."

Vincie nodded. "That must have been obvious to him."

"It was. He tried to bluff and then he lost his temper; but finally he stepped down and said he would see Brown to-morrow at ten. As I came here, I left an urgent note for Bohm, asking him to put a man on Withers at once, in case he tried a bolt."

"But suppose Bohm doesn't come in?" I asked.

"By a bit of luck I was able to make sure that that couldn't happen," he replied. "I saw Inspector Kay in his little car after that. He was coming home, and as he was wearing an ancient dinner-jacket, I assumed that he had been dining somewhere. Actually he had been to Mrs. Davey-Renny's, and looked as full of himself as a dog with two tails. He promised to run home, change, and watch Withers's house till Bohm's man came on. But I really don't think Withers will bolt."

"To come back to the question of the rose," I said, "your little discovery about it is plain enough proof that Mr. Jolson told us a lie."

"Ah, you saw that?" he murmured. "Topping memory you must have."

"More than I have," said Vincie. "What was it Penny saw, or heard?"

"You both heard it. Jolson said he saw Morgan sniffing at the rose, Mercer. Or words to that effect."

"So he did. It beats me entirely. But he may have found Morgan dead, and got the wind up."

Power rose. "I don't see how it was done, or why," he said. "All I can be sure of is that Jolson told that lie."

"It's a twister," Vincie sighed. "And, like Voce, I'm for bed. One thing I am sure of now, and that is all; that's Bone's decency, and loyalty to his dead rival. He must have known that he might be suspected, on the strength of his presence in the lane that morning. He knew Jolson had a packet of the drug found in the case. But he neither told Withers of his knowledge, nor hinted at it to Voce."

"Which suggests that he didn't believe Jolson guilty of killing Morgan," I said. "He didn't even like the idea of his memory being blackened when Jolson was found dead."

"Who would believe that little shrimp was able to knock out a man like Morgan?" said Vincie. "I know even little men are troublesome when they go berserk, but I can quite understand Bone's incredulity."

He was on his feet now too, and looked at Power, who yawned, then assumed a dreamy expression.

"Well, to-morrow I must repair fresh gaps in my ignorance," Power said. "From roses to pathology. Good night."

CHAPTER XXII

UNTIL then, Mrs. Jennifer's maid had treated us with deference, or indifference; it is hard to say which. But the next morning, when we went down to breakfast, she stopped us excitedly to say that Mr. Bone had been locked up.

"What, Mr. Bone, the artist?" Vincie demanded. "And what do you mean by locked up?" I asked.

"Locked up by the police, ma'am," she replied at once.

"When was this?"

"Late last night, they say, ma'am."

Vincie and I exchanged horrified glances, and Power coming down the stairs at that moment, we communicated the surprising news to him.

"You're sure?" he asked the girl. "What was it for, do you know?"

"No, sir, that I don't. It was the milkman told me, and he didn't know himself, only he said it was at Mr. Withers's house."

She hurried off to the kitchen for our food, and we went into the dining-room, and sat down. At the moment our breath had been too much taken away to allow us to speak.

Power was the first to recover.

"Local police, if anyone," he said; "Hollick is an ass. I am sure Voce wouldn't authorise an arrest after what you told him."

"You asked Bohm to have a man put on Withers's house," I said. "He, the constable I mean, may have—"

"Just a minute!" said Vincie. "Didn't you say, Power, that Inspector Kay had promised to keep an eye on it?"

"Yes, but Kay is an experienced officer, and knows Voce is in charge of the case, Mercer. I'll run over to the station the moment I've finished breakfast, and see what's up. I am sure Bone isn't the guilty man. Of course, he may have got lit up, and made a confession. Drunk men sometimes do, when they have a thing on their minds, and get fuddled."

We all made sketchy breakfasts that morning, but Power's was really impressionist. He even left half his first cup of coffee, and ran out, to the surprise of the maid who was coming in with fresh toast.

"Now," said Vincie, when the door was closed again, "this is fierce. I do hope our information hasn't put wrong views into the heads of the police. With all his faults, I like that little man."

"That would be mad," I protested. "Why, unless they take it that Bone told the story of the packet to transfer the onus to Jolson—"

"But there was no need for him to mention it," Vincie interrupted. "He kept it dark before, though that was not to his interest."

"You ring up the police station," I suggested "Power may be too busy to come back and tell us."

"Not on your life!" said my husband, taking a cigarette from his case. "The police will be busy too."

I did Power an injustice, for he was back within half an hour, his pipe going well, and an amused look on his face. When we saw that, our fears were allayed.

"Is he really locked up?" I demanded, as he sat down.

"He was. They let him out with a caution early this morning," he replied. "It was Kay who arrested him after all."

This was astonishing news. Vincie spoke for us both when he said he hadn't known Kay was such a fool.

"Not a bit of it," said Power. "He was hanging about at my request, waiting for a constable to come on duty, when someone rolled up the street, paused on the other pavement, and then there was a crash."

"A shot?" I cried.

"Glass," said Power. "Half a brick through the window of Withers's drawing-room. Kay, of course, charged across at the man and brought him down. It was Bone. He stank of drink, and had another half-brick in his left hand. So Kay, seeing the constable coming up at a run, handed Bone over to him, and told him to lock Bone up and come back."

"Oh, is that all?" I said, relieved. "Did Withers come down?"

"He did. Kay says he refused to charge Bone, but the police decided to let Bone stay in the cells and cool off. This morning they gave him some strong coffee and told him to go home."

Vincie shook his head in a puzzled way. "Any explanation why Bone went off the deep-end like that?"

"Two!" said our friend. "It seems that Mrs. Davey-Renny has fixed it up with Kay. He must have heard that; and then it seems pretty obvious that he called on Mrs. Davey-Renny when he heard. Either then, at her house, or from some other source, he got to know that Mr. Withers was at the back of the bucket-shop that did him down."

"A double blow," I remarked sympathetically.

"At any rate, Mrs. Mercer, the result was that he rushed home, filled up with gin and other drinks, and half-bricks from the bottom of that broken wall near the White Horse. I presume his idea was to bring Withers out, and then assault him."

"I only hope that the association of ideas won't lead the police to think of Morgan's death," I said. "Bone was a bit lit up that morning too. Do you think he could possibly have talked to poor Morgan with a half-brick?"

"No," Power said decidedly. "A half-brick would have left a more obvious mark on the abdomen. It's too hard and edgy not to."

"Well, it was very good of you to hurry back to tell us," I said. "Are you going out again?"

"Yes, to Bone's. I want to see him. I want this kept dark till Mr. Withers has seen Brown, and put his financial intentions on paper. He does not know yet why Bone threw the brick; merely heard that he was drunk."

"How will you quiet Bone?" Vincie asked.

"I'll tell him that I am going to have a stab at getting his money back too," Power said, "that's all."

"But will Withers have enough to satisfy all demands?" I asked.

"I bet he has," Power assured me. "He's been running this show for some time, and Bone's little bit isn't very much. He has an income of about two hundred and fifty a year, or had, and put three thousand of his capital into these rubbishy shares. He was not well-to-do, like Jolson, but would feel the loss more. Even a sober portrait-painter isn't likely to earn much nowadays."

Mr. Power was going on to town when he had seen Bone, so we sat in the garden and got on with our work. When the maid was just bringing us out our "Elevenses," who should turn up but Mr. Bone himself. We sent the girl for another cup, and made the little man sit down.

He looked fairly respectable now, though he had the embryo of a black eye, where Kay's charging elbow had rammed him, and other dying signs of a thick night.

"I suppose you heard I'd made a fool of myself," he grunted, as we greeted him.

"Righteous indignation sometimes takes that form," Vincie told him. "Someone swindled you, and you had a go at him, I heard."

Bone nodded. "It was that—" Here, being more of a gentleman than Sibbins, he looked at me, and added: "That fellow Withers. Mind you, it was he put me on to those shares, and never said he was the swine behind the circular."

"If the swine stood in front of their circulars," I suggested, "I don't think there would have been so many buyers. Did you see Mr. Power? He thought of calling on you."

Bone nodded. "Mr Power has been extremely kind," he said. "Do you know, without being asked, he has volunteered to try to get my money back. Do you think he can?"

"I think he will," said Vincie. "Much better than having it published and the newspapers making a song-and-dance of your natural indignation."

"Oh, much," said Bone. "I promised him not to mention it outside. You're friends of his, of course; so that's different."

"Quite," I agreed, "and if Withers makes no charge, the thing will die down."

The maid had now come with a cup, and Bone drank his tea this time without distaste.

"But fancy Withers being a crook," he said.

"You never call a financier a crook till he's been tried and condemned," I suggested. "But never mind. I have an idea that Withers will go away soon."

"Not before I get my money, I hope," he said, with some alarm. "I'll mention that to Inspector Voce. I am to see him at twelve."

"Mr. Power was to interview Withers before that," Vincie reassured him. "I think you need not worry. I suppose Voce wants to see you about the other case?"

Bone nodded. "I think so. Really, I don't see why. I had an alibi, you know, if anyone was silly enough to suspect me."

"Perhaps they thought you had called in that morning to see Mr. Morgan," said Vincie. "You didn't, of course?"

Mr. Bone's round-eyed wonder convinced us that he hadn't. "I didn't feel very well, that morning," he said euphemistically. "I thought I would go for a walk and get some fresh air. I cut up the lane, and on towards the country a bit." Then here he looked at us earnestly—"the walking rather joggled my brains. I had a headache."

"Walking *is* trying when you have a headache," I agreed.

He looked at me gratefully. "So I went back, and when I was near the end of the lane, I saw Withers."

"You didn't hear any sound from Morgan's garden when you were in the lane, going or coming?" I asked.

"Not a sound, Mrs. Mercer. If I had, I would have told the police about it when they questioned me."

He looked at his watch and got up. "Thanks for the tea," he said, "and for what you've told me. I can't afford to lose that money. Now I think I had better go to my appointment with Inspector Voce."

He bowed to us in a rather nervous way, then turned as if to go.

"Oh, I suppose you heard about Mrs. Davey-Renny and Inspector Kay?" he asked, wheeling about again.

"Yes, we did," I said. "But only this morning definitely."

"A nice fellow," said Mr. Bone bravely, "and, I should say, a very competent officer." He dabbed his eye tentatively where the elbow of the competent officer had jabbed it, and went off with a very straight back to the gate.

"The British bulldog looks as if he had fixed his teeth in the right leg again," Vincie murmured, as we watched the little man go. "And it isn't Bone's."

"You mean Voce?" I asked.

"Yes. Unless Withers was more than a mere share-pusher, we seem to have to fall back on Jolson."

"I know Voce has practically refused to look elsewhere since he came," I said. "But Mr. Power may breeze in with some fresh idea yet."

"That's the point," said Vincie. "It may just happen that Power is considering means rather than men. His talk about mugging up pathology hints that it was the method of the murder that interests him. I can see he is still as puzzled about it as we are."

We settled down to work again, and there were no further disturbances that morning.

We had had an idea that Power would go on to town. He generally consulted good authorities when in doubt, and was in touch in town with one or two famous pathologists. But this time he came home for lunch, and looking sufficiently cheerful to suggest that Mr. Withers had made the great renunciation.

In fact, we forgot to tell him about Bone's visit, and rushed him with questions about the bucket-shop scandal.

"One at a time, please," he said. "Did Withers turn up? Yes. Was he sticky again? Yes, at first. He was inclined to argue with Brown about Morgan's joint responsibility in the matter of that share holding, and when Brown seemed incapable of fighting him on the right lines, I had to open fire again."

"Score a bull?" I asked.

"Several," he replied. "In the first place, I made it clear to him that I was now acting for three people; Sibbins, Mrs. Davey-Renny, and Bone. Mrs. Davey-Renny I represented since she had come under suspicion in the Morgan case, and it was up to me to show that at least one other resident might be suspected. Old Brown opened his eyes at that. I think he would have told me that this was irrelevant, only that he was so furious with Withers."

"It was a bit body-line," Vincie said.

"More than a bit, my son, and meant to be. I went on to say that, whatever the rights and wrongs in the matter of Morgan's purchase of shares, I felt that the right place to debate it was in one of His Majesty's Courts, and that was that."

"Did Withers wilt?" I asked.

"He did a little. But Brown then backed me up. He was, he said, prepared to take legal action, and I added that I knew Mr. Bone would also be prepared to engage me to take separate legal action on his behalf. 'And I am sure you do not want that, Mr. Withers,' I said, 'apart from the fact that it must involve another question'."

"You didn't say what?"

"Not I. Brown saw the point too, and of course he is a pedantic old lawyer, and normally ready to stand by the legal rules. If Withers hadn't been nasty at first, he would have dissociated himself from that remark of mine, I am sure. As it was, he sat mum."

"Withers has a passport, I suppose?" Vincie said.

"I believe so, but it seems Voce gave him a hint or two. He knows quite well that measures have been taken to see that he cannot get out of the country. He's still a suspect, you know."

"In face of the evidence against Jolson?" I asked.

"From the point of view of getting a verdict from a jury against the late Mr. Jolson, Mrs. M., what evidence is there? First, the undoubted fact that Jolson visited Morgan that morning. But that does not prove he killed him. Secondly, that cocaine was found in Morgan, and Bone avers that he was shown a packet of it that Jolson carried in his pocket. Apart from the fact that Bone is also a suspect and might wish to clear himself in that way, proof that Jolson had cocaine prior to the murder is no evidence that he used it on Morgan."

"Perhaps not legally," I said.

"Well, no verdict is of any use that does not come from a jury, after a legal process," Power replied. "Again, if Bone is as innocent as the dawn, what he says proves nothing. The prosecution, the defence, and the jury, would require proof not only that Bone saw a packet alleged to contain cocaine, but that the packet did contain cocaine. And beyond that, it would be necessary to prove that the cocaine in the packet was of the same nature, and was mixed with the same, and in the same proportions of adulterant, as that found in Morgan's body."

"Oh, blow your pedantry!" said Vincie. "Then nothing could be proved against Jolson at all?"

"No, not in court; though we may think what we like, and know what we know," said Mr. Power.

CHAPTER XXIII

"To go back to our friend Withers," I said, "what exactly is he prepared to do? Unless you have got him on paper, he may wriggle out yet."

"He *is* on paper," said Power. "Trust us lawyers to see to that. I got up to telephone to my partners in town, asking them to prepare for action, and Withers sat down and did a little writing to our dictation. So that's that."

"Exactly what?" inquired Vincie.

"He is taking back the shares held by Morgan, and Bone, at the price paid. Mr. Brown is accompanying him to Birmingham this afternoon by the two-thirty, and he's not going to leave till he has the money. Judging by Withers's acceptance of that proposition, he has the money in the bank. But I can assure you that, if our conference had taken place at the North Pole, there would have been another Arctic tragedy, and two explorers wiped out."

"He was furious?" I asked.

"Murderous," said Power. "As the story-books say: 'His face was distorted with rage.'"

"But honestly?" I said.

"Honestly? How would you feel if you had sweated a fortune out of other people, and were going abroad to retire on it, when one of them conked out, and the police told you to stand to while they poked about? Not to speak of a nosey lawyer butting in and making you put the money back. I think I should be cross myself."

"Do you know, Vincie," I said, noticing the gleam in Power's eyes, "I shouldn't be surprised if he hasn't been encouraging Voce to believe that Withers slew Morgan. With the mercenary idea of holding him up and screwing the money out of him."

"For my clients," said Power, thoughtfully. "I simply hate to think that Sibbins will profit by this act of justice, but there it is. I might add that I did not at first take the view that Withers was necessarily innocent. I had my doubts. But I admit that Voce's suspicion gave me an opportunity to straighten out the financial side, if I may put it that way."

"The inquest will be resumed soon," Vincie said, after a moment. "I wonder what will come of it?"

"I have no idea," said Power. "Voce knows better than I do that no one will bring in a verdict that Jolson killed Morgan. They may—that is the jury—see a parallel in Jolson's death, and decide that the dog did it. By the way, I have received a copy of the pathologist's report from Voce; which was very decent of him. But, like me, he sometimes gives away with one hand so that he may take back with the other."

"In other words, he wants your views?" said Vincie.

"I think so. As you know, my client Sibbins, Charles Gailey Sibbins, has been out of it for some time. That left me with the mere job of collecting his inheritance, so that he can spend it as fast as possible. I have put that in train, thanks to Voce's misunderstood warning to Withers. All that is left is to co-operate with Voce, out of goodwill, if I can. That is what I propose to do."

"You are going to mug up pathology, prior to dissecting the report?" I asked.

"I have found a lazier, and a more effectual way," said Power. "I hope to bring a pal, who is also a tame pathologist, here to dinner to-morrow night. We'll have a slap-up dinner and a talk. You are both invited."

We met Mrs. Davey-Renny later in the day, shopping in Malpertuis. She invited us to have an ice with her, and was tremendously enthusiastic about Power.

"He rang me up, you know," she said, "and told me. Quite too clever! I don't really need the money, you know, but I should have hated to see that oily man get away with it."

"And, of course, you're getting married," I said softly.

She laughed. "Yes, there is that. He's so keen on farming; heaven knows why! But farming is such an expensive luxury now. This windfall would just do for a little farm, do you think?"

Vincie replied out of the fullness of his ignorance.

"Oh, rather. Quite a big one, I should think."

"But I believe there is stock," she murmured. "So many things as well as the land. Never mind. If I do get the money, I'll buy it as a surprise for him."

"Lucky lad!" Vincie commented. "By the way, we saw Bone. He took it extremely well, though obviously heart-broken."

She looked sympathetic. "I am so sorry. But I did love hearing about the naughty brick he threw. I suppose he was a bit squiffy?"

"Quite a bit," I agreed, "and full of heady indignation, which helped."

"My young man was quite worried because he accidentally put his elbow in Mr. Bone's eye," she said. "Is it black?"

"Tending that way," said Vincie. "Tell the inspector that Bone bears no malice. He spoke highly of him."

"He ought to go away, and do some work," she said slowly. "As long as he hangs about here with nothing to do, he'll tipple. I really believe he has talent, if he would stick to his job."

Voce had gone to town, and taken Bohm with him. We went home and began to work. Having had so many people to see, and so much to discuss, I had fallen behind with my chronicle. Now—for nothing seemed likely to happen till Power's pathologist came down—I was determined to catch up. Incidentally, I was wondering what the critics would think of it when it was done.

There are three main types of critics of detective fiction, I find. There is the man who uses his brains, and is not averse from tackling a problem which is intricate. He ought to satisfy any decent author, even when his opinions are adverse. Then there is the man who likes action and is not particularly critical of the quality, or verisimilitude, of the detection. Last comes the critic who calls all detective stories "thrillers," but admits that he can't be bothered using his brains on stuff like that. Any attempt to be realistic or logical he firmly puts down. I wonder why so many high-brows go bald-headed in favour of thick-ear fiction. You find the same in the cinema; people of intellect whose whole eyes are given to gangster films and children's cartoons. Is it a kind of inverted intellectual snobbery?

Next day I went on again. Power had left early for town, and only work could have kept me from finding the day forty-eight hour long, before the specialist came down, and satisfied our curiosity.

At four, Vincie came and took my typewriter away from me. "Your eyes are already bulging like little apples," he said unkindly, "and this last page is more mistakes than words. Run upstairs like a good woman, bathe your face, remove your frown and wrinkles, and try to look human! Or go and ask Mrs. Jennifer what's for dinner. She's been making tremendous preparations."

Dr. Terpis, who was Power's oddly-named friend, arrived with him at half-past six. He made us both think what a jolly science pathology must be. He was no more than thirty, fat, red-faced, with a perpetual smile, and a horse-laugh which broke out on the least provocation.

I judged from his talk that he was interested in puppet-shows. He had made a puppet-show himself and all the figures, and told us all about it. And he was now writing a farce for them, and he told us bits of it, and laughed uproariously at the simple jokes and knockabout business he had invented.

Power says he has as many letters after his name as in it, but they threw no shadow on his conversation.

When dinner began I could see that he liked his food, and understood it. He beamed at every course as it came in, and more than beamed on it. It was as good as eating yourself to watch his gastronomic pleasure.

"Well, that was good grub, Power," he said when he had finished. "I know now why you came down to the country, to make a beast of yourself."

Power laughed. "Mrs. Jennifer does us pretty well, Terpis," he agreed. "I had it recommended to me by the Mercers here. I shall be glad to have your opinion on the coffee."

Terpis's opinion on that was favourable too, and at last we moved to the drawing-room, and the men lit cigars, while I enjoyed my cigarette.

Power knew quite well that we were dying to hear Terpis on Morgan, so he started his friend on the Commedia dell'Arte, and wasted half an hour of our good time before he pulled him up and said he supposed he had had a glance at the copy of the report.

Dr. Terpis nodded. "Old Gladsty's? Why, yes," he said. "I must say it is always a treat to read anything of Skinny's. Bit dry, you know, but the meat's there all right. And careful! Skinny was born a maiden aunt. But what a way for that man to die."

Power raised his eyebrows. "We're all novices here, my son. Is it at all likely that Mr. Morgan died of a blow in the tummy?"

"Or what passes for it, in the presence of ladies," said Terpis, with his horse-laugh. "My dear fellow, is it any more strange than that a man should pass out after taking a bathe on top of a heavy meal?"

"I know. But now you have read the report, does it bear out the theory that Morgan's sniff of dope had nothing to do with his death?"

"Of course it does. The stuff isn't prussic acid, Power. And what he took wasn't much."

I leaned forward. "Did Mr. Power tell you about the little man who was butted over a quarry by his dog?"

"Oh, rather," said Dr. Terpis genially; "but Power's such a dreadful liar, you know. Congenitally incapable, and so on."

"The inquest was in the papers," I said.

He nodded. "Very likely, Mrs. Mercer, but it isn't any entertainment to a bloke like me to read about post-mortems. 'We makes 'em,' as the author's valet told the book canvasser."

"Well, it's true," Power laughed. "Jolson had a big dog and it had the bad habit of bouncing. The Mercers saw it bounce at its owner in the garden here, and the jury took the quite reasonable view that it bounced for the last time when Jolson was admiring the view from the upper edge of a gravel-pit."

"The incident is interesting, without being very relevant," said Dr. Terpis, looking at the ash on his cigar. "Minus the gravel-pit with the view, that sort of thing happens ten times a day where there are large pets."

"The relevance lies in this, Dr. Terpis," said Vincie. "The late Mr. Morgan's abdomen, we have all agreed, was about on a level with the head of the Great Dane—at least, when slightly lowered."

"Tum-tum, or head?" asked Terpis.

"Head. Now you have read the book of words. We are all anxious to think that the Great Dane charged at Mr. Morgan, butted him, and so slew him."

"Why anxious?" he demanded.

"Well, he was a decent little man, and is now dead—Jolson, I mean."

"Was he a decent little man?" said Terpis inquiringly.

"So everyone says. We really did not know much of him."

"Well, views on what is decency differ—especially nowadays," Terpis observed judicially. "Using the word decency in its old sense, I should fault Jolson on it, if your theory is correct. Here he had a dog. It butted a gentleman who had had a breakfast too big for safety in the circumstances. He lay down and died. The owner of the pet, knowing quite well that the dog had only been doggish, did not ring for a doctor, or warn the police, but simply faded away, leaving the corpse in the garden."

"That," said Vincie, "is a side to the question which has troubled me a little. But there was a lady in it."

"In the garden?"

"No, the case. Five men or so here were suspected of being in love with her. Morgan, quite unjustifiably, was suspected of worse. One local bounder seems to have found his fun in circulating nasty rumours which exasperated the rival lovers."

"Why, this is right outside my garden," said Terpis. "Cadavers, not cupids, are my subjects."

"The point is this," I put in. "Mr. Jolson was one of the lovers, or, we had better say, suitors, and he was not only an also-ran, but rather conscious of it. It seems pretty well established that he went round that morning to have a row with Morgan. Not a scrap. He was too small for that. Just a row. In fact, they may have had one and the dog may have thought he was protecting his master when he rammed Morgan."

"I see what you mean," Dr. Terpis remarked. "Mr. Jolson may have felt that he might be suspected of killing Morgan, because he had gone there to have a row with him. A man with guts and a little common sense, would, I think, have rung up a doctor all the same. But a little weed, recovering from a fit of bad temper and an inferiority complex, might not. So far I am with you."

"The qualifying 'so far,' Terpis," Power observed, "suggests that there was something in the pathologist's report which does not quite square with our theory."

"I suppose the report is frightfully detailed, and full of technicalities?" I asked.

"It was almost Greek to me," said Power. "I was amazed to find how carefully these blokes do their stuff. And how much they can read from what they see. It reminded me of a radio photograph of my jaws I saw once at my dentist's. With a glass, I could see brown shading here and there, and tiny blurs. But my dentist nearly made an epic poem out of them."

Terpis laughed. "Well, if someone will provide me with a sheet of paper I'll do my best to draw for you a section and outline of the skull of a Great Dane."

"Then you understand the anatomy of animals?" I asked.

"The biologist must study the dumb animals as well as the talkative ones like himself, Mrs. Mercer." Terpis smiled at me as Vincie fetched a writing-pad of mine. "Thanks. That'll be big enough."

He was a quick but neat and careful draughtsman, and in five minutes he had handed us a drawing of the "profile" of a Great Dane's skull, and a cross-section of it.

"Here is the contour of your battering-ram," he said. "Now give me another sheet while you count the bumps on the dog's dome."

While neither of us saw the point Terpis was trying to make, both Vincie and I studied the drawings with interest and respect. The human skull looks knobbly enough when despoiled of skin, flesh and hair, but the Great Dane's dome, as he called it, was stranger still.

Power looked over our shoulders. "Alas, poor Yorick!" he quoted. "Did you really look like that when bald."

"By the way," said Terpis, still sketching busily, "the head would be inclined somewhat downward when the dog butted. He would save his nose at the expense of his frontal bone."

CHAPTER XXIV

Dr. Terpis asked for our sheet, placed it over the other, and told us to look over at what he proposed to do.

"Now here," he said, "I propose to draw an outline of a gentleman, shall we say as an advertisement for one of those electrified belts which are supposed to give him new health and vigour."

As he spoke, he drew the outline of a man who, from what we had heard, must have developed something of Morgan's elderly spread.

"A bow window, but of the shallow type," he went on. "Increasing years, and the lack of exercise due to his arthritic knee, would have eventually made it more visible still."

"That's about right," said Power. "Morgan wasn't actually a fat man."

"I gathered a hint of his proportions from the report," said Terpis. "I now come to the vulnerable area which must have suffered that morning. My drawing is not to scale, but we can guess the proportions reasonably well."

"Now I get you," Power murmured.

Terpis grinned. "Ladies and gentlemen, if you are trying to deduce the size of a hammer from the area of a bruise, accurate measurements of the bruise are the first essential. We have those in the report."

"I did see that part," Power agreed.

"The second point is to decide on the relative depth of the bruising, and its relative severity over the whole area of the bruise," Terpis went on, "and that may indeed enable you to decide that it was not caused by a hammer at all, or by its edge, or side, or top, nor the face of a hammer. The face of a hammer is practically flat."

"Ah, the dog's—" Vincie began.

"Are you lecturing to this class or am I?" Terpis demanded. "I am? Good. I am a better lecturer than listener. Now here I shall mark the measurements of the impacting surface of the skull of a normal Great Dane. I allow, of course, for the curvature of the male figure, and its relative elasticity when forcibly dented."

He added to his diagram and then wrote down some measurements from the report, and I kicked Vincie, who showed signs of disturbing the seance with further questions.

"As you will have observed," Terpis resumed, "owing to the muzzle and other prominent cranial features, the lowered head of the dog is neither flat nor smooth. When you are struck with a fist, the resultant bruise is deeper and more severe where the prominent knuckle-bones impact on your skin, than where the more depressed finger-bones touch. Looking at the dog's skull we can more or less accurately decide the size and type of bruise or injury it would inflict."

As he now paused for a comment, I let Vincie remark that it was all clear as mud. "If you hit a man with a blackthorn, you make a different kind of mark; not the type you inflict when you bean him with a sandbag."

"Exactly. To be brief, ladies and gentlemen, there is not a hope that the injuries observed by, measured and reported on, by Skinny—by Professor Gladsty, I should say—could have been inflicted by the head of a Great Dane, or any other dog."

"So that's a wash-out too," Power said.

"Forward with the cigars, and I'll tell you," Terpis said. "I can only deal with facts. The Great Dane may have butted Jolson to Kingdom Come, but it did not inflict itself on Mr. Morgan."

Power brought the box of cigars, and Terpis cut and lit one, with care. "I smoke 'em a bit stronger than this," he said, "but the flavour isn't bad."

"Thank you," said Power. "The Corona people will feel flattered. But we want your opinion of the case. It's more valuable about that."

"Right. I'll go on. It may be that you would find an expert ready to go into the box and swear that my conclusions are all wrong. You can always find an expert to do that. In the Sunday papers, as you must have noticed, it is enough for a man to write that he saw Henry Irving in *The Bells*, in the sixties, for another man to write that Irving never acted in *The Bells* in the sixties at the theatre mentioned."

"True, but irrelevant," said Power. "Get on with it."

He was having a bit of his own medicine now, and did not like it. We smiled; having been kept on tenterhooks by him often enough.

"I merely say that, subject to correction, which may itself be incorrect, I interpret Skinny's report as meaning that the injury to the abdominal walls was caused by a smooth, curved object, with no knobs on. He even gives the supposititious measurements of this hypothetical object; also of the area of it which impinged on Mr. Morgan's bow window."

"A smooth curved object?" I said wonderingly. "I wonder what that could be?"

"It seems to me to have been a weapon which we all carry about with us," Terpis said, puffing at his cigar. "The seat of intellect, if we have any; the garden where grow the hair-follicles, if not."

"You mean the head?" said Vincie.

"I do," said Dr. Terpis, "and in support of the theory I can tell you an anecdote of my schooldays; even if Power calls it irrelevant."

"Tell us, and never mind Power!" I said eagerly.

"Well, when I was eleven, I was not very big, and I was certainly neither muscular nor plucky. Further, I had none of those silly ideas about what is fair play and what is not. A school-fellow of fourteen, a bully, and burly with it, proposed to punch my head. Not only to avoid the punch, but with a view to incapacitating my enemy, to give me time to fly, I lowered my head and dashed into his waistcoat. It was most effective. He lay gasping and gurgling. I fled."

"He's got it," said Vincie. "It was Jolson then. He got his rag out and butted Morgan in the tummy."

"It is all here," remarked Terpis, recovering his lowest sheet and showing us the last diagram. "The wretched little ram must have got the fright of his life when he saw Morgan collapse."

"And die," I said soberly. "How beastly! No wonder he was afraid. And naturally he hadn't meant to kill the man."

"Talking of killing," said Power slowly. "Would that blow be instantaneous death, Terpis?"

"No," said Terpis gravely, "it would not, in my opinion. I don't think he lived more than four or five minutes after he received the blow. Did it appear that anything had been done for him by the man who must have been his assailant?"

"What exactly do you mean? Jolson wasn't a doctor, but a retired bank manager. I doubt if he knew the first thing about first aid."

"Quite so. But there is one thing the average man flies to in an accident. On the rugby field when a man is injured in any spot, his fellow players at once massage his tummy. It may be concussion, but that is what they do. The amateur civilian more wisely opens the patient's collar and shirt."

"I see," said Power. "No, there was no sign that any attention had been given to Morgan."

"Doesn't that hint that the murderer was in a state of muddled panic?" I asked.

Dr. Terpis smiled. "Well, I shouldn't call him a murderer exactly, Mrs. Mercer. There was no premeditation, and it would hardly occur to the silly little man that his method of attack would lead to Morgan's death. If it was intentional, there would be no panic."

"Possibly Morgan was in a state of coma before he died," Power remarked, "but the blow would be extremely painful before he lost consciousness. Surely someone in the house would have heard a noise—a scream say?"

"Not necessarily," Terpis remarked. "The wind would be knocked out of the man, and though he may have groaned, and probably did, a low-pitched sound is not heard so far away as a high-pitched one."

"I agree," Power observed. "By the way, if I did not understand everything Professor Gladsty wrote in his report, I did realise that, even if he stressed the nature of the 'weapon' which caused the injury, he did not hint that it was a human head."

"No," said Terpis. "He wouldn't. Skinny is a splendid pathologist, but forensic medicine is not really his job, and he is rarely consulted in criminal cases. That side would not interest him. I can assure you that the old soul would utterly ignore the personal equation. If Morgan had been a soccer player, he might have thought of it."

"Does he play?" I asked.

"No, but he used to, and he's one of the directors of Barnfield United. One or two footballers have been killed in much the same way as Morgan; in accidental collisions, of course."

"If Mr. Morgan was in pain, it seems odd to me that even a panicky man should not have tried to help him," I said.

"Panic," observed Terpis, "has no rules. It's the one premise you cannot base any logical conclusions on, Mrs. Mercer. Real panic makes some people deaf, dumb and blind."

"What about his hat?" I said suddenly, for women are more concerned with trifles than men.

"Whose hat?" said Dr. Terpis.

"Mr. Jolson's," I said. "The one he wore that morning."

"Oo-er," said Vincie. "What about that?"

Power nodded approvingly. "Minus one to me; plus one to you, Mrs. M. As it wasn't a crash helmet, that's very relevant."

Dr. Terpis smiled. "Yes. Or was he a no-hatter?"

"He wore one when he came to see us," I said.

"I shall make inquiries about that," Power told us. "If you are about to spar with a man, you may remove your hat. If you are so mad with rage that you stoop to butting a man, it is hardly likely."

Vincie is never jealous of me when I make a score, but, of course, he likes to even up when he can. And a sensible wife will encourage her husband so to do.

"To carry the matter a little farther," he said, "what about Jolson's neck, my dear fellow?"

Power held up his hands. "Two up, and none to play for the Mercer family," he remarked. "Your turn, Terpis."

The doctor smiled. "The neck is certainly as relevant, if not more so than the hat," he commented. "The jar to neck and head may have contributed to Jolson's mental confusion."

"Very well," said Power. "Whether Jolson wanted an alibi or not, it is an incontestable fact that he slipped out of the garden and walked off to a distant village, where, presumably, he had something to buck him up. I think inquiries should be made there."

"Would there be any bruising on Jolson's head?" I asked.

"There might be, especially if it came in contact with a waist-coat button."

Power growled. "Unfortunately, some days elapsed before Jolson was even suspected. No one examined his sconce for signs of a collision, and the fall down the gravel-pit did the rest."

"I suppose," said Vincie, turning to Terpis, "there is no possibility that the damage was inflicted by a knee, which is fairly round and smooth, when doubled up."

"It would be effective, but it must be ruled out. Skinny's report makes that clear to me."

Vincie thanked him and rose. "I am going to see Mrs. Jennifer and ask her a question," he said, and went out before we could ask him the nature of the question.

"My tame sleuth-hounds are very keen," Power told Terpis. "There's one gone off on a strong scent."

We discussed the case at large till Vincie came back ten minutes later. He waved a hand to us as he came in, and showed every sign of being pleased with himself.

"Point one practically settled," he said. "For once Mrs. Jennifer betrayed some interest in a common crime. It occurred to me just now that middle-aged gentlemen in the summer-time often walk about with their hats in their hands. Convention I suppose forbids them not to have a hat; heat induces them to carry it. It is like the ritual of the folded gloves and unfurled umbrella."

"What did Mrs. Jennifer say?"

"She confirmed my suspicion. Mr. Jolson often promenaded in the town, carrying his smart Homburg in his hand; sometimes waving it gently, and occasionally fanning himself with it."

"To-morrow," Power announced, "Terpis goes back to town. You and I, and your husband, Mrs. Mercer, will go to the village and hear if Mr. Jolson bought anything more than a drink or two."

Dr. Terpis remarked that he did not see why Scotland Yard was kept up at such a cost. "Just get your people on the job, and there you are. The great unpaid!"

"By the way," said Power, "I ordered Terpis's dinner, but forgot his bed. Would you ask Mrs. Jennifer if she will be so kind, Mrs. Mercer?"

I rose at once. "Did you ever collect trilobites, doctor?" I asked.

"Never," he said. "But, of course, I know what they are."

"Then," I said, "I can safely tell Mrs. Jennifer that you are a student of them. They are the things which seem particularly to have earned her respect."

CHAPTER XXV

DR. TERPIS left next morning after breakfast, and we were sorry to see him go. However, he promised to look us up in town later on.

At ten, we three set out to drive to the village of Plymly. We parked the car on the edge of the village green, and looked about for an inn.

"The Waggoneers' Arms," a nice bit of black and white, stood on the farther side of the green, and we went there at once. The landlord, a bullet-headed, but not unintelligent, man, informed us at once that we should have to wait a couple of hours.

"We don't want drinks—only information," Power told him. "I suppose there is nothing against our sitting on the settle out here for a few minutes and asking you a few questions?"

There were, of course, several things, such as the waste of the landlord's time and the fact that we were non-paying guests, but the man suddenly grinned, and assented. Power gave him a cigar, and that settled matters.

"I want to know something about a visitor to your inn some time ago," Power began, when we were all smoking. "His name was Jolson, and he was accidentally killed near Malpertuis by a fall the other day."

"Oh, him!" said the landlord, looking less puzzled. "The police was asking about that t'other day. Wanted to know if he had been here, and if I served him. I told them I ought to know Mr. Jolson, seeing it was his bank I have my account in."

"Oh, then you knew him?"

"'Course I knew him, sir, though it's some time back he left the bank. He'd come out here sometimes to have a chat."

"Good. Now the police were asking you, no doubt, about a particular day. You remembered that visit?"

"Yes, I did. He come in looking very hot and bothered, and said he had been stung by a wasp that had got down his clothes. My missus she got a blue-bag for him."

"Did she apply it?"

"No, sir, she didn't," the man grinned. "He asked if he could go upstairs to the bathroom, and he wouldn't have the blue-bag either."

We all exchanged glances. Vincie put the next question. "Refused the blue-bag? What did he want, washing-soda?"

"No, sir, not that either. He said as how his mother always used arnica for a wasp sting. I said I'd never heard of it being any good that way; but we always have arnica for our boy, who plays games, and the missus give it to him, and he goes upstairs with it."

"He had the dog with him?"

"Yes, sir, he had. Quiet beast that, for all its ugly looks. I kept it by me in the bar."

"Was he wearing his hat when he came to you?" I asked.

"Wearing his hat?" the landlord looked hard at me. "Swinging it in his hand, as he always did that I remember, when it was warm."

Power got up. We all saw that a cross-inquisition on the landlord's part was imminent, and were not anxious to stay for it.

"That proves it," said Power gravely. "A fatal habit this hot weather. A touch of sun and you get giddy and aren't so sure of your footing."

A false light broke on the landlord's mind, as Power had intended it should. "Was that the way of it, sir?" he commented. "Come to think of it, it's very like. I never did think that dog pushed him over the gravel-pit. Giddy; that's what it will have been."

We thanked him warmly and retired in good order to the car.

"Bravo!" Power congratulated us when we were off again. "You both struck lucky. From a medical point of view I believe that arnica has no real value, apart from the fact that it is used to massage the part. Jolson came here with a stiff neck, went to the bathroom and massaged it. I think we can acquit the imaginary wasp of a malicious attack."

"What now?" I asked. "Voce should be told."

"I'll drop you at the Old Rectory, and go in search of him," Power said, "and, of course, give him the gist of Terpis's argument. But I am not at all sure that Voce will be able to do anything about it. He'll see the point as we do, but Captain Hollick may not want to be convinced that 'dear old Jolson' was a homicide as well as a suicide."

"You really think he committed suicide?" I said.

"I am inclined to believe so," he remarked. "If he'd killed a man, not with premeditation, but certainly as a result of letting his temper get the better of him, he would not want to go through life with the memory of it. But proving things on the strength of imponderables, with the very ponderable bulk of the local chief constable against you, will be the devil of a job."

"It will just be another case of the killer being known to the police, and no action being taken," Vincie admitted. "There must have been at least ten in the last five years, Voce told me once. And, of course, there is not much point in getting a verdict if the man is dead."

"You won't get it any way," said Power. "I have a strong suspicion Bone won't be so sure about having actually seen a packet of 'coke,' if he is brought into the witness-box at the inquest. By the way, it is pretty obvious now that the rose was never in Morgan's button-hole until he was dead."

"I agree," I said. "It isn't even the question of its being too large, as I suggested at first, but it would have shown signs of a rough-and-tumble."

"I expect Morgan had put it on the seat beside him before Jolson called," Vincie suggested. "With a gammy knee, I don't suppose he got up to greet an unwelcome visitor. He probably did so later, when he saw that Jolson was a bit off his rocker."

Power nodded. "That's it. For some reason or other, Jolson stuck it in the dead man's buttonhole. Now why?"

"I pass," said Vincie, and I had to echo him.

"At a venture," said our friend thoughtfully, "there is the chance that Jolson decided that the presence of an undamaged flower in the man's coat would suggest to the police that there had been no scrimmage, no violence."

"Good," said Vincie. "That's an idea. As it was, the whole thing almost escaped notice. If it hadn't been for the trace of 'coke' on the rose, they might have assumed that the death was natural, since the organs would not have been sent up to the pathologist for examination."

"You mean that Jolson was sufficiently calm, when he saw that Morgan was actually dead, to stage a natural looking death?" I asked.

"Well, he was calm enough to sprinkle some dope on the rose, to give a possible appearance of death from that cause," Vincie said.

"I am not so sure," Power remarked. "The traces on the rose were very slight."

I felt sure by now that no one would ever penetrate the mystery of the presence of the dope. "I wonder why Jolson admitted to us that he had been in the garden that morning?" I said. "It's inexplicable."

"I don't think it is," said Power. "Unless you killed someone in a desert, or on top of the Pole, you could never be sure that you were not seen by someone. Jolson must have been worrying dreadfully about that possibility. Did the police know, and pretend not to, giving him rope to hang himself? Would it not be wiser, while there was still a possibility that Morgan's death seemed natural, to tell the truth? So he came on to you, and let it out. It isn't the first time it's been said that the truth, within limits, is the best defence."

He dropped us at the Old Rectory, and went off to look for Voce. We had hardly settled ourselves in the garden with our writing-pads, when Captain Hollick came in, and walked across the lawn to us.

Although he smiled and bowed very politely, he had an air of constraint which was very illuminating. It said, as clearly as if he had voiced it, that everyone in Malpertuis was doing very nicely, thank you, till we arrived, and wanted to join in.

In fact he regarded us as a member of a small country tennis club might regard a visiting player, who told him that the court was shorter than regulation size, and the net not at the right height. They enjoyed playing the game that way, and were not grateful for hints on the correct procedure.

He took a chair and a cigarette, coughed dryly, and remarked that he supposed we were enjoying the wonderful summer. "Though, secretly, I suppose," he added, "you are both pining to get back to town."

"We thought of stopping over for the inquest," I said. "We are so interested, you know."

"I am sure you are," he said, "but I'm afraid it will only be a very formal business."

I thought of the Mikado's song: "It is the law; it is: I made it so," and smiled: "Really?"

He nodded. "The fact is, Mrs. Mercer, our coroner is, like myself, a stickler for correct procedure. There's nothing more injurious to the processes of justice than an official disregarding the statutes laid down for his guidance and attempting to turn an inquest into a criminal trial."

"But I suppose he does attempt to get at the cause of death?" said Vincie ironically.

But Captain Hollick was too much in earnest to notice that. "As far as lies in his power, of course. But there are cases, and this threatens to be one of them, where it is impossible for a coroner's jury to decide on the evidence what was the exact cause of death."

"It has happened," I said. "But don't the police carry on, regardless?"

Hollick frowned. "They are at liberty to do so if they think fit," he said. "In this case there is a strong presumption that, if Mr. Morgan died by violence, it was inflicted by the dog. I think you were among the first to see that and the verdict on dear old Jolson certainly confirmed your views."

Simultaneously, Vincie and I made a resolution not to tell him what Dr. Terpis had said. We were not supposed anyway to know the contents of the pathologist's report.

"But how will the jury swallow the dope?" I asked.

"As it does not seem relevant to the inquiry," Hollick muttered, "I do not see that it need be brought up. The cause of death is at issue only. Mr. Morgan did not die of cocaine poisoning, nor is there any evidence that it contributed in the smallest degree to his death. So its presence may be fortuitous."

"And Mr. Jolson's account of an incident in Paris a mere yarn?" Vincie asked. "What did the packet contain—indigestion powders?"

Hollick looked displeased. "The whole question of there having been such a packet in Jolson's possession is dubious. Mr. Bone is a charming man—I had a little chat with him this morning—but, like all artists, somewhat imaginative."

"You think it was that?" I asked.

He nodded. "In addition, we all know that the good fellow is rather, shall we say—Well, perhaps I had better not say it."

"We noticed that," Vincie replied. "In fact it was too obvious not to."

"Quite. He's a very nice fellow in spite of his weakness. Naturally in my chat with him this morning I had to touch on the point you are making, the—er—hypothetical packet."

"Has it got as far as that?" I inquired.

"Well," he looked away from me, and frowned, "our good friend Bone seems more than a little hazy about it now. I pressed him rather for details of the occasion when this yarn was told him by Jolson, and he admitted that he had been—er—celebrating a birthday or something, and may—he did not go farther than may—have muddled up the matter with something he had read. I was able to help him there."

We exchanged glances. Vincie interpreted them in speech. "I am sure you did it very gladly."

Hollick looked at him suspiciously. "I. Oh, yes, of course. I want to get at the truth. It just occurred to me that I had read a magazine story somewhere, called, I think, 'In the Rue de la

Bonne,' in which a dope vendor had approached a tourist, much as Bone described it. Bone thought he had read the story too."

"But how interesting, and what a coincidence!" I cried. "Do go on."

"In fact," Hollick hurried on, as a man does when the ground is slippery, and he is anxious not to trip up, "allowing for the drink Bone had taken and subconscious memories, as they call them, and so forth, I have a shrewd suspicion that the tale and the packet were—er—so to speak, evolved from Bone's inner consciousness."

"How well you simplify things," Vincie said admiringly. "It's quite an art."

Hollick looked embarrassed. "That being so, and Bone appearing rather unwilling to admit at the inquest, when resumed, that he either saw a packet alleged to contain dope, or alternatively dramatised and made a romantic story of something which only existed in his confused mind—"

Vincie hastened to cut short what threatened to be the longest sentence on record. "You decided not to call him, and he fades out of the picture. Is that it?"

"That," said Hollick, after some hesitation, "is, more or less, it."

"And what," I asked, "will Chief Inspector Voce say to that?"

Hollick looked so uncomfortable that we knew Voce had been a snag.

"I saw him this morning, and he has sent his sergeant up to London to lay the facts before the Public Prosecutor. The question of criminal proceedings, as you no doubt know, lies with that official. They are never undertaken without a great deal of thought and care."

"Then you do not believe in Jolson's inferiority complex and its consequences?" I asked.

Hollick laughed a very military laugh. "My dear Mrs. Mercer, science is a useful thing; psychology, though still in the experimental stage, is no doubt valuable in certain hands. But the idea that feeling small (if Mr. Jolson ever did feel small—which is a moot point) makes a man commit murder to recover his prestige is *too* laughable!"

"You are giving us an example of the *ignoratio elenchi*," I said.

Hollick frowned and looked puzzled. "If you care to put it that way," he remarked, making Vincie turn away to hide a grin. "At all events, no one down here would believe such a thing for a moment. I think I am safe in saying that the jury will return an open verdict."

"No doubt they will," I said.

"As for the cocaine, which is not to be denied, even if it did not come from that romantically acquired packet," he added, more easily, "who is to say, if it comes to that, that Mr. Morgan had not once come into possession of a small quantity of the stuff."

"What about his known intolerance of it?" I asked.

He smiled triumphantly. "My dear Mrs. Mercer, even Bone's muddled story suggested that Jolson kept cocaine, but did not use it. If he did so, why not Morgan?"

"Why not?" said Vincie. "But what became of the receptacle he kept it in?"

"No packet was found on Mr. Jolson either," said Hollick. "So I do not see the point of your remark."

He rose, added that he must get home to lunch and hoped that the weather would hold.

"For the rest of your short holiday," he said.

CHAPTER XXVI

WE TOLD Power all about the Chief Constable's visit when he returned.

"He is not going to encourage a prosecution," Vincie added. "That's quite clear, and he has persuaded Bone to back him up."

"He is right, from his own point of view," Power replied. "I have seen Voce. He has talked it over with Hollick, and assures me that the man does not believe a word of the theory that

Jolson killed Morgan. It turns, of course, on a subject which fills Hollick with amusement. He is temperamentally incapable of understanding mental kinks. That being so, it would be ludicrous to expect him to urge a prosecution, or, since Jolson is dead, legal proceedings to follow the inquest."

"But the Public Prosecutor is independent of him," I said.

"Yes. But he will consider several things: local views, the likelihood of getting a verdict and now, of course, Bone's backing down. It is a question if the jury here would understand the point of Bone's story, if he were willing to tell it. But if he is not called, or if he was put in the box, and blew hot and cold about it, it would be fatal."

We were not disappointed, of course, for we both saw that Jolson had not visited Morgan with homicide in view; but we were curious to know what Morgan made of the last evidence Power had procured.

"What did Voce think of Jolson's stiff neck?" I asked.

Power smiled. "It appears that he got that information about the arnica from the pub, but hadn't worked it into our pattern. He felt that it had some meaning; only the publican's remark about going up to the bathroom to apply the arnica might have hinted at any part of the body."

"He sees it now, of course," said Vincie.

"Certainly, when I was able to give him Terpis's interpretation of the pathologist's report. In return for that, he told me that the analyst's report, on the stuff collected from the grass round the seat in Morgan's garden showed that it included considerable traces of a white powder, which turned out to be adulterated cocaine. More than that, some had got into the fibres of Morgan's clothes, though there were signs that they had been roughly dusted off."

"What about Jolson's clothes?" I asked. "I suppose he did not tell you that."

"He did," said Power. "He knows he and Bohm will have to pack up and go home, and the business of the cocaine won't be allowed to emerge. The right-hand waistcoat pocket of Jolson's suit showed traces of the stuff too."

Vincie uttered an exclamation. "My dear fellow, surely you, or someone, said when Jolson was picked up at the bottom of the gravel-pit—"

"I know," Power interrupted, "and that was quite right. Only, it seems that Jolson was wearing a cheviot-cloth suit when he called on Morgan. He had on plus-fours, and a sports jacket, when he went over the top."

"But doesn't that convince Hollick?" I asked.

"That was my remark to Voce. He replied that there was no reason why Jolson should administer dope to Morgan, or any way in which he could have done it. That is in Hollick's opinion. And he said no jury in Malpertuis would deduce a murder from a few specks of white powder in a dead man's pocket. That is the only point on which Voce agrees with him. and if Bone rats, as he's going to do, it's hopeless."

"Thank heaven for luncheon," said Vincie. "Let's go and swallow our defeat with something tasty to take the edge off it."

"Let's!" said Power. "Meanwhile, I asked Voce to drop in to-night. We may hear what Bohm got at the Public Prosecutor's Office. The sergeant was to ring Voce up as soon as he could."

"Heard any more of Tressy Withers?" I asked, as we were eating our fish.

"Lovely news," Power replied, with a grin. "He has repaid the money, but he hasn't heard yet from Voce that he can slide out if he wishes. So he is in town and when last heard of, was in a bar; punishing strong liquor, and emitting strong language."

That was satisfactory news, and pleased us very much. Bone's defection pleased us less, but the little man bravely called on us at three, and did his best to explain.

It took quite an hour, and was most humiliating for the poor dear. No tippler, however hardened, can ever quite like describing to others how bemused he often is. It reminded me of Addison's story of the band of hard-swearing gentlemen who did not realise the accumulated and horrific effect of their profanity, until a man behind a screen took it down and read it to them en bloc.

"I'm rather a dreamy fellow too," Bone said at last. "I mean to say, realities and dreams get sort of mixed, you know, and I suppose I got thinking about what I had heard; of the dope, and so on."

"And of Jolson, and knowing Jolson had really called on Morgan," I said helpfully. "I know."

He was backing out anyway, so it was merciful to steady the step-ladder for him.

"You must have been pretty tight that day," Power said candidly.

Mr. Bone coloured. "I am afraid I was," he said. "Not that I can swear Jolson did not say something about dope. I won't go as far as that. Or something about a Paris café; and I'd been reading a story about dope. That may have been it. I am frightfully sorry to have misled you."

"Oh, I don't think you did really," Power remarked with faint irony. "It's just that you can't be sure, and you don't like to blacken dear old Jolson's memory, if there is any doubt about it."

"In any case, there was the dog," he said, "I bet the dog did it. As Cap—I mean to say, the brute did bounce and bump people."

"Think no more about it," I said. "I suppose you will not be called to give evidence at the inquest?"

He got up. "I? No. Why should I? I really know no more about it than yourselves." He hesitated a moment, then looked at Power. "Mr. Power I am particularly sorry I let you down, because you have pulled off that business for me. I should have been in Queer Street, I assure you, if Withers had bunked with my money."

"I'll send you an account, and that will square it," said Power. "And don't worry about letting me down. My clients have ended up on velvet."

For the first time that afternoon, Mr. Bone smiled. When the maid brought our tea out into the garden that afternoon, I told her that Chief Inspector Voce would be in for coffee in the evening.

"My compliments to Mrs. Jennifer," I added, "and will you tell her that Mr. Voce considers her coffee better than any he ever got in Vienna. I am having a pint of cream specially for him this evening."

"No hot milk, ma'am?"

"None," I said. "*Café Americain*, please." Voce came in after dinner, in very good form considering the set-back he had had. I refused to let him speak till he had lapped up a cup of hot coffee and cream, and lit one of Vincie's best cigars. Then I made a sign to Mr. Power.

"Well, Voce," said our friend, "is there any secret about the P.P.'s decision?"

"No, sir," said Voce, puffed at his cigar luxuriously, and added, "we go back to town to-morrow, sir. It seems Captain Hollick was on the wire to-day to our Commissioner, and the P.P."

"He would!" said Vincie.

"He advised against any proceedings, and that finished it. Not that the P.P. cares a hoot about Chief Constables," Voce added. "But I had to admit through Bohm that I did not see how we could carry a jury with us on the evidence we had."

"But you do believe in it?" I said.

Voce winked slowly. "It isn't what I believe, or what the P.P. believes and it isn't what Captain Hollick believes. If a doctor can't give a patient a certain drug, he doesn't prescribe it. The job of the P.P. is to see if a prosecution, or court proceedings, can be initiated with any chance of success. There is nothing the public likes less than our pointing the finger at anyone, and then having to apologise for it. A lost case does us more harm than no case at all."

"Hard luck," said Power.

"We're used to it, sir, and the P.P. is used to it. He throws out dozens of cases every year. You see, a jury will believe that Mr. Jolson called on Morgan, accept the possibility that he was in a jealous rage, and, perhaps, also the inference that he had a sore place, and put arnica on it at the pub in Plymly."

"Or they might rather believe in the wasp."

"As you say, madam, they might believe in the wasp. One thing you wouldn't get them to agree to is the dope business."

"But you can prove Jolson carried dope," said Vincie.

"Yes, but I can't tell a jury, who know nothing more of complexes than they do of comets, that Jolson was carrying defiance to the world in his waistcoat pocket. It wouldn't make sense to them. Even Hollick, who is an educated man, is too normal to understand the abnormal."

"I agree," Power remarked. "If they did understand that, you would still be faced by the administration of the dope, which none of us has yet got to the bottom of. If we could explain that, you might get a verdict; though it is doubtful even then."

"Very," said Voce, watching me appreciatively as I reached for the jug of hot cream, and Vincie for his empty cup. "I suppose none of you will wait for the inquest now?"

Vincie laughed. "No. We'll get back to town. My wife will want to get on with her story, and I have several people I ought to see."

"And you, Mr. Power?" said Voce. "Thank you, Mrs. Mercer, I never tasted coffee like this."

"Not even in Vienna?" I asked.

"I've never been there," he said.

"As for me," said Power, "I'm a working man, and must get back to the old job. But, no doubt, we'll run across one another some day, Voce, and here's to our next meeting."

We all raised our coffee cups.

CHAPTER XXVII

While I am sure we both regretted leaving the flesh-pots of Malpertuis, we realised that there was no more for us to do there. Mr. Bone came to see us off. Captain Hollick did not. But he was relieved, I am sure. Inspector Kay came to say good-bye before we left, and brought Mrs. Davey-Renny rather diffidently with him.

Then we were home again, and I sat down to get on with my work, and Mr. Power settled to his, and there was a great peace.

But it was not a peace that we were fully able to enjoy. I know I worried and worried, secretly, over the problem which we had all had to leave in the air, and Vincie admitted that he had a dream about it. This, however, was not very helpful.

He imagined that he was in Morgan's garden, and suddenly he saw Mr. Jolson come in. Simultaneously, a great black cloud overshadowed the sky, and there was a blast of icy wind. Mr. Morgan suddenly held his hands to his middle, and appeared to be numbed by the cold. Mr. Jolson stared up at the sky, from which a few white flakes were then beginning to fall.

"Well, if it isn't snow!" Vincie said to himself. "Snow in summer."

Mr. Morgan was soon covered with white flakes which dried and turned into dry powder, and Mr. Jolson called his dog and ran away, swinging his hat in his hand.

"It's time you put the whole thing out of your mind, Vincie," I told my husband. "When you have nightmares, you kick!"

"You lie, woman!" he said. "I neither kick nor bite. But I am afraid I am not a prophetic or useful dreamer."

When the accounts of the resumed inquest on Mr. Morgan appeared in the papers, we were not surprised to note that Mr. Bone was not among the witnesses.

Professor Gladsty was. He gave his dry evidence with a degree of dessication unusual even at inquests. As he had been asked for a report on the cause of death, he did not mention the cocaine, but concentrated on the abdominal injuries.

Asked if they could have been caused by a fall on some rounded object, he agreed that they could. He added that the death would not immediately follow the injury, and admitted that it was just possible the dead man had moved to the seat after receiving it.

He gave several instances of men having performed prodigies of physical effort after receiving terrible injuries.

He was not pressed for further details, and presently the coroner summed up. From his extremely sparse speech, it was taken that Mr. Morgan had received injuries of a nature which could not be clearly explained. But there had been no evidence to show that these injuries had been inflicted by a second party.

The police had gone into the matter very carefully, but without reaching any conclusion on which to base a prosecution.

At the same time, it was his duty to say that the police did not rule out the possibility that someone unknown had inflicted these injuries. If anything further came to light in that connection, or if further evidence suggesting the possibility of homicide turned up, it would be for the authorities to reopen the matter.

"As you are no doubt aware," the coroner added, "our deliberations are merely directed to finding the cause of death. Prior to, or during, or after our investigation is concluded, the police are entitled to take whatever steps may be desirable to further the ends of justice. Our business here is separate and distinct from any duty that may fall upon the police."

And then he left it to the jury.

The jury were some time coming back to court. They had not found it easy to agree on the exact terms of their verdict (though whitewash was the basis of it). It was to the effect that Mr. Morgan had died following abdominal injuries, but how, or by whom inflicted, the jury were unable to say.

The coroner accepted it with a word of approval, and the inquest came to an end.

"So that's that!" said Vincie. "Hollick will be pleased."

"In spite of his wangle, of course," I said. "He made the more practical decision. If nothing had been covered up, the result would have been the same; plus doubts of Mr. Jolson's guilt, which would have been distressing to his friends."

Vincie sighed. "You call yourself a writer of detective stories, Penny, and can't even produce a workable theory about the dope."

"You must always remember, my dear," I said patiently, "that I do not believe amateurs ever solve crimes. Help, or hinder, the police, as the case may be, but never solve the real problem."

Mr. Power did not write or call for a long time after that, not even to comment on the inquest or verdict. The incidents which had caused us so much excitement at the time, gradually began to fade from our minds. Even my book was just a recital of actual events, and I find that I have more interest in what is imaginary than what is true.

I think it was a month later, and the book was done, and sent to my publisher, when Power unexpectedly came to see us at tea-time. He had three stalls for the most crowded and popular play in town that evening, and asked us to join him.

We agreed on condition that he joined us at dinner somewhere.

"How long it does seem since we were all at Malpertuis," I said, presently, hoping against hope that Power might have heard something since.

"Ages," he agreed. "That reminds me, I ran across Voce yesterday."

"Where?" I asked.

"Lunching at Scapati's," he said. "He was looking well."

"Good," said Vincie. "I am sure he, for one, doesn't worry his mind about that case any longer."

Power smiled. "He didn't mention it anyway, till I did," he remarked.

"And when he did, he felt with me that there was no point in reopening it now."

I stared at him. "Of course not, Mr. Power. Unless you dreamed a dream, like Vincie; only not such a silly one."

"Well, I just told him what I thought," said Power, taking another cigarette. "Hollick is a boneheaded fool, but I began to take his view before I left Malpertuis. I mean to say, what with Jolson conked out, and no one to lock up."

"You mean you had a theory about the dope?" I said.

"Have, not had," he replied. "Voce agrees with me that it does cover the ground, but I'll tell you what it is, if you like."

"If we like!" I cried. "If you don't, we'll both fall on you and assault you! When did you get this idea?"

"Two days ago. I was talking to a client of ours, who lost an arm in the war. He was lying in great pain somewhere near Thiepval and an R.A.M.C. man, in a great hurry to get to the dressing-station forward, heard him groan and stopped for a moment in his rush to put a tablet in his mouth. He had the sense to send back—"

"Just a moment," Vincie interrupted. "Is this part of your history of the Great War, or a side-light on the great Malpertuis mystery?"

"Oh, my aunt!" said Mr. Power. "Successful argument is based largely on the capacity for making your opponent see analogies. But if he happens to be a woolly-headed, vacuum-brained—"

"Go on," I said. "Vincie hears quite enough about that from me without your butting in."

"No man more richly deserves it," said Power. "But to get back to my subject. Here we had little Jolson butting Morgan in the tummy in a frenzy of rage, and then frozen stiff with horror when he saw he'd knocked him off."

"He lived for a few minutes, Terpis said."

"Quite, and that added to Jolson's horror, for he had not really wished to kill Morgan, or to inflict pain on him. He simply lost his head, and used it. Now he sees what he has done; he does not know even then that Morgan will die. But his first impulse must be to stop the pain, which is almost as distressing in its appeal to his ears, as it must be to poor Morgan's tummy. What is he to do?"

"Anaesthesia!" I cried.

"Well, the little donkey has a packet of cocaine in his pocket, and if it can't be guaranteed to help a dying man, it does obviously quiet an aching gum. And it is all he has at his disposal which he can use. He takes out the packet and tried to make Morgan take it. Morgan, of course, won't. His teeth may be clenched with pain, apart from disinclination. But he must be drawing in deep breaths and inhaling some of that finely precipitated powder. Jolson dusted him, and himself, afterwards, and by that time knew that Morgan was dead. He had to fly."

"Then what about the rose?" said Vincie.

"I take it that he saw that Morgan did not look as if he had died from anything but natural causes, Mercer. One of you, I think, suggested that the rose was placed by him in Morgan's button-hole to hint at the absence of a struggle. The traces of dope must have got on to the rose, either flying on to it from Jolson's hands when he picked it up, or from the shower that ensued when he tried to force Morgan to take the stuff. Even Voce agrees that it is the only possible explanation."

"But he does not propose to do anything about it?" I asked.

"Of course not," said Power. "But it pleased him all the same, for he had stuck to the line of the one suspect all along."

THE END

www.ingramcontent.com/pod-product-compliance
Lightning Source LLC
Chambersburg PA
CBHW031015190726
48286CB00003BA/851